Over Our Spilled Blood

The Diviner's Legacy: Book Four

E.K. BARNES

MORE BY E.K. BARNES

THE DIVINER'S LEGACY SERIES

WHEN THE DIVINE ARE DEAD

IN THE CASE OF OUR FATE

WHILE WE SHATTER APART

OTHER WORKS

THE INTENSITY OF SILENCE

TO
10-YEAR-OLD ME
I GOT YOU THIS FAR

TABLE OF CONTENTS

CONTENT WARNING CAN BE FOUND AT
https://linktr.ee/ekbarnesauthor

"Let no man despise thy youth."

— *1 Timothy 4:12a*

OVER OUR SPILLED BLOOD

1 // I AM ALONE
SAVANNA

Mom began carving scratches in the cheap plastic handle of the oven, her stick-on nails threatening to break. She didn't seem to notice how her lip was bleeding from chewing too hard. Instead, her dull blue eyes above the bags of her lower eyelids seemed to be lost in thought.

I sat at the small round table, which had taken up most of the free space in our small kitchen for as long as I could remember. Attempting to ignore the tension in the air, I scratched at an old scratch-and-sniff sticker I'd placed in the center of the table almost a decade ago. My eleven-year-old sister, Ursula, blew a breath of air, puffing out her cheeks. Her arms were crossed, her brown eyes watching my broken nails fail to rip the sticker out of its permanent location.

What a metaphor.

Mom and I had come straight home from the women's center after the on-call doctor told us the pills didn't work. I had thought a ninety-six percent success rate would be enough to fix this. My mom did too. But instead, we were sitting in our kitchen on New Year's Eve panicking about what to tell Dad.

My mom is Catholic and devoutly pro-life, so I was surprised when she gave me permission for the pills. But a whole surgery? She couldn't stomach it. The entire time we were talking to the doctor, I thought she'd throw up on my shoes. We were out of options as far as she was concerned. As a minor in Indiana who had zero friends with driver's licenses who could drive me across state lines, I didn't have a choice but to go along with what she wanted. Except, I knew she didn't want this for me. She'd said it before. That's how I talked her into the pills. I'm fifteen, a sophomore in high school, and a junior varsity cheerleader. I'm also a martial artist. Not to mention that as a Fated One, my first child will apparently be born with a target on their back. None of those things mix well with being eight weeks pregnant. Dad was gonna blow a gasket.

"This is a child that fate wants," Mom had said through tight lips on our way home. The rest of the ride had been shrouded in deafening silence.

Fate could go screw itself.

I wondered how the Fates fit into her idea of God and the Holy Trinity. Did she see the Fates as types of cherubs or angels? Or did the Fates represent a physical manifestation of God's will? Either way, she was bending to the ridiculous notion that she was going to be a grandmother in her thirties. Somehow, I didn't think Dad was going to be quite so malleable to this higher power's plan. I really hoped Mom wouldn't try to paint me as the Virgin Mary. I wasn't a virgin, and this wasn't the Son of God I was carrying. It was just, I don't know, an Immortal One? Unfortunately, they were proving to be immortal from the womb, which makes no sense, considering last I checked, the current Immortal One was still immortal.

That's the weird thing about this entire situation. There can only be one Immortal One in the world at any one time, and according to Maria, the current Immortal One, the next Immortal One has to be born before she loses her ability to not die. Clearly, this baby didn't get the memo.

I pulled out my cell phone to check my messages. I'd had it on silent for the last two hours, missing a bunch of random texts from my friends. There was one at the top from Jay-Jay. *You okay?*

I puffed out my cheeks, huffing in annoyance. Couldn't people just leave me in peace? I slid the keyboard out, typing, *Still pregnant,* before hitting send. The number of concerned messages I had been getting over the last two weeks was annoying, especially since not a single one was from the person I cared the most about. I knew it was ridiculous to be bothered by Bradley's nonexistence in my message history since his family lived in the Stone Age when it came to cell phones, but he could have at least called.

"Is Bradley still in Tennessee?" Ursula asked as I set the phone on the table.

I nodded. I'd barely seen him since Maria told me I was pregnant. When three pregnancy tests later confirmed it, Bradley and I talked for hours on the phone until I fell asleep. His family left town for the holidays the day before Christmas Eve, so I was alone in breaking the news to my mom. In fact, I chickened out about twenty times because Christmas just didn't seem like the right occasion for bad news. Plus, I wanted to wait until Dad was out of the house.

I never got to tell Bradley I was taking the pills. We'd talked about the possibility, but with him out of town, I wasn't able to call him. The doctor had told us it was better to take them sooner rather than later, so I did without notifying him. I felt a little guilty about it, but since they hadn't worked anyway, there was no point in getting totally worked up. Plus, it was probably a good thing he was gone, since Dad couldn't march across the street and murder him. Not that he could.

Bradley could self-heal, although he didn't seem to heal in the same way I did. That was probably because he wasn't the one pregnant with the death-defying baby. But in theory, while I was with child, we couldn't die, which was probably the only perk out of this whole mess. Even if we could, I'd still have to remind Dad that killing Bradley would kill me. Literally.

I peered at the time on my phone. Dad was gonna be home any minute. My stomach churned with anxiety, which, coupled with the random bouts of nausea I kept experiencing, wasn't good. I forced myself to swallow some of the bile rising in my throat. This conversation wasn't going to be pleasant.

"Do I really have to be here?" I pleaded, peering at Mom.

She barely glanced at me before refocusing her gaze on the fridge's blinking water filter light. "Yes," she said without removing her teeth from her lip.

Ursula briefly drummed her hands on the table, her gaze shifting between us. After a few seconds, she scraped her chair back, getting ready to stand.

The doorknob turned.

My sister quickly lowered herself in her chair as Dad opened the front door. I couldn't see him with my back to the front of the house, but Ursula's gaze seemed to follow him as he whistled his way through the living room.

"I don't smell dinner," Dad noted, his coat rustling. I pictured him shrugging it off and hanging it on the coat rack. His footsteps thudded into the kitchen. He had to be right behind me now.

Mom's gaze left the fridge, landing on Dad.

"What's wrong?" he asked.

Ursula's eyes shifted once again between Mom and me. Nobody answered. I was physically shaking at this point, blood rushing through my ears. Dad took another step forward. This time, I could see his arm from the corner of my eye.

Mom swallowed, her eyes glistening. "Milo." She dipped her head, her teeth dislodging from her lip. "We have a situation."

Mom motioned to me with her eyes, and I immediately felt self-conscious. As I avoided their gazes, I dug my nails into my skin.

Ursula tried to break the tension. "Hey, Dad! Do you want some Jell-O? I made Jell-O today."

Her attempt didn't work. I could practically feel his stare burning through my skin. Or maybe it was just a hot flash. I don't know. Was that normal?

Dad's gruff voice broke through my anxiety. "Ursula, I'd like a moment alone with your mom and sister."

Ursula hesitated, glancing at me before standing, rounding the limited space between Dad and the wall to get to the stairs. Once I heard a few footsteps stomping the carpet, Dad slammed his fist on the table, causing it to rattle. I jumped, my phone vibrating across it before landing on the floor.

Mom joined him tableside as his voice rumbled, "That no good, good-for-nothing boy knocked you up, didn't he?" Some of his spit landed on my arm.

I closed my eyes, surprised at how easily my tears came. Dad always tried to paint Bradley as some horrible monster, but I'd known true monsters, and Bradley wasn't one of them. My throat burned as I tried to control the sobs.

"Where is he? I want to talk to him," Dad demanded.

Mom tried to be the voice of reason. "Milo, they're out of town. They're not going to be back for a few more days," she said in a tone that was probably supposed to relax him. It didn't.

"I told you this was going to happen!" Dad roared.

I hugged myself tighter. Was it possible to hug myself so tight that the problem would just go away?

"How does a fifteen-year-old get another fifteen-year-old pregnant anyway?"

"Pretty much the normal way, Dad," I croaked, my eyes barely open enough to see his foot come down on my phone. It shattered as he shoved the table away from me. There went my one lifeline. My blood ran cold.

Clenching my teeth, I opened my eyes a little further, daring to meet my father's as he sputtered out another shout. "That bastard talked you into it!"

I stood, my fists clenched. "No, Dad. Maybe I'm just a whore!" In hindsight, that was probably not the best choice of words, but that didn't excuse what came next.

His palm met my cheek before I had time to blink, the force causing me to stumble into the antique cabinet lining the wall. My elbow dove through the glass.

Mom screamed at Dad, but I was done with this conversation. I didn't even want to be in it in the first place. My cheek and elbow stung as my feet steered me around the corner and up the stairs, nearly tripping over Ursula in the process.

"Did he hit you?" Ursula asked, her eyes wide as she ran after me. I didn't answer, making a beeline for my bedroom and slamming the door in her face. I flipped the lock for good measure before my back hit the door. My legs gave out. Sliding to the carpet, I let out a cacophony of sobs, my chest heaving. I knew my dad was going to be mad, but I never thought he would hit me. He'd never reacted like that before. Not outside the ring, anyway. It was like he'd forgotten who his true enemies were.

My sister pounded on the other side, causing it to shake, but I ignored it for the most part. Through my blurry vision, I pulled my left arm forward and tried to twist it to get a better look at my elbow. I could barely see the glass poking out of my skin through the tears. Yanking the pieces out, I watched the part of the wound I could see disappear. It made me cry harder.

This was real. This was happening. And there was nothing I could do about it.

I wished Bradley were with me. I wished we'd had more time to talk about it. A few hours in the middle of the night a week and a half ago wasn't enough. I needed him here. I needed him to convince me this wasn't the end of the world because it felt like the beginning of the end. Like, this moment led to only one end—complete and total destruction. Which sucked.

As much as I'd tried to convince Bradley over the last year that he wasn't doomed, here I was spiraling into the same black hole he was always landing in. And damn, for once, could he be the strong one? For once, could he sit here with me in the pain and hold me through it? 'Cause I sure as hell wasn't strong enough.

My parents were still screaming at each other when the tears slowed. Dad had gone on a rant, starting with, "Ever since the Chambers family moved across the street..." and never ending his point through Mom's constant interruptions.

"We need to be there to support her, Milo. This isn't a problem that's going to go away just because you don't like it," Mom interjected.

I shook my head, attempting to tune them out. For the first time in my life, I wished I were a normal teenager with smaller problems. I wished I were a normal fifteen-year-old whose biggest problem was whether her eye makeup was on point. I wished I didn't have powers. I wished I didn't live in a family who knew what it was like to live on the run. I wished I didn't spend all these years training to fight when the real enemy wasn't something I could kick in the face.

The only thing I didn't wish to be different was Bradley. Even in an alternate reality, I couldn't imagine my life without him. So would this have happened anyway? Were we destined—outside of mystery and magic—to bring another life into the world at such a young age? Or could we have had a different life? One where everyone was happy and nobody tried to leave the other every time something got hard?

I know him not being here wasn't his fault. It was the holidays, for crying out loud. Lots of families left town. Hell, even Marcie's family had run off to Florida at her grandparents' expense. The sad thing was, I didn't even know the Chamberses had made plans to leave. It didn't make sense for them to travel only a few days after their daughter's suicide attempt. Not to mention Bradley's and my news. I thought for sure they'd still be here out of paranoia at the very least. But Bradley said his grandpa had called about something urgent, something that made it a requirement for their entire family to pile into their twelve-passenger van and drive out of state. All I can say about that is I hope it was worth it. I hope it was worth abandoning me.

"Are you okay?" Ursula whispered through the door.

Out of tears, I shook my head, then reached to unlock the door. As soon as the lock clicked, there was a force on the other side, shoving me. I squirmed out of the way as she poked her head through before sliding in and shutting the door. Ursula met me on the floor, sidling next to me and wrapping her arms around my right arm, stretching to prop her chin on my shoulder. Her dark eyes peered up at me as I wiped my dripping nose with my free arm.

"I must look deplorable," I said, sniffling.

She lifted her chin from my shoulder to shake her head. Letting go of my arm, she reached to run her fingers through my hair before grabbing the ends and twisting them into a small braid. "I've always thought you were the strongest person I knew, and I still do." She licked her chapped lips. "I just wanted you to know that." Holding my hair in one hand, she stretched to grab her cell phone out of her pocket. "I called Mya Lindt, and she gave me Mrs. Chambers's cell phone number." She offered the phone to me. "It's saved in my contacts if you want to call her."

I stared at the phone for several seconds before snatching it from her open palm. "Oh my God, thank you, thank you, thank you," I said, struggling to contain my gratitude. I flipped it open, inputting the PIN she used for everything to unlock it. Scrolling through her contacts, I quickly found the number labeled *Mrs. Chambers* and hit call. Ursula continued to braid my hair as I anxiously waited through the dial tone.

My heart stuttered when Mrs. Chambers answered. "Hello?"

I opened my mouth to speak, but my words stuck in my throat. I barely squeaked them out. "Um, is it possible…" I cleared my throat, restarting. "Can I talk to Bradley?"

Mrs. Chambers's tone softened. I realized I never said who I was, but she must have recognized my voice. "Of course, sweetheart. Hold on a second."

I swallowed, the tears returning as I listened to several muffled voices and some rustling. I could barely hear Bradley's mom say, "It's Savanna, honey. Why don't you take this in the other room?"

Bradley's voice was on the other line in a heartbeat. "Savanna? What's wrong? Is something wrong?"

The sobs broke through once again. It took a few seconds to regain my composure enough to respond. "I just want you to come home."

OVER OUR SPILLED BLOOD

3 MONTHS LATER

2 // I TAKE SETH TO CLARK KENT'S FRAT HOUSE
SERENA

Seth dug the toe of her shoe into the dirt, rolling her ankle as she peered at the large Greek letters on the stone building in front of us. "This is a frat house," she complained, her fists shoved so far down her jacket pockets that she stretched the fabric.

I shrugged, moving toward the painted cement steps, my hand reaching for the metal railing. "You don't complain when we're on rooftops in the middle of the night, but as soon as I take you to a frat house on a weekday in broad daylight, you object," I teased.

She stopped messing with the lawn and huddled close to me, hissing, "The darkness gives us an advantage." Her eyes scanned the area, searching for hidden villains. Doing vigilante work with Seth was fun, but sometimes, I think she got a little too paranoid because of it.

I rolled my eyes, jogging up the first few steps. "We're not here to stake the place out. I told you. This is just a quick little visit to see an old friend. We're gonna need all the help we can get." I stopped at the top set of stairs, smiling at the names painted in purple and gold on the concrete. I tapped one of the names with my foot.

Seth scowled. "Him?"

"Yes, him," I said, annoyed with her disgust. Ever since Seth kissed me last December and I temporarily scared her off, it's been a constant battle setting boundaries. She knew I only wanted to be friends, and she'd been good about respecting that, but she wasn't always the best at hiding her jealousy. There was really nothing going on with me and this guy anyway. He liked me, sure, but nothing was ever going to happen between us if I could help it.

She followed me up the rest of the stairs to the large wooden double doors, dancing anxiously on her toes. One of the doors opened, almost smacking me in the face. Seth yanked me away just in time.

"Oh. Sorry," said a guy, blinking down at us. His apologetic expression suddenly turned to one of suspicion as he shifted the stack of books in his hand. "You two don't look like you belong here."

"We're just visiting her brother," Seth blurted out.

I rolled my eyes to the overhang. Like he was gonna believe that.

The guy smirked, his pale eyes studying me. "Who's your brother?" I racked my brain, trying to remember the rest of the names on the cement stairs. Which one sounded the most... *brown*?

I was about to answer with "Sandeep," but Seth cut me off. "Calvin Brown."

Well, at least he had Brown as his last name. As if that was going to get us anywhere. I internally groaned, trying to keep my composure innocent.

As expected, the guy wasn't buying it. "Calvin doesn't have any sisters." Yep. Should have guessed a frat brother would know that. I bet Sandeep had a sister.

"You know what? Screw this," I huffed, attempting to push past him.

He blocked my path. "No can do."

Okay, that was it. Time to stop playing nice. "You have no idea who you're dealing with!" I clenched my fist, snarling at him.

Seth tugged my arm as the guy snorted, unimpressed. "How old are you?" He glanced at my beat-up car parked at the curb. The orange paint had been flaking off for years. It was almost steel silver now, blending in with the pavement. The engine was completely unreliable, which was probably why my aunt was so eager to get rid of it. "Sixteen?"

"So what if I am?"

He shook his head, letting the door slam closed. The automatic lock clicked behind him. "Look, I'm already on probation. So why don't you and your friend skedaddle?"

Probation? What the hell did that mean? I continued to glare at him. When we didn't move, he stepped around us, heading toward the street. Seth stopped tugging.

"He's going on my list," I muttered when he was out of earshot.

Seth made a derisive noise, stuffing her hands back in her jacket. "Can you get us in or not? 'Cause I want to go home," she whined.

I waited for the guy to leave my line of sight, then quickly swept the area for other curious eyes. There was no one. And oh! I glanced at the overhang. No security cameras. Even better. Placing my hand on the door and holding my other hand out to Seth, I gritted my teeth, preparing myself for the pain.

My powers hadn't been right since, well, the *event*. Even a whole year and a half later, it still felt like my organs were being squished whenever I walked through a wall. I cringed in anticipation of the pain as I led Seth through, gasping in relief when we were inside. Seth shot me a concerned look, but I'd trained her well enough to stop asking me if I was okay. I pulled her to the right, trying to take the steps as quickly as I could without being seen. The common area had been devoid of students, but that didn't mean it would stay that way.

Calvin had told me in one of his many emails exactly where to find him if I needed him. That was back in September. Clearly, I hadn't needed him before now. To be fair, this trip wasn't about helping me. It was about crushing Priori Labs.

When we reached the upper hallway, a half-naked guy with a towel wrapped around his waist was moseying along the corridor, scrubbing his teeth furiously with a brush. All three of us froze, ogling each other, before the guy shrugged and entered a nearby room. Seth let out an audible breath. "That was close," she whispered. Thank God for towel guy's nonchalance.

Quickly, I paced five doors down, stopping in front of the fifth door on the left. "This is it," I said, rapping the knuckles of my free hand on the wood, hoping it was loud enough for him to hear but not loud enough to alert any other curious tenants.

The door opened to reveal Calvin in a polo shirt and khakis. A pair of reading glasses somehow altered the face I was once privy to seeing at least once daily in the school hallways.

"Hey there, Clark Kent." I smiled, shoving past him and into his room, continuing to tug Seth with me. Her grip tightened around my hand.

Calvin turned, removing his glasses and rubbing his eyes.

"Shell-shocked?" I asked.

He groaned, blinking rapidly. "I—What are you doing here? Don't you have school?"

"It's spring break," I said, plopping down on his messy twin bed, joining a pile of... well, I couldn't tell whether they were dirty or clean clothes. At least they were all tops. Not a pair of boxers in sight. Didn't want to tempt the ancestors in adding to their backlog of retributions for me.

Seth continued to stand, refusing to drop her guard. I appreciated her protectiveness, but she didn't seem to understand how much of a threat Calvin wasn't. "Didn't your brothers tell you?" I asked.

Calvin kicked the door shut. "To be honest, I barely know what day it is. This German class is killing me." He dropped a pencil that was behind his ear onto a stack of papers and books littering his desk.

I kept smiling. He was too easy to tease. "Es tut mir leid, ich verstehe das nicht." In English, it roughly translated to, "I'm sorry, I don't understand."

He snorted. "Of course you can't relate."

"Pays to grow up in a multilingual family."

"I *am* in a multilingual family."

"Oh, please. You can barely read Hebrew."

I knew I'd won when he landed in his swivel chair, puffing out his cheeks in exasperation. Calvin and his family were Jewish reform, but I'd heard him speak Hebrew about as much as he'd heard me speak Romanes. I found out very quickly he didn't know that either. Typical didikai.

After a few seconds of defeated silence, he asked, "So, what made you come here? And"—he turned away from us, but there were no windows that direction—"did you drive that old beater all the way here?"

I laughed. I'd sent him pictures of my car from almost every possible angle when my aunt gifted it to me back in January. He'd spent weeks teasing me. "Hey, don't make fun of Gertrude. She is clearly in distress."

"Clearly," he mocked. "But really, what's up? You're not running away from home, are you?" He eyed my hand in Seth's, which, at this point, was pretty much being crushed to death. "Or have you come to your senses and decided to let someone actually date you?"

I pulled my hand out of Seth's grasp with my powers, flexing it as she blushed profusely. "No. As a matter of fact, I'm here on a mission."

"A mission?" He reclined in his chair. "This oughta be good."

"I'm serious," I said, trying to pull Seth down on the bed with me. She refused to bend her legs properly, instead tripping sideways and nearly faceplanting on the floor. I rushed to clear some space for her, moving the bedding and clothes aside before she had time to get too mad at me. She sat in the new space as I explained, "We already have it all mapped out. All we need is people."

He must have heard something slip in my mind because, all of a sudden, he got really angry, his face turning red. "Priori Labs?" he nearly shouted. "No. Not this again." Calvin and his telepathy were the whole reason I got pulled out of the last mission against the lab. He was like a protective older brother, always getting in my way.

"No, wait." I waved my hands, trying to distract him from my thoughts. "No. This isn't about that. Well, it is, but it's not about infiltrating them or going on any suicide missions. I promise."

He still looked uneasy, but the red was starting to drain from his face. "Go on."

I took a deep breath. "Bradley's grandpa reengineered the cure for type one diabetes at the end of December. For months we've been working with diviners from around the nation who have the power to manipulate the quantity of objects. It's taking a bit longer than we'd like because we can't just use any diviner with that ability. They have to also have a working knowledge of how medicine and biology function in order to properly replicate the ingredients. We've been mass-producing this stuff right under Priori's noses. They don't know a thing."

Calvin leaned forward. His eyes narrowed. He didn't say anything, but I could tell he was impressed. My thoughts would have told him if I was lying.

I continued, "The problem now is that we can't get it FDA approved. If we try to run it through government sanctions, we'll be caught. That means we can't get it to the people who need it the most. Without the FDA's approval, it won't be covered by anyone's insurance, nor can it be distributed without a national emergency. We have to back-alley this."

"So you need bodies," Calvin inferred.

I nodded. "Bradley's grandpa's free any time this week to teach people how to properly inject the serum. But there are rules. If you see more than four cars in their driveway, just keep driving. We can't have too many diviners in one place without it looking suspicious. The captivators can sense large gatherings of power, and it'll look suspicious. His grandpa can't leave their house to meet you, either, because we're worried he'll be tracked or followed. There's a history of the Krauses threatening him, and we're trying to minimize the danger we could be putting him in. The only way Bradley's grandpa's getting in or out of their house is via teleportation, which isn't exactly a power we have access to at all times. He's here in secret, and we have to keep it that way."

Calvin narrowed his eyes, drinking in my explanation. I waited for him to nod at me and continued, "I don't think I have to say this, but no talking about this to anyone, and that includes written, text, and email correspondence. If you have a question, try to contact one of us in person. That way there's nothing to trace. We haven't seen evidence that the captivators are watching Bradley and Savanna's families, but after what happened at the football field, I'd be surprised if they weren't somehow attempting to surveil them."

Calvin swallowed, nodding, his face growing paler. "I'll try to swing by when I have some free time." He grabbed a rubber band ball from his desk and tossed it between his hands. "So, how are you planning to distribute it?"

I was prepared for the questions. Everything had to be perfect if we were going to pull this off. "Jay-Jay and

I have been working on hacking some of the largest medical databases in the country, trying to gather a list of people who've been diagnosed. Once we have that, we'll be pulling groups of diviners together. Each group will have a teleporter assigned to them. The teleporters are responsible for getting everyone where they need to be. We want to make this mission go as smoothly as possible."

Calvin stared at me for a second, dumbfounded. "You've been hacking medical databases? How are you doing that without being caught? That's extremely illegal."

I shrugged, knowing full well I was accessing information a lot of people would hate me for having. But what were the alternatives? "I already had Priori's list of insulin-receiving patients from over a year ago. It's really just a matter of getting the other insulin distributors' information. Don't worry. It's not just us. We have diviners on the inside too. In fact, we've already gifted diviner nurses and doctors with vials." Bradley's trip to Rukeli's hadn't all been for nothing. Connections to other diviners turned out to be crucial. Khayr's sister, for example, was a doctor in Chicago.

Seth spoke for the first time since we entered Calvin's room. "The only people we're not helping are the people getting diagnosed after our mission. This doesn't eradicate type one diabetes—it just cures it for the people who have it now."

I waved a hand in her direction, dismissing her comment. "We're hoping after we diminish the number of people in need of insulin, Priori and other distributors will be forced to actually distribute the cure. I mean, come on. They're villains. They'll probably just take credit for it just so they can be seen as the heroes. They have the power and the resources to do it too. They're not gonna continue to pretend the cure doesn't exist. There'll be too much proof. I mean, think about it. It's genius."

Calvin shook his head, his mouth open in awe. "Anything from your mind is automatically genius."

I smiled, smug. If there was anyone I could count on for liking my nonsuicidal plans, it was Calvin.

3 // MY BIRTHDAY SUCKS (EXCEPT FOR THE POWERS)
BLAKE

My brother's a stupid head. That was my only explanation for everything bad happening. It'd always been.

I didn't remember a time when my brother didn't mess something up. For a long time, he was never home when he was supposed to be. Dad would yell at him in the middle of the night while Jesse and I lay awake and listened. Sometimes Mom would come into our room and apologize to us. She'd read us a bedtime story and promise to bake us cookies in the morning if we slept. I always pretended, though. Who could sleep when Dad and Bradley were slamming doors?

Another time, Bradley and his friends lit a bunch of firecrackers in the backyard. It wasn't even the Fourth of July. They just wanted to blow stuff up. Dad wasn't home to tell them to stop, and Mom was running errands. They didn't quit until the cops came. After that, Mom said she wasn't allowed to leave us home alone anymore. I thought that was a good idea.

But then Bradley just spent more time at other people's houses. One time he took Paige to a party at his friend's house, and when they came back, Paige had nightmares for a year. She would wake us up with her screams almost every night. I don't really know what happened except that Mom took them both to a funeral later that week. I guess one of the pastor's kids died. But that wasn't the worst. The worst was when Bradley's friend shot Jesse. And then Jesse died too.

People died around my brother.

It's probably why I expected this to be my last birthday. Our family was always talking about how much danger we were in, and it always had to do with Bradley. I tried to pretend I wasn't listening. I played video games with my headphones on to tune out some of their words. I thought if I could pretend long enough and hard enough, the danger would pass. But now Grandma and Grandpa can't leave the house without a teleporter.

I know Grandma and Grandpa were living here for a good reason. Grandpa made the cure for type one diabetes. But everyone was desperate to give it to the people who needed it because of Bradley.

See, Bradley got his girlfriend pregnant. Apparently, the baby is some sort of super baby the bad guys want. So, everyone has been hoping if they give away the cure, the bad guys will be so distracted that they won't have the time to focus so much on the baby. Also, Mom's been wanting Bradley to take the cure so they can't mess up his insulin again. The last time they did that, Bradley made all the adults' powers disappear. If the adults can't protect us, then it would just be us fending for ourselves. And that doesn't sound good at all.

I'm not really sure how babies are made. My teacher sent a permission slip home asking my parents if they'll let me attend a meeting about puberty soon. I guess it has something to do with that, but Mom won't tell me, and Dad said as he was signing my slip that babies only happen when people love each other very much. That doesn't make sense though, because I don't understand how Bradley can love Savanna if he can't even love me. We've been brothers for all of my ten years but he's always ignoring me. He doesn't even feel like my brother.

You know who did, though? Jesse. But he isn't here. And he never will be.

Today is supposed to get me a ticket into their supersecret diviner club. Except, I'm not sure I want to be a part of it anymore. I used to feel left out, and maybe I still do, but the thing about having powers is it means I now don't have a reason to not help my brother. I don't really think I want to help my brother destroy anything else. I don't want to be the reason bad things keep happening.

Also, this birthday sucked. It sucked less than last year, but it still sucked. Most people have friends to invite to their parties, but I don't have any. Not since Bradley made our family move all the way to Indiana. Diviners usually throw huge parties, especially on their tenth birthday, but again, because of Bradley, we weren't allowed to have so many diviners in one place. Not even the Lindts come over as one big family anymore. It's usually only a couple of them at a time. So I'm stuck with the people who live in my house, which isn't special.

I remember Paige's tenth birthday party. The house was so full of people, we could barely walk around. The backyard was almost just as bad. It was both chaos and energy. I remember the police showing up. After that, the volume in the house lowered. There were a few diviners out back who started shouting about freedom. People gathered around the bonfire as a man made Paige stand on a chair, demanding we celebrate her as loudly as we wanted.

"Make some noise," he rallied.

Then people started screaming and throwing stuff. A fight even broke out about who could scream the loudest. Some of them hit and kicked and threw punches at each other, and nobody broke it up. They just cheered them on and gave advice on how to throw a better punch.

Mom was always telling us not to fight, so it blew my mind that she was letting these boys beat the crap out of each other. When I asked her about it, she just said that it was an honorable fight. That the reason they were fighting wasn't to harm each other, even though they both came out with broken skin and bruises. I didn't understand it. I still don't. But if I could have a party like Paige's, then maybe I would.

The front door opened, but I barely looked from my video game to see who it was. I already knew it was Bradley coming home from his job at Wich Wharf. Dad had made him get a job back in January, which didn't turn out to be hard because one of the two diviner families that moved here after the news about the baby broke owned a chain of sandwich shops.

Bradley had been working the lunch shift instead of his usual afternoons during spring break, so he'd missed a good chunk of the "party."

"Any powers yet?" he asked when he passed me. I shook my head, pressing a few buttons on my controller to dodge an attack. The thing about diviners getting their powers on their tenth birthday was that the timing wasn't an exact science. Some diviners woke up with new abilities. Some didn't get them till right before they went to bed.

Something landed over my hands. I moved to get rid of it so I could focus on my game.

"The Porters made you a card," he said.

Those were the people who ran Wich Wharf. I didn't understand why they called it that. What the heck was a wharf anyway?

The Porters moved here from New Orleans. I guess their original shop was once a front for a safe house before Hurricane Katrina, which was how Maria knew about them. She was the one who sent them here. Well, them and the Sullys. The Sullys were from San Diego. I think she chose them because both families had a daughter Bradley's age, and she wanted them to keep an eye on him. Again, another change caused by Bradley.

I paused my game, tossing the controller onto Rebecca's lap. She had the card in her hand, but I didn't look at it. "Mom said we could have cake when you got home. I want cake." I stood, but Bradley was blocking my way.

"Savanna called." He dangled his new flip phone in my face, holding it by the strap. "She said you were rude to her."

I shoved him, and he stumbled a step. It was just enough that I could pass by.

"Hey!" He followed me to the kitchen. "If you have a problem with me, take it up with me. Don't take it out on Savanna."

"Is that why she left?" Mom entered from the dining room, smiling at me. "Need me to cut the cake?" I nodded and she reached for a knife before eyeing Bradley. "She told me her father was on his way home." My family started to gather around us, sensing cake was about to be served.

"Her dad's down in Greenwood all day for an open house," Bradley told Mom. "She called me in tears because Blake told her she didn't belong here."

"I didn't say that," I argued, grabbing the first plate of chocolate cake. "Mom said only family could come, and she's not family."

"Blake," Mom warned, but I shoved the biggest bite of cake in my mouth so she couldn't have a conversation with me.

Bradley stared at me with his jaw half-dropped. Then he swung around to face Paige, who was standing behind him. "You consider Savanna family, don't you?"

Sage answered instead. "In a found family sort of way, sure."

Paige scoffed. "I would if you'd marry her."

I rolled my eyes, swallowing the chunk of cake. Paige thinks everybody should be married.

Mom pointed the tip of her knife at them. "Nobody is getting married. I don't even want to see a ring until you turn eighteen. That goes for both of you."

"Well, that's hypocritical!" Paige shouted, waving her arm. "You and Dad got engaged when you were seventeen."

Mom lowered the knife, placing it on the counter. She looked down, taking a deep breath. "Your father and I have talked about this. That is the agreement we made. That is not meant to trap you. That is not meant to control you. That is not meant to punish you. We want you to be able to stay kids, and while that isn't proving to be possible, the least we can do is refuse to sign marriage consent forms. It's illegal in this state to get married as a minor without parental approval, and we will uphold that. That is not changing for any circumstance." Her eyes flickered to Bradley before she grabbed the knife again. "Now who else wants cake?"

Paige crossed her arms, bobbing her head from side to side. "Well, I'm marrying Kevin as soon as I'm eighteen."

Sage snorted. "In your dreams." Paige shot her a look and Sage explained, "You just started dating last week. Also, I'm pretty sure he only agreed to go out with you because he feels bad for you."

"Take that back," Paige snapped. Something smashed against a wall in the living room, shattering. From what I could see, it looked like a vase.

"Girls," Mom warned. Sage grabbed a plate and stormed off. Mom eyed Paige. "Maybe we need to do some meditation after this." Seth nodded enthusiastically, swiveling her head between the two.

Paige glanced at the wall. "I'm fine," she muttered, stretching her hands. "Totally fine." She didn't sound fine.

I took another bite of my cake as Rebecca walked to where the vase had broken and waved her hand over it. The pieces floated back together as if they were never apart. She picked the vase up and set it on the coffee table.

"I will not blow up the house. I will not blow up the house," someone said. It sounded like Paige but somehow different, like she was speaking in an echo chamber. I looked at her. She was still staring at the wall, flexing her hands. Her mouth was closed.

"God, I hope she doesn't crack again," someone else's voice echoed. Who was that? I looked around the room, searching for moving mouths, but the only person speaking was Bradley, who was asking for a smaller piece of cake. I caught Seth staring at Paige, her nails digging into her crossed arms. Had she said it?

"Cake, cake, cake." This time the words came with an image of my birthday cake before it had been cut. I looked down to see Tuesday making her way to Mom. Her lips were moving. She was actually speaking those words.

"What if Savanna and I got married?" Bradley's voice took over. "She would be like family. She already is family. I mean, how could she not be? She's carrying my child. At the very least, that's honorary. Who am I kidding? I'm fifteen, I'm not even old enough. I can't even work more than three hours on a school day. Besides, I can't picture us married. I mean, I want to, but I can't even picture us with a kid, which is mind-boggling because that's actually happening. I'm not gonna be a good father. I'm not. We both know it. We can't be parents. We don't want to be parents. And if we can't be parents, then we definitely can't be married. Or do I have that backward? Whatever. It doesn't matter. That's not my focus right now. It can't be." His voice faded as he walked into the dining room. He wouldn't say that all out loud, would he? Nobody commented on it.

"I think your grandparents are still taking a nap." Mom sighed, putting the knife down. Her mouth stopped moving before more words echoed in her voice. "I don't want them to miss Blake getting his powers. It would be such a wonderful opportunity for them. They never got to see the others get theirs." She wiped the frosting off the knife.

Paige pushed past Seth to grab a plate, then marched off to the dining room. "Rude," someone said. Seth did the same without the pushing-past-anyone part. After a few seconds, everyone had gone into another room except Mom and me.

I put my plate down. Most of my cake was gone. "M-mom?" I asked, unsure of myself. I was expecting to feel pain when I got my powers, but there was nothing. Bradley had been in pain when he got his. Rebecca had screamed when hers came in. Surely this wasn't it. "C-can you think of something?"

Mom froze for a split second before setting the newly cleaned knife down. "Sure, honey. What do you want me to think about? A color? A number?" She leaned over the counter, propping her elbow so her hand could hold her head. The color blue flashed in my mind, then the number *64*.

"Uh," I said, hesitating.

"Is he trying to read my mind?" I heard. "Did he hear something? Oh God, this is it. I can't believe Chastain is missing this. His parents are missing this!" Her eyes glanced at the ceiling as she thought this, but then she looked back at me and smiled encouragingly.

I sighed. Maybe it would be better if I waited until Grandma and Grandpa woke up and Dad got home from work so they wouldn't have to miss it. I could pretend I was hearing thoughts for the first time then. I shook my head. "Never mind."

I started to walk away, but her voice called out to me. "Blake, can you read my mind?" I froze, then slowly turned around.

Mom's smile was as wide as her face. "I know you heard that."

Dang it. She tricked me. "Y-you didn't say that out loud?" I asked.

She shook her head. "My baby boy is all grown up."

4 // GRANDPA TEACHES SAVANNA TO STAB AN ORANGE
BRADLEY

Grandpa had pulled a living room chair to the front room a few days ago, and he now sat relaxed, his back to the curtained windows. When diviners first started showing up for his lessons, he positioned himself on the carpet. It took four of us to get him back on his feet. After that, we'd made him sit in an actual chair.

Savanna and Ursula had perched themselves on the love seat. I watched from the corner as Savanna tentatively picked up an orange from the coffee table. Ursula already had one, tossing it between her hands.

"We use oranges for this lesson because the peel works a lot like human skin. It protects the fruit. Now, what I want you to do is take a syringe"—Grandpa picked one up from the pile he'd arranged on the table—"and hold it at a ninety-degree angle against the orange." Ursula eagerly reached for one, holding it at a thirty-degree angle. Grandpa waved his hand. "No, no. A ninety-degree angle. That means straight."

Ursula held the syringe away from her orange. "If it means straight, then why did you use the word angle?"

"Because it's still an angle, sweetheart," Grandpa replied, diving into a mini math lesson as he demonstrated a variety of angles, eventually explaining the need for the syringe to form an angle like a square against the orange. This only confused Ursula further, since the orange was round and had no straight edges.

Savanna hadn't even tried. Her eyes were on me, but her gaze seemed distant. I knew she was worried about going back to school on Monday after a two-week break. She had lost a lot when the news started spreading at the end of January. She was let go from the cheerleading squad, which was what had spurred a lot of the gossip. Now she was barely speaking to most of the other cheerleaders, including her friend Angela. I think the biggest thing that was bothering her, though, was how people suddenly looked and treated her differently. Before all this, her teachers admired her motivation and willingness to learn. They respected her kindness and generosity. She was who some people would call Miss Perfect. Now everyone looked at her with pity, treating her like she'd lost her potential. She was a cautionary tale whispered in the hallways or a product of a poorly built system... instead of an actual human being. I'd heard on more than one occasion a snide remark about us being Romani. As if that had anything to do with it. It wasn't like Savanna was the only pregnant person in school, but that didn't seem to matter. Maybe it was because people didn't expect this for her. As if some of the others somehow deserved it because they did drugs or slept around. It wasn't like people didn't say things to me too, but I saw the inequality in how people treated us. If I didn't see it, I heard about it. Because of that, I knew how much worse it was for her.

The administration had us in a Teens as Parents class, TAPs being the acronym. It was full of other teens who had or were having a baby and operated more as a support group than anything. We would have joined at the beginning of the semester, but Savanna hadn't been ready to tell people. In hindsight, it was obvious why. She wanted to hold all the judgment at bay for as long as she could. But when Savanna fell at cheer practice one day in late January, Marcie panicked and spilled the secret to their coach, who told Savanna she couldn't keep her on the team for safety reasons. That's when the gossip spread through the school like wildfire. That was when we transferred to the class.

TAPs is awkward for me. Mostly because it's full of girls who often tell horror stories about their babies' fathers, some of whom were older and out of high school. There was only me and one other guy in the class, which further proved their points about men. I don't blame them. It's easy to look at our situations and want to run far away. Maybe it's easier for undivine men to leave because leaving seems to erase the responsibility. There are few reminders of what has happened. But for the divine, we experience a break in our ability to use our powers correctly that lasts as long as the pregnancy. It's like the baby drains Savanna of her abilities then actively tries to take mine, as if it doesn't get enough juice from its mother. My dad isn't a diviner, so I didn't know anything happened to guys too until it was happening to me. To make things worse, since Savanna and I are fated, if I purposefully tried to leave, I started experiencing obnoxious symptoms like uncontrollable coughing or nausea or pain. Running wasn't a choice for me.

But I didn't feel trapped. I mean, yeah, I felt like we were at a standstill or an impasse where there was nothing we could really do but wait for the inevitable. In a way, I felt trapped because we were sitting ducks with go bags prepared not for sudden hospital visits but in case we needed to run. But being here with Savanna… this wasn't a trap. I'm scared as hell. But the side effects were never keeping me from leaving. The fierce, strong, and smart woman sitting across the room from me was more than just some girl I fell in love with. She was my anchor. Or… she had been.

I still don't really know what to do about our situation. It's not something I can undo. We never officially got back together either, and I think all this drama was why. Everything's been so awkward the last few months. Whatever I've tried didn't seem to make her feel better. Somewhere along the way, she lost the ability to trust or rely on me. I've tried to keep myself open and available, but lately, all our conversations seemed to be one-sided. She needed someone to vent to. So I listened.

We couldn't feel each other's feelings like we had before. Not in the literal sense, anyway. So she couldn't feel the love I still had for her, which was probably why I was glad Grandpa had reengineered the serum amid all this. It was the only thing big enough to distract us.

Well, it was distracting for me. Savanna didn't seem all that focused.

She twiddled a syringe in her hand, gazing at the clear liquid inside. It wasn't anything important. Just water. But still, something about it caught her attention. She frowned, blinked, and cleared her throat. "Um, Mr. Chambers?"

Grandpa looked up from a syringe he was filling. "Darlin', you can call me Grandpa. We're practically family." I leaned my head against the wall. At least *some*one considered her family.

She shifted uncomfortably on the couch, running her full hands against the length of her dress, trying to pull it closer to her knees. She gave up, the fabric bouncing back to her midthighs. "Is diabetes genetic?"

I flinched at her question. I couldn't help it. I hadn't thought of the possibility that the baby might inherit certain things from me. Probably because I barely thought of it as my child. I was too busy seeing it as a force of diviner nature or another Maria to really consider it as anything else.

Grandpa set his syringe and vial of water on the table. "Does it matter?" He gestured to all the supplies. "Granddaughter." Her blue eyes misted at the title. I already knew that her own grandfather refused to speak to her. Not that she saw him that much anyway. Grandpa leaned forward, and Savanna shoved the syringe against the orange to free her hand. She wiped at the tears. "You are a spectacular joy. To answer your question, yes, it *can* be genetic, but lots of factors come into play. Tons of people develop diabetes with no history of it in their family tree. On the off chance, God forbid, our entire operation crumbles, we lose access to the cure, and your baby has it, we'll just have to play this old-school."

"But…" Now her chin was trembling. I peeled myself from the wall, preparing to comfort her, although my stomach churned. Savanna had an unsettling habit of making diabetes sound extremely undesirable. And not like how I thought of it—the needles and the carb counting—as undesirable, but how others saw it. Like it was a negative trait. Like if they could choose between me and a version of me without the illness… let's just say I wouldn't be the first choice.

Tears streaked down her cheeks. "That's not what I meant. I'm sorry. I just…"

I stopped walking, waiting for her to explain. She sucked in a tiny breath, then blew it back out. "I'm not afraid of this baby dying. They can't die."

Reality hit me. I'd forgotten for a second that even if the baby developed diabetes, they would never die from it. In fact, diabetes was the least of their problems, if it was even possible for them to have it.

"I'm just"—Savanna paused to gulp—"I want to be aware of the things that could cause them pain so I can tell whoever's going to be taking care of them when I'm gone."

My heart skipped a beat. When she's gone? We'd been fiddling with the idea of adoption, but I thought we had agreed it was impractical, especially since we couldn't go through a legitimate agency. It was too much of a risk to place the baby in an undivine home that couldn't protect it. The best protection we had was Rebecca and Maria, although I suspected Maria would stop being useful the second the baby was born.

Ursula shot her sister a piercing stare. "Don't say that."

Savanna turned her attention to her sister, her vocal pitch shooting higher. "I'm just trying to be realistic!"

"No, you're trying to be a martyr!" her sister shouted, standing, her fists at her sides. "You're acting like you and Bradley are the walking dead!"

This wasn't about adoption at all. "Wait." I finally inserted myself into the conversation. I waited for Savanna to meet my eyes, but she didn't. Instead, she dug her nails into the orange peel. "You think we're gonna die?"

Grandpa looked from me to Savanna, his expression uncertain.

Savanna took a while to answer me as she peeled the fruit. "I think the countdown started the second the condom broke."

It felt like someone had reached their hand inside my gut, grabbed whatever organ they could find first, and tugged. Hard. I shouldn't have confessed that to her. I knew it was just gonna be held against me. I'd apologized numerous times for not knowing condoms expire or that they broke when you kept them someplace warm like a pocket or a wallet for too long. It wasn't like anyone had given either of us a lesson on proper condom usage and storage. Adults always just said, "Be sure to use a condom," and then hoped for the best. Everyone on television seemed to keep one in their wallet, so... that was what I did. And besides, I thought it hadn't broken until I was trying to take it off. But if her doctor's math was correct, that was the day it happened—the Saturday before Thanksgiving break. This was my fault.

"We're not gonna die," I said, seething as I fought myself to stay in the room. My hands shook. "Maria said she wasn't gonna let us die."

"Maria isn't even going to be immortal in a few months!" Savanna shouted, slamming the orange and the syringe on the coffee table. "She can't protect us!" It took her a few seconds to stand, but when she was upright, her blue eyes bore into mine—angry and fierce. She took a step toward me. When I automatically backstepped, she paused. "We're gonna be dead by the end of the year, and you need to accept that."

I set my jaw, glaring back at her. I knew what this was about. For months, Savanna had been rejecting any help that had come our way. She didn't like to feel weak or helpless. And yet, diviners still flocked to her, insisting they'd protect her. It was practically Alyssa Sully's and Victoria Porter's job. Their families traveled halfway across the country to act as backup. Everybody else was either family or close friends who, as always, had no intention of letting anybody die. All the other diviners? They only cared about us because the baby carried the life force and abilities of the next generation of diviners. Without that baby, diviners would cease to exist. Everyone cared more about the baby than they did about us.

"What do they have to be worried about?" Savanna had complained one day, pacing our living room. "The baby is immortal." While the baby's immortality wasn't going to run out, at least, not for another sixty or so years, ours had a much sooner expiration date. And yet, the main goal—the one everybody was invested in—wasn't to keep us alive. The main goal was keeping the baby out of our enemies' hands. Still, Maria had insisted our lives would be protected. We would be cared about too. But even I knew we were an afterthought. We would come second.

Grandpa stood, rounding his chair to stand in between us, holding out his hands. "Kids—"

"I'm not a kid," Savanna snapped, breaking our eye contact to turn her furious gaze on him.

Grandpa hesitated, studying her for a second. Most adults would have argued with her like they'd been doing since December. At first, she'd agreed with them. We were too young. We were just kids. But the further she got in the pregnancy, the less she seemed to believe that. After all, most kids didn't have babies.

As if on cue, Hanna popped in, gasping in exhilaration from wherever she had come from. She fanned herself excitedly. "Philadelphia can officially be checked off our list." She ran to the wall dividing the front room from the dining room, having to bypass Ursula. Sage and Alyssa had spent countless hours creating a checklist of the country's two hundred largest cities, barely fitting them all on a large section of stick-on whiteboard paper. Hanna couldn't reach Philadelphia to cross it off. Paige and the twins had been crossing off the cities at the top of the list telekinetically. When she realized it, she spun on her heels. "One hundred and five hospitals. Can you believe it? It took *forever.*" She flopped onto the couch, exhausted.

Grandpa was still focused on our predicament. He cleared his throat, nodding. "Okay." His eyes darted between us. "I know neither of you signed up for this. I know what y'all are going through is real tough. But I don't want either of you biting each other's heads off. That ain't gon' solve the problem. I don't know much about this diviner stuff, but I know what you've been handed is an impossible situation that you have little control over. What you do have control over is how you treat each other, how you talk to each other, and how you treat yourself up in here." He pointed to his temple. "I don't want anyone worryin' 'bout death when y'all got a life to live. Right now," he clapped his hands, rubbing them together the way my dad always did when he was eager to get something done. "We got a job to do. We got somethin' we *can* control. We got lives we *know* we can save. We can't do all that with you two arguin' 'bout the future. We gotta focus on the present. So let's learn how to administer this cure. Let's save one point six million people in the comin' weeks."

Grandpa nodded to Hanna, acknowledging her announcement. "I know it doesn't look it, but one hundred and five is some real progress."

The twelve-year-old's face lit up. "I know! We've already supplied more than four hundred hospitals, but according to Serena, it's only six percent in the country. Also, the San Diego safe house is working on disguising the cure as insulin and making it look like it's coming from their normal suppliers. So not only are we curing the people who are actually in the hospitals, but we'll be helping people in their own homes, and they won't even know it." She jumped out of her slump, suddenly energetic again. "Khayr also wants to find a way to help homeless people with diabetes. He thinks we're missing a lot of them on our lists. But don't worry. He's got ideas. That reminds me." She grabbed an untouched orange from the coffee table and peeled it with her fingers. "I gotta go meet one of the San Antonio groups." In an instant, she disappeared.

Ursula's upper lip curled into a sneer. "Are they shooting coffee directly into her veins now?"

Nobody answered as Savanna glumly sat back on the couch and picked up her abandoned orange and syringe. "Ninety-degree angle?" She asked tiredly, holding the needle correctly against the fruit.

Grandpa nodded. "Yes, dear. Then you…" He trailed off, watching her draw the plunger back a little to reveal she hadn't drawn blood, or fruit juice in this case. "Now," he reminded, "some doctors have stopped doing that part because I guess there have been some new studies about aspirations being unnecessary, but I was always trained to aspirate." She nodded and slowly pushed the practice water inside. Grandpa gaped at her. "I was under the impression you needed lessons."

She shrugged, setting the empty syringe and the orange back on the table. "I've watched Bradley do it a million times, although the angle thing is different."

5 // TELEPORTING DOESN'T AGREE WITH ME
SERENA

Mya and I never looked like sisters. She's a miniature version of Mom with her light brown hair and emerald eyes and has a habit of trying to convince people that we're anything but Romani. Just last week, I heard her friend ask what it was like when we lived in Cuba. Cuba! We're Americans for crying out loud. We haven't even been outside the country. To top it off, Mya, who doesn't speak a lick of Spanish, just went with it. She didn't even blink. She just made up an entire story, spewing some bullshit about communism and Fidel Castro. I don't even know how she learned about Fidel Castro. She's twelve.

"I'm almost thirteen," she'd said to our parents before we left. I had rolled my eyes. If anything, her reminder only hurt her argument. Mya had been begging them for weeks to let her try out for next year's eighth grade cheerleading team. I thought maybe she might have an inkling of a chance at convincing them if the whole thing with Bradley and Savanna hadn't happened. But now the chances weren't even slim. They were zero. Negative.

Mom already had a problem with girls kicking their legs high. It's like she lives in the nineteenth century, always complaining about parents who let their daughters, I don't know, do things they actually enjoy. When Mya tried to use history to her advantage by talking about the cancan dance, I knew she was in for it.

"That dance was invented by prostitutes!" Mom had whisper-shouted.

"And now it's a piece of world culture," Mya had argued. I had rolled my eyes, prompting a glare from my sister. "Back me up on this."

I shook my head. Mom was one of the most stubborn people I knew. Plus, I knew how her mind worked. If she'd said anything more to Mya about that dance, she'd say it promoted… *things*, because Mom never liked to use the word sex. Then she'd get in a tizzy about how the gadje world invites immorality, as if sex and immorality had anything to do with each other. Mom never tried to get in the way of her students' business. In fact, she would smile and listen to their complaints and give advice. But if it was one of her own children coming to her about the same problems or complaints, her reaction always made it seem like the world was about to end.

I figured Mya would know this, considering she was the telepath and not me, but she just kept throwing argument after argument back at Mom until Mom finally said what was really bothering her. "You are not going to end up like that Huckleberry girl!"

That Huckleberry girl. Mom couldn't even say her first name. Somehow, Mom had gotten it in her head that Savanna being a cheerleader is what led to her getting pregnant at fifteen. I was pretty sure it had more to do with her being head over heels obsessed with our idiot godbrother. I always thought they were having sex, but Bradley was tight-lipped about it to the point where I was beginning to think he was asexual because what guy doesn't brag about having sex?

"Why does Mom have to make everything I want to do sound like it's a gateway drug to being a slut?" Mya groaned, kicking at the turf on the high school football field as we waited for the rest of our group to meet us.

I ignored her, catching sight of Victoria Porter's car pulling into the parking lot near the entrance. If I had the power to change Mom's mind, I'd be allowed to do all sorts of things I wasn't supposed to. Now I just did them in secret.

Victoria stepped out of her silver sedan, her tall black platform boots making her look like a giant. I was surprised to see Rebecca step out of the passenger's side, considering Mrs. Chambers wasn't exactly a fan of the Porters. It was something about Mr. Porter being a little too snoopy about her business, but to an outsider, it was easy to assume her annoyance with them was because the Porters are witches. Technically, Victoria's dad is the only one of them who is a witch in the literal magic-making sense. But still, Victoria dresses the part—all goth and slightly scary. Reds and blacks seemed to be the only colors of clothing she owned. Her box braids even had little red beads in them. As Afro-Romanies, they all had a little bit of magic woven into their practices. We all did, even if we didn't all call or consider it magic.

As they approached, I felt a rush of cold air behind me and swung around to see my ex holding hands with a blond-haired, green-eyed twentysomething stranger. My heart skipped a beat as heat rushed to my cheeks. I was expecting Hanna to guide us, not a handsome older guy.

"Who's your boyfriend?" I asked Kase, eyeing the stranger's shirt. It seemed to cling to what I assumed were impeccable abs.

Kase reached for my hand, ignoring my implication. "This is Remy. He's from the Atlanta safe house."

Instead of taking Kase's hand, I reached for Remy's. He smiled, nodding his head politely. "Hello. Nice to meet you."

My jaw nearly dropped to the floor. I was expecting a Southern accent if anything, but instead, his words flitted out his mouth in a clipped British or Australian. As Mya grabbed my hand, I stomped her foot, meaning to hit Kase's. My eyes flashed to him. "Liar."

"Ow!" Mya slipped her foot from under mine, hopping on her left for a few seconds.

"I'm not *lying*," Kase insisted, leaning forward.

"No way's he from Atlanta."

Remy glanced between us. "I'm from New Zealand, actually."

New Zealand? God, I loved his accent.

His eyes followed Victoria and Rebecca as they made their way across the field. "Am I the only adult in this group?"

I winked, swinging our arms. "Teenagers run this city. It's the only way we get anything done around here."

Kase thought he had to correct me. "Not true. They just outnumber the adults."

I glared at him. He didn't even live here anymore.

Rebecca reached us first, rushing to join hands with Mya. Victoria was in no rush, dragging her feet like we weren't on a time crunch. I turned to Remy, trying to make conversation. "So, what's the plan?"

Remy swung his large leather satchel from around his back to his left side, removing the top to show me the inside. It was full of vials and syringes and little notecards someone had spent an ungodly amount of time furnishing with light blue and silver ribbons. "There are thirty-three hospitals in the San Antonio area. We're in charge of six. We're finding we have more luck convincing doctors than patients. You would be surprised how many endocrinologists have believed us. We've had to switch tactics since some diviners had been met with resistance from patients who thought we were drugging them. The endocrinologists understand the research more." He tapped at a handful of pamphlets stuffed between the edge of the bag and a carton of vials. He gazed at the five of us, Victoria having reached us by then. "I'm concerned, though, that they're not going to believe a group of teenagers." His green eyes stopped on Rebecca, the youngest of our group.

Victoria snorted, digging a small velvet pouch out of her pocket and dangling it by the strings. "Why do you think I brought this?" We all stared at it, confused. How was a bag of… was that a hex bag? Yeah, how was a hex bag going to help us convince anyone to believe us? She stuffed it back in her pocket. "Don't look at me like that. It's just a bag of persuasion dust."

Mya's green eyes widened. "Wait. Persuasion dust? That's a thing?" She let go of my hand and Rebecca's, eagerly reaching for the bag before it disappeared. "Can it convince my parents to let me cheerlead?"

I grabbed her hand, yanking her back, but her eyes were focused on Victoria's pocket.

Victoria shrugged. "Sure."

"There's gotta be a catch," I said, narrowing my eyes. People with that much magic at their fingertips would surely be ruling the world if it were that easy.

Victoria reached for Rebecca and Kase's hands to complete our circle, smiling crookedly. "It doesn't work on the same person twice." In an instant, she disappeared from sight.

My gut was tugged and twisted as if someone had shoved their fist inside me and was moving it around. I screamed at the nothingness that enveloped me. Colors swirled around the black spots in my vision. Bile rose in my esophagus, burning my chest and throat as my lungs lost their ability to gasp for air. I realized we must have been teleporting because when I struggled to wrench myself loose, my feet only hit air. I panicked, gripping the hands that held me tighter to keep myself from falling.

I'd once read somewhere that when people get electrocuted, their muscles seize up. They're unable to let go of the thing that is killing them. That was what this felt like. If I let go, I'd be dropped to my death, but if I didn't, I'd die anyway.

The wind stopped, and I tumbled onto the pavement, screaming. I was barely able to feel my skin scrape the cement over the agony that twisted my insides. My stomach lurched, vomit pouring out of me. If anyone had told me teleporting was going to be like that, I wouldn't have agreed to come.

Feet skittered away from me, then toward me. I heard Victoria's voice first. "Jesus."

"Are you okay?" Mya asked, her hands trying to turn me toward her.

I pulled away, clutching my stomach, my screams turning into airy sobs as I struggled to catch my breath. I kept my head down, trying to angle it away from the vomit as well as the prying eyes. Nobody else had felt that, I realized, struggling to gather my thoughts. I shoved my fingers against my cheeks and lips, rubbing the tears and vomit away. I was tired of being the weak link. I was not getting kicked off this mission.

Sucking in a deep breath, I stood, waving away anyone who tried to help. "I'm fine."

Remy didn't look like he knew what to say as he stammered. "I-I think… m-maybe… w-we should…" He glanced at the others, his eyes begging for guidance.

I crossed my arms. "Sucks to be the only adult, doesn't it?" God, I hated that I had just puked my guts out in front of this New Zealand hottie.

Remy cleared his throat, his eyebrows angrily drawn against each other. "We should keep you stationary for a while. I'll assign you and"—he scanned the group, before pointing to my sister—"her to this hospital."

I glanced at the sign, which had the name of the hospital in large silver letters. When I looked back, Victoria had her arm extended, a black satchel materializing in her grip. It looked just like Remy's, with the exception of the gloomy color. She dropped it to the concrete, then held her free hand to create another one of her little velvet bags. When I didn't make a move to grab the satchel, Mya did, inching toward Remy so he could fill it with supplies while Victoria sprinkled a bit of her magic dust into the new bag.

"Don't let the wind catch it," she said, "or there'll be trouble." She smiled cheekily through her makeup, holding the pouch out to me. I snatched it, grumbling my thanks.

Remy handed a piece of paper and a few pamphlets to me as Mya covered the satchel. "Dr. Gil Crawford is the head of internal medicine here. I'd start with him. Who knows? This could be a short stop." I glanced at the list of patients I'd previously pulled from the database. It was unlikely most of them were still here. Whoever's idea it was to go to the doctors instead, well, kudos to them. "We'll meet you back here when we're done."

Remy and the others huddled together, joining hands. I tried to catch Kase's eye, but he was ogling Victoria in the way that he used to ogle me. I guess goth chic really turned some guys on. I scowled. Dating her would mean he would be dating someone his own height, and that bothered me. Victoria was a literal upgrade.

I blinked. In an instant they were gone, leaving me with a growing sense of unease. Out of the corner of my eye, I caught Mya reaching for the pouch. I yanked it away. "No way. I don't trust you with this stuff. If we don't end up using it, you're gonna waste it all on Mom and Dad for that stupid cheerleading obsession you have."

"It's not stupid," Mya whined, stomping her feet.

I rolled my eyes, spinning to face the hospital entrance. Here went nothing.

Mya followed me to the front desk where I asked if I could speak to Dr. Crawford.

"Do you have an appointment?" the receptionist asked, staring sternly through their thick glasses.

I stood my ground, attempting to remain confident. "Yes. Yes, I do."

The receptionist turned to their computer, tapping a few buttons on their keyboard. "Name?"

I glanced at Mya. Lying was so much easier when I had a telepath on my side. My sister's forehead scrunched for a second before her green eyes brightened. "Ariel Graham," her voice echoed in my mind.

I forced a smile, leaning over the desk and repeating the name. The receptionist nodded, pressing a few more buttons, then pointed in the direction of a waiting room. "I'll page him to let him know you're here."

We walked to the waiting room—an area that looked more like a doctor's office waiting room than the ones I'd seen in hospitals. Maybe it was because we weren't in the emergency wing.

"I didn't know doctors actually had offices inside hospitals," Mya noted. "I thought this was a place people go for last resorts."

I read the plaque on the wall that listed all the doctors in the wing, noting their specialties. "I think these are all specialists. People probably need a referral to see them." I remembered some of the doctors I'd seen in Indianapolis after my surgery and again after my "mental health crisis." Some of them had offices, but most of the time, they had met me at my bedside.

Mya stared at the large cross on the wall with a red ribbon swirling around it. "Is that supposed to bring good fortune?"

"What do you mean?" I asked, wishing I were the telepath instead of her.

She frowned. "Don't a lot of bad things happen here? Like, people die in hospitals all the time. It's full of sick people and bad energy. Is the cross supposed to offset that somehow? Like, clearly it doesn't heal people, but I don't know, does it suck some of the bad energy out?"

I studied it more closely, pondering her theory. Our parents preferred the idea of angels over crosses. Little cherub figurines were displayed in many corners of our house. To them, angels meant more in the means of protection than the God or "savior" who was continually used as an excuse to harm our people. Our parents believed in God, sure, but in an agnostic way. They placed their faiths more in superstition than anything. God was not generous in my experience. They did not always heal the sick. They let people die. When they didn't let them die, they let them suffer. And yet, there this cross was, its weight on the wall somehow equal to the weight of an ominous sensation around me, like I was being watched somehow. It was rude, really. A god sitting on their throne, watching the world devolve into chaos and doing nothing. I guess that was why we were here. It was *our* job to do something to help stop the anarchy.

Dr. Crawford didn't enter the waiting area for a while. When he did, I already had the persuasion dust in the palm of my hand ready to go. I refused to waste any more time in this place. Holding my palm face up, I stood on the chair, blowing the dust in the doctor's face. He blinked in confusion as I dusted my hands. "We're here to deliver the new cure for type one diabetes." I motioned for Mya to hand him the stuff as I leapt to the floor. I grabbed a pamphlet of information. "It's gone through all the necessary testing," I began, opening the pamphlet and pointing to the brief explanation of the serum's history from the eighties. "I suggest you start administering it to any patients who may need it." I handed him the pamphlet as he nodded, his mouth agape, his eyes in a daze. I started to walk away but turned on my heel. I wasn't sure how long the dust would last before he stopped taking suggestions from me. Victoria had said it only worked once. Did that mean he would only do one thing I told him? Or did that mean I had a set time to convince him of everything I needed to convince him of? "Oh, and I wouldn't charge for it. God knows"—I pointed to the cross on the wall—"these people have spent enough money on this disease."

I backed away, letting him process the information. Mya left the bag behind, rushing to follow me out the nearest exit. When we were outside, I heaved a huge sigh of relief. Now all we had to do was wait for Remy to return with our next assignment.

6 // I Wait for My Islet Cells to Regenerate
BRADLEY

We were sitting at our usual lunch table in the cafeteria once again debating the pros and cons of me taking the diabetes cure. Savanna was trying to use the old "what affects you affects me" excuse, although she had grumbled it half-heartedly, her chin in her hands. There was a time when Savanna would have probably injected the cure in me herself when I was off my guard. I mean, the fact that we had the cure in the first place was because she'd stolen a vial from one of Priori Lab's lawyers. I'd always thought she'd done it for selfish reasons. She wanted me cured because she cared about herself. But I knew she cared about me.

My diabetes wasn't something that affected her. Even with our connection, she didn't experience my symptoms. She never felt my highs or lows. If my pain was significant, she could sometimes feel it, but a single needle prick? A quick blood sugar check? Nothing.

It was the same when she was on her period. I didn't feel her cramps or anything else people feel when that happens. These had been some of the exceptions to our connection. With the pregnancy, everything was now irrelevant. There wasn't a physical, emotional, or telepathic connection affecting us at all. She knew that. I knew she knew that. My diabetes wasn't her problem. Taking the cure was all on me.

Would my diabetes still physically affect her if it killed me? All this time, we'd been told either of our deaths would end the other's life. But was that still a thing while Savanna was pregnant? I mean, we were both basically self-healing. Sort of. If only the whole healing thing would work on my pancreas, I wouldn't have to make the decision at all.

Don't get me wrong. I wanted to take the cure. I wanted to have a working pancreas. I wanted to stop having to wear my continuous glucose monitor and insulin pump. I'd take the cure in a heartbeat just to stop having to worry about my blood sugar levels every damn second of my life. So it's hard to explain why I hadn't yet taken it.

Maybe it was because people were constantly trying to make my issue their issue. It was like they all wanted me to take the cure so they didn't have to feel responsible for me anymore. They made me feel like a burden. Maybe it was spite, but the more they made me feel that way, the more I wanted them to stay feeling that way.

Dr. Lamb thought I was punishing myself. "Do you think you might not be taking the cure because you don't feel like you deserve it?" she'd asked in our last session.

Ugh. *Deserve.* There was that pesky little word that kept popping up in our sessions. Even Frank had used that word with me on multiple occasions. I'd learned over the last year and a half of therapy that my C-PTSD made it difficult for me to have self-compassion. I never really understood it. How did self-compassion get anyone anywhere? How did they learn from their mistakes by feeling sorry for themselves?

"You're trying to undo something that you cannot undo," Frank had said during one of our study hall sessions a couple of months ago. "Do you think refusing to take this cure is going to undo your mistakes?"

"Undo?" I had scowled. It was a ridiculous suggestion. No, I was not refusing to take this cure because I thought it would "undo" anything. The past can't be undone.

Frank had groaned. "You once came into this office and argued with me about whether you were good or evil. Do you remember what side of that argument you were on? You've told me before that you don't think you deserve nice things."

"Yeah. I've told a lot of people that. It didn't make it less true," I argued. I didn't deserve nice things. I didn't deserve this cure.

"Bradley, for the love of the gods." Victoria's gloomy groan jerked me out of my memory. She kicked her feet off one of the table's support brackets, the table shaking as she did so. She set her nail file next to her tray.

"My family didn't relocate eight hundred miles to keep you safe only to let you undermine our efforts."

Serena scowled and rolled her eyes. "Ugh. Like we needed your family's help."

Victoria ground her teeth, shooting an angry look at Serena. "The captivators can't sense or see Savanna while she's under my dad's protection spells. We're the only reason she can walk outside her house."

"Big whoop," Serena mumbled, sliding her chair a few inches from Victoria.

Savanna reached for the necklace around her neck, clutching the tiny potion bottle with the strange mixture of small rocks, herbs, and dirty liquid. There were a few different crystals strung on both sides of the bottle. When she was first given the necklace back in January, she used to complain about it being an eyesore and would stuff it in the bottom of her backpack. When Victoria saw she was refusing to wear it, she threatened to have it fused to Savanna's skin. Savanna had to be *wearing* it for its magic to work. Carrying it in a bag didn't have the same effect. She still didn't start wearing it regularly until she stopped cheering and started showing.

Savanna dropped her hands, releasing the necklace. Her palms rested flat on the table as she addressed Victoria. "When does Bradley get to wear one?" She didn't look at me as she said this, but to be fair, she'd been avoiding my gaze on and off for months. It sucked because as much as I wanted her to know we were in this together, I couldn't seem to get her to believe that.

Victoria's dark eyes turned to glare at me, her jaw set. "Bradley's job is to take the cure before I stab him with it myself."

I slid my arms under the table, trying to minimize the amount of exposed skin in her presence.

Savanna rolled her eyes, still holding her chin in her hands, her elbows propped on the table. "That's not gonna happen."

"You don't think I can take him?" Victoria asked, cocking an eyebrow.

Serena snorted, capping a bottle of water. "Oh, please. Anyone can take him."

"Hey." I held my hands out. They were talking about me like I wasn't sitting right there.

Serena smiled, pointing at Jay-Jay. "Except for maybe Jay-Jay."

"I see you ladies woke up and chose emasculation today," Jay-Jay said, dropping his barbecue chicken drumstick on his tray.

Savanna shook her head. "No. That's not what I meant. I meant that Bradley isn't taking that cure. You and Alyssa"—she pointed to Alyssa, who was sitting quietly on the other side of Serena—"are new here, so you probably haven't picked up on this, but Bradley doesn't make decisions that are good for him."

I froze as Jay-Jay coughed up a piece of his food. Pounding his chest, his eyes watery, he shot me a nervous look. "Shots fired."

I sat there for several seconds, attempting to unlock my muscles. I moved my fingers first, then my arms, my legs… As soon as I had control of my feet, I stood, my fists clenched, and made a beeline for Frank's office.

I knew Savanna was right. I'd said it before. But there was something about hearing it come out of her mouth that was different. It angered me. Not because she was wrong, but because… I don't know. It came from the same place all her other anger about our entire situation was coming from. There was a lot I couldn't do about most of it. But this one…

Frank had a forkful of salad in his mouth when I opened his office door. The minute he saw me, he spat it all out. "You couldn't knock?"

I shut the door behind me. "I'm sorry I couldn't give you and your salad more privacy." He frowned, and I changed the subject. "Do you have a vial with you?"

Frank dabbed at his lips with a napkin. "I have a leftover one from the pack your grandfather gave me to give to the nurse. I kept one in case there was ever an emergency…" He glanced at the pile of stuff on his desk. He opened a few drawers before closing them as he searched. "You gonna take it?" he asked, rolling open another drawer and shuffling a few papers.

"Maybe," I said, dropping my backpack in a chair and zipping open the pocket I kept my backup supplies in.

"Aha!" Frank exclaimed at the same moment he held up a vial of the cure.

"Awesome." My words came out a little too unenthused as I reached for it.

"You don't seem excited," Frank noted, rolling the drawer closed.

I sucked in a breath, plunging the syringe through the aluminum seal. "Savanna thinks I don't make good decisions. I'm proving her wrong."

"Glad to see you care about *one* person's opinion."

I scowled, hating that everyone seemed to be making this decision for me. I hated that it was never going to feel one hundred percent like it was my idea. And it made me feel gross, like nobody liked me the way I was. Like taking this cure would be some kind of trade-in for them. Like somehow it would make me this new and improved person and not just… me as I am. I was just getting the hang of all the calculations. I finally got my A1C under seven percent, which is what my doctor had wanted me to aim for, and now all that effort felt… worthless. It was like learning the Pythagorean theorem in math class when I was pretty sure I was never going to use it in real life.

I lifted my shirt, not feeling like explaining all that. I rarely had to give myself insulin via a syringe anymore, since my pump usually did all the work. I didn't have to avoid all the areas I'd recently used as injection sites.

Picking a spot at random, I squeezed my eyes shut and pushed the needle through my skin. The sharpness stung as my thumb pressed the plunger. The room-temperature liquid was barely noticeable as it raced under my skin and rushed through my bloodstream. Unsticking myself, I tossed the syringe in the trashcan next to Frank's desk. Then I grabbed a tissue to apply pressure to the spot since a small amount of blood had seeped through. I sat down, waiting to feel different. I didn't want to unhook my pump until I knew for sure that it had worked.

Frank twiddled his thumbs for a second, watching me, before grabbing his fork and returning to his salad. "You let me know if you start feeling funny," he said, flipping a page of a binder in front of him. I leaned over to see what he was looking at as he stuffed a heap of lettuce into his mouth. It was some kind of decorative pink form in a plastic cover, vis-à-vis ink filling in half the blanks on the page. Frank muttered unintelligibly through his food as he opened a drawer to search for something. I leaned a little closer to read the text before realizing it was a list of people that were going to be in Frank and Dr. Lamb's wedding party.

Frank noticed me reading as he procured a vis-à-vis marker from a drawer. "Melinda's got me approving, adjusting, and vetoing wedding stuff this week," he explained. He started to write a few names in the groomsmen category, all of which I didn't recognize. They must have been his friends from the police force. He tapped the top of the marker against the blank spot for best man. My heart stuttered for a second when he glanced at me. Was he seriously going to ask me to be his best man?

"When is Savanna due again?"

I slumped into the nearest chair. Of course, he wasn't going to ask, not that I wanted him to. All anyone seemed to care about these days was Savanna and the baby. It wasn't that I didn't care about either of them, but I was tired of every conversation getting redirected to our… situation. The diabetes cure was being rushed around the nation not to cure a bunch of people, but to distract and hopefully weaken Priori Labs. The captivators couldn't focus on Savanna and me when their lab was financially crumbling. Plus, everyone wanted me cured so the neo-Nazis couldn't use my meds against us like they had a year and a half ago. All this was being rushed in time for the birth. I looked down at my pump, my hands searching for the power button. We still had four months, but time seemed to be speeding up. Was she really already that far along?

"August ninth," I answered, unhooking the tube from the circular canula on my stomach. I still didn't feel different, but Grandpa had mentioned it could be up to twenty-four hours before the cure would start taking effect.

"It needs time to repair the damage," he'd explained months ago. "Islet-cell regeneration doesn't happen with the snap of a finger."

I didn't care about the wait time, so much as I wanted to be done. Four months suddenly didn't seem like as long a time as it had. My grandparents had already been relocated to one of the safe houses. Probably the one in Nashville.

Frank let out a relieved breath. "Okay, good. Melinda reserved the date before everything went down and I just wanted to make sure—"

I cut him off without meeting his gaze, unhooking the pump from my jeans. "She already checked with me months ago. That's one plan I didn't ruin."

I glanced at the screen on my pump again and suddenly had second thoughts about removing it. Tracing the edge of the cannula on my stomach, I remembered I'd just changed it that morning. And if for whatever reason I needed to reconnect, I didn't want to waste it. I decided to wait to take it off when I got home.

Frank slowly closed the binder. "You have to stop saying that."

I blinked, confused, as I lifted my head to meet his gaze. What was it that I had said?

"A little advice from a guy who's about to get married." He raised his eyebrows, pausing briefly as if he were waiting for my permission to continue. I didn't give him any. He kept talking anyway. "There is no 'I' in 'we.'"

"There is in 'relationship,'" I retorted.

Frank shook his head, failing to hold back a grimace. "My point is that a relationship takes two people. There are two people making decisions, and those decisions affect the other person. Excuse the cliché, but it takes two to tango. This can't all be your fault."

My throat tightened as I averted my eyes, focusing instead on a framed engagement photo of Frank and Dr. Lamb. My eyes watered and I dipped my head behind my hand, my fingers rubbing my forehead. "We're not like you," I choked out. This wasn't fair. I didn't know how to make him understand, not without spilling details Savanna would kill me for sharing. Even if she couldn't read my thoughts anymore, she had a way of just looking at me and knowing I had betrayed her. Of course, that was her usual look these days.

"You can't feel when the other is turned on," I mumbled, squeezing my eyes shut so I didn't have to see his face. I was hoping that one phrase would be self-explanatory enough that I wouldn't have to give any more details.

"I am failing to see how that's any more your fault than hers."

I opened my eyes, refusing to look at him. Instead, I focused on my bouncing knee. I really didn't want to talk to Frank about sex. "It can get really intense sometimes. It's hard to tell whose feelings are whose. I just…" I rubbed my right eye with the palm of my hand, blurring my vision. "What if her feelings weren't really her feelings? What if she was just projecting mine back at me?"

Frank puffed out his cheeks, then let out a quick breath of air. "You think it might not have been consensual?" he asked, his eyebrows so high, they caused his forehead to wrinkle.

I didn't answer. I had thought that it was, but what if it wasn't? I mean, I had also thought the condom hadn't broken, but that clearly didn't turn out to be true.

The day it happened I was about to leave for Tennessee to spend Thanksgiving break with my grandparents. For once, we were alone while my family was running last-minute errands for the trip. I had this overwhelming feeling like I didn't want to leave her, even if it was just gonna be for a week. The moment I saw her, the feelings were intoxicating. And sure, she was kissing me back, and she seemed like she enjoyed it, but sometimes our feelings felt like a drug, and if she was high on mine, what did that mean?

"I think if you really want to know the answer to that, you need to talk to Savanna," Frank said, interrupting my downward spiral.

"If it wasn't for me and my stupid feelings, she wouldn't be pregnant," I said.

Frank shrugged. "Maybe. But playing the what-if game isn't going to undo it. I think you and her need to sit down and have an honest conversation about it."

"How?" I dropped my hand, slamming it against my leg. "We can't be in the same room without her saying something passive-aggressive. You know she thinks we're gonna die?"

Frank traced his bottom teeth with his tongue, his eyes narrowing. "You don't?" My heart stuttered. Did he agree with her on this? "I don't mean to alarm you, but there's a reason Markus Porter made that amulet for Savanna. There's a reason why his family and the Sullys are here. That's why I asked about the due date—because I wanted to make sure Melinda and I would be in town for backup. We're anticipating a fight. We're assuming the captivators and Dr. Sauer and whoever else is on board will do anything to get their hands on that child, including disposing of you and Savanna. We're not playing around here, and I think the sooner you accept that, the sooner Savanna will stop fighting with you. You two need to get on the same page, and quick."

7 // BEDTIME STORIES AND OTHER NATURAL SOLUTIONS
WYSTAN

The parking lot was packed as it always was on Tuesday afternoons. Cursing under my breath, I pulled my car into an empty space in the boonies, killing the engine. I glanced in the rearview mirror, readjusting it so I had a clear view of my sleeping child. I was sure she didn't know how much I had sacrificed to drive sixteen hours to Kansas and back to get her. Griselda would be pleased, but she wasn't the one who had to answer a call from their ex in the middle of the night.

"You need to come get her!" Miranda had shouted over the screams. Apparently, Daphne had been having nightmares since she turned six on Sunday. She kept begging her mom to let her see me.

"If she comes back with even a scratch," Miranda had warned as she handed our daughter off, "I will be suing for custody." She knew she couldn't win, not with Griselda in the process of establishing a school for the gifted. We all knew Daphne would fare better there than at the local school my ex had sent her.

I peered at the tinted window on the fifth floor where Griselda's office was. She no doubt had sensed us coming. Two matronae in the same city were impossible for intuitives like her to miss.

I tried to be as quiet as I could while I opened my door. Kids were much more bearable when they slept. My daughter was no exception. I had worked hard to lull her to sleep with visions of puppies and unicorns on the drive back, only to realize during our separation she had come to be fascinated by fairies and trolls instead, having had an incident with a neighbor's vicious dog.

I popped the trunk, attempting not to shake the car too much, and shouldered her duffel. When I closed it, I nearly jumped out of my skin. Daphne was standing by her door, a fabric doll dangling from her fist. She squinted against the sunlight, peering at me. She still had her pajamas on, having refused to change before we left. Frowning, she turned her head and blinked rapidly. "Something bad is happening."

I swallowed, following her gaze, but couldn't see the proof in her statement. It was foolish to ignore her. Daphne had never been wrong in her six years of life.

I reached for her hand, clutching it along with her doll, and began our journey through the large parking lot.

We found Griselda on the main conference room floor. She hadn't sought us out as I had assumed she would. That was a bad sign. I led Daphne to a bench, dropping her duffel next to her after she hopped onto it.

After digging out a box of crayons and a drawing pad, I handed them to her. She made a face, curling her upper lip in disgust. "I don't want her to know I'm here." She hugged her doll to her chest as I dropped the materials back into the bag.

Griselda smirked, peeling her gaze from the closed conference room door. "Wise little matrona." She crouched to Daphne's height, peering into her green eyes. "Can she sense you when you draw?" Her fingers tapped the sketch pad, a slow smile spreading across her face.

Daphne nodded vigorously. "I can see her when we do the same things." She pointed to the pad. "She likes to draw. A lot."

Griselda's eyes flashed, her hands curling around one of Daphne's. "Fascinating."

I cleared my throat, unsure what to make of their conversation. Who could my resilient and powerful daughter see when she drew? A spirit, maybe?

"You'll have to stay and be my little spy," Griselda said, chuckling.

Daphne pulled her hand out of her grasp, shrugging before digging through her bag for something else to do. Griselda stood, brushing her slacks.

"What's going on?" I asked, nodding toward the door.

She grimaced. "They've been in meetings all day. Something about a significant drop in revenue." She raised her eyebrows, flashing me a knowing look.

I leaned against the wall. "The diviners?" I guessed.

She averted her eyes to stare at the door some more. "Either our clients are dying at a drastic rate, or it wasn't a mouse that tripped the wire at the office." Her accusing green eyes flashed back to me.

I shrugged, attempting not to show my defensiveness. "They never found a body, and the cameras were destroyed in the explosion."

Griselda narrowed her eyes, stepping toward me. I stood my ground. "Some diviners can teleport," she said. "I would know. I killed one myself last year, and I saw one at the Chamberses' house last Christmas. It would explain why the power here has been fluctuating lately. Diviners seem to be popping in and out of the city." She was inches from my face, her tall frame hunched.

"You think they found a way to make copies of the cure?" I asked, keeping my voice steady.

She tilted her head and hissed through her teeth. "I think they're trying to distract us. We need to distract them back."

She stepped away from me, approaching my daughter instead. Crouching, she danced her fingers on Daphne's knee. My daughter stopped dressing her doll to meet Griselda's gaze.

Griselda smiled. "Tell me more about Rebecca Chambers."

Daphne tapped her chin thoughtfully, glancing at the ceiling. She'd lost several teeth since I'd last seen her.

There were gaps in her cheeky grin as she giggled at a memory. "She drew a picture of me." Her finger slid into her mouth, tugging at her lower lip. "It's so pretty."

"She can see you too?" Griselda asked, leaning in with intrigue. I slid Daphne's duffel toward me, reaching for her art supplies as she nodded. I didn't like the idea that the diviners' deadliest weapon could see what my daughter was doing. For all we knew, their matrona had been spying on her for years. No wonder she was having nightmares.

A few loose papers fell from the sketch pad. Grumbling, I bent to pick them up but stopped when I saw what they were. An opened envelope and a detailed drawing of my daughter stared back at me. My eyes darted to the address on the envelope. "They know where you live!" I shouted, waving the envelope at my daughter. She cringed, biting her nail. "They would attack your mom. Do you want that?" I hissed.

Daphne's eyes filled with tears.

"Oh, hush now," Griselda whispered, sliding herself onto the bench and pulling my crying daughter onto her lap. She held her all mother-like, swaying to quelch her cries. Griselda didn't seem perturbed at all by this news, but then again, she never wanted Daphne to live with my ex. Miranda held our daughter back from greatness. With Griselda as her teacher, she could be so much more.

"I've been doing some research on your little friend," Griselda murmured in her ear. "I know how to keep your mommy safe." Daphne sniffled, quieting her cries. I picked up the drawing, examining the details. It almost looked like a black-and-white photograph. The sun shone through the translucent curtains of her bedroom window in the background, giving it an unbelievable realism. Daphne was holding a toy pony, raking a tiny hairbrush through its mane. I smiled dubiously to myself as I remembered what my daughter had said about being able to see Rebecca. Rebecca Chambers must also like horses.

"Once upon a time," Griselda began. "There was a girl named Liesel Keller. She lived in the town of Asperg as a lowly gypsy. She would do magic tricks for the villagers, conning them out of their money. One day, the villagers had enough of her wicked ways. They deported her and the rest of the gypsies and put them in prison. There, Liesel spent her time plotting her revenge. One day, another gypsy girl named Magdalena arrived at the prison. While there, Magdalena gave birth to a powerful baby—one that held the key to protecting the villagers from their magic tricks. The guards took the baby for protection, but Liesel snatched it back and broke out of the prison. For decades, Liesel hid the baby from those it was born to protect. When Liesel died, she was supposed to reincarnate far away from the baby. She would've lost all her memories and started life as a new person."

Daphne had her thumb in her mouth by that time in the story and yanked it out to interrupt. "Like me?"

Griselda stroked Daphne's chest-length brown hair. "Yes. Just like you, my little matrona."

Daphne furrowed her brow. "But she didn't follow the directions."

Griselda shook her head. "I think she did at first." She tapped Daphne's nose, which resulted in a giggle. Smiling, Griselda continued her story. "You see, there was a boy who was born the day she died. His name was Jesse Chambers."

Daphne recognized the last name. "Like Rebecca Chambers?"

"Exactly." Griselda nodded. "But his body was weak. He died very young." She frowned, but I suspected it had little to do with a child's death. "I suspect Liesel's spirit planned it. She needed an older body—somebody who could find the child—now a woman—and keep the villagers and their descendants from finding it. She had an opportunity to transfer her spirit to Jesse's sister. Rebecca was not born to be a matrona."

"Is that bad?" Daphne asked, her green eyes widening.

Griselda smiled. "If you believe the story of our ancestors, it is very bad for her." She paused. "Do you know the story of Onora?"

Griselda's green eyes flashed to me, and I grimaced at the insult. Every captivator knew the story. It was made into a children's fairy tale. Daphne had my sister's copy on her bookshelf at home.

Daphne nodded excitedly, clapping her hands. "There once was a girl named Onora." She quoted the opening line from memory.

"She lived in an old village in Wales," Griselda continued to quote, but then she jumped to the interesting part of the story. "Onora wanted to share her abilities with the people of her village. She did not like being singled out. It made her lonely to have zero friends who were just like her. So, she asked the gods to spread her power, and they agreed. For almost two years, her village was the most powerful in the kingdom. No one could conquer their land. Then, one by one, the people of her village began to ramble and hallucinate. They believed things that were not true. Disloyalty and mistrust spread through the village, causing men and women to die. Soon, there was no one left in the village but Onora. When she asked the gods why she was alone, they said, 'That is what happens when an ordinary druid is given powers that don't belong to them. You should have asked about the consequences.'"

I smiled, understanding where Griselda was heading with her theory. "If the diviners are trying to distract us," I said, "Rebecca will exact our revenge for us."

Griselda glanced at me, agreeing with her smile, before returning her attention to Daphne. "Rebecca has stolen powers, my dear. She will be punished for her crime."

Daphne pulled back, attempting to slide off Griselda's lap. "But that's why I came!" She raised her voice. "She keeps sharing her nightmares with me!" Her fist hit Griselda's shoulder as she began to wail. "I want her to stop!"

Griselda grabbed my daughter's wrists, locking eyes with her. "I will make them stop," she said from behind clenched teeth.

"Dr. Sauer can give you some medicine," I said, even though that wasn't entirely true. I licked my lips. I had to be careful not to lie to her. She could sense every lie. All the doctor could do was sedate her. The serum from the Maria Project he used to dampen the diviners' powers didn't work on captivators. It certainly didn't work on the matronae. I rephrased my statement. "Dr. Sauer will be able to give you something."

She stopped struggling. Vagueness was always the key to a good truth. He would be able to give her something—it just may not be the something she needed.

The door to the conference room opened, Cyrus Krause emerging from the room. I straightened my posture as he glowered in our direction. "General."

He scowled, walking past me to stand in front of Griselda, who slid my daughter off her lap so she could stand. "Sir." She nodded, brushing the wrinkles out of her slacks.

He glanced at her badge, then back at her. "Your father would not have let this happen, Miss Day." He spat her name, saliva landing on her blouse. General Krause was a short and plump man. Although he was intimidating to most people, Griselda was an exception. She towered over him, her stony expression refusing to waver.

Cyrus kept talking. "When we lay off a fifth of our staff, I'll be sure to let them know you're the one to blame." He wagged his fat, wrinkly finger. "It was your idea to negotiate with the Chambers kid instead of shooting him and his friends on the spot. If I were the suspicious type, I'd say you were on their side." He paused briefly before continuing his rant. "I'll tell you what. The next time I see one of those *diviners*"—he snarled—"I'll put them down myself."

Griselda crossed her arms, lifting an eyebrow. "Well, you know what they say. Keep your friends close and your enemies closer," she quipped. Before he could counteract, she added, "The diviners are about to get what's coming to them. You'll see what I mean soon."

"You better turn this around, Day, before I—" He cut himself off, running a finger under his chin in a slicing motion before thumping down the hallway.

I snorted as he disappeared around the corner. The conference room began to empty of people, including the general's son, who shot us a warning glare as he passed. The idea that the Krauses held all the power at Priori Labs was absurd. We had our own foothold.

8 // THE CHARM OF SAINT SARA E KALI
SAVANNA

When did high school get to be so nightmarish? I had two months left in my sophomore year, and all I had to show for it was a retired cheer uniform and these ridiculous—

I groaned, tearing the obscene artwork from my locker door. "Who did this?" I shouted at the passersby, crumpling the paper into a ball. A boy and his friend laughed from across the hallway, and I threw it at them, my satchel slipping from my shoulder in the process. "*Juno*? Really? Like you couldn't be more original?" I spat. I swear, that movie was ruining my life. It didn't help that Bradley ran track and field… just like Michael Cera's character.

I squinted through the sea of students, catching sight of more "art" on Bradley's locker. I had to get to it before he saw. Nobody was allowed to mess with him but me. They had no right.

One good thing about being visibly pregnant? People parted like the Red Sea when they saw me coming. I scrambled to rip the pages from his locker, glancing wildly between both ends of the hallway, hoping he wouldn't see me.

"Need some help?" Serena popped out of nowhere, and I jumped, bumping into another student.

Regaining my composure, I nodded, tearing at the paper. There were several spots where the paper refused to separate from the glue. "God, what did they use to stick this with?" Serena started to pick at them, standing on her tiptoes.

I noticed something poking out of the vents. When I ran my finger against the edge, whatever it was fell out. I inadvertently screeched, jumping back as it hit the floor. Serena paused, holding her hands up like she had been caught committing a crime before looking down. It was a condom, wrapped in all its foil glory. Serena bent to pick it up, examined it, then pocketed it.

"Ew! You don't know where that's been!" I blurted.

Serena shot me a look of disbelief. "Did you really just scream at an unopened condom? No wonder you're pregnant."

"Shut up," I grumbled, my face heating as I dug my nails underneath the glue on Bradley's locker.

Serena continued to pick at another piece before she froze. "Wait. You don't think whoever did this stuffed his whole locker with those, do you?"

"I can open it and find out."

I froze at the sound of Bradley's voice as Serena glanced behind me. The baby kicked, and I sucked in a breath. My hand was halfway to my stomach before Serena grabbed my forearm, pulling me out of Bradley's way. I exhaled, trying to calm my overactive heartbeat as Bradley began to twist the dial. Nothing would calm it. As his finger lifted the tab, I heard a snicker behind me. A hand curled over my right shoulder, someone's arm bending around the back of my neck. Bradley had barely opened the locker and yet dozens of condoms had already spilled out. He struggled to close it, several of the foil packages getting stuck in the creases.

Angela's voice was in my left ear. "We lost the competition last weekend."

Marcie had told me as much. She was worried my ex-teammates would retaliate and wanted to warn me. All week I'd been getting nasty looks. I thought that was the brunt of it, but I guess they'd been biding their time.

"We could have won if he'd just kept it in his pants," Angela snarled.

My throat burned as she shook me before releasing. I didn't know whether to cry or scream or hit her. I wanted to do all the above as she sashayed away, but I couldn't move.

A girl from our Teens as Parents class lifted my satchel from the ground in front of my locker, narrowing her eyes at Angela as she passed. My arm stung as she approached, and I glanced down to see Serena's nails digging into my arm. She was trembling, her furious brown eyes refusing to lose their mark on my ex-friend.

She didn't loosen her grip until Angela rounded the corner.

The girl from my class handed the satchel to me, briefly glancing at Bradley with an uneasy grimace. He wasn't looking at us, his eyes distant as he stared at the locker next to his. "Cheerleaders think they gotta know everything. They don't know what it's like to not have the world revolve around them," she said, shrugging before heading in the opposite direction.

Ever since I was kicked off the team, everyone else has treated me like I was never truly part of the squad to begin with. I loved cheering, though, and I missed being part of a team that had my back. So when people insulted the cheerleaders and classified them into stereotypes, it still felt like an insult to me.

I winced, glancing back down at my arm as Serena let go. I watched as the broken skin closed on its own. Bradley's fist hit the metal locker, and I flinched. Without glancing in our direction, he mumbled something about having to get to work before rushing off. My eyes couldn't help but tear as he went.

Serena bent to gather the fallen condoms before offering them to the few students left in the hallway like she was the health teacher on all those television shows that supported safe sex over abstinence. I was beginning to think schools like that were a myth. If a principal caught her, she'd be pulled into a meeting with her parents for sure. They treated condoms like they were drugs here.

"You better get rid of those," I warned her.

"What do you think I'm trying to do?" she hissed, tossing one at a girl who refused to take it. She still had several when the hallway cleared, so she unzipped her backpack and stuffed them inside.

I nervously tucked my hair behind my ear, searching for administrators. "What are you gonna do with those? You don't even need them." I bit my lip, realizing my mistake as soon as the words were out of my mouth.

She briefly paused before roughly zipping her bag and slinging it over her shoulder. Her eyes were glassy, her teeth gritted. "They're not just for preventing pregnancies, you know. Besides, some of us would give anything to be you right now," she bitterly shot back. "If my choices were between never having kids or having one now, I wouldn't hesitate. The teasing I could handle. Having a man never want to marry me because I can't give him children, I can't." She started to pace away.

"That's ridiculous!" I shouted after her.

She stopped, turning on her heels. "Maybe. But so is my life! So is all of ours!" She spun back around, disappearing in the direction of her mom's classroom. I couldn't believe she was actually suggesting it was better to be me. The audacity. What about being pregnant at fifteen and having a target on my back was appealing?

My phone buzzed against the textbooks in my bag. I struggled to dig it out before it went to voice mail. I waited for it to ring again, holding it in my hand. If it was who I thought it was, they'd call back. Sure enough, "Dad" flashed across the screen. "I'm coming!" I practically yelled as I answered.

"You do not need to use that tone—"

I ended the call, huffing in annoyance. I wasn't sure which place I preferred—school or home. They were equally tense, especially on days like today when everyone seemed to have it out for me and Bradley. And the worst part? I couldn't even talk to Bradley about it. We were never alone together. Anything I said to him would turn into gossip. Even surrounded by people, I felt alone.

Resigning myself to my dad's perpetually bad mood, I dragged my feet over the tiles and toward the exit.

Dad was visibly fuming in the car as I slipped in the back seat next to Ursula. "You been crying?" Dad asked, twisting to see my face. He was still shaking, his tone furious.

I wiped beneath my blurry eyes. "No."

"I'll kill him," Dad said like he did every day, turning back to pull the car out of park. I didn't even argue with him this time. It wasn't worth it.

Ursula held out the palm of her hand, a silver charm forming in it. I recognized it immediately and burst into fresh tears. I once had a charm just like it when I was little. Our mother had bought it for me from a Romani metal maker during our visit to Saintes-Maries-de-la-Mer the year after Ursula was born. We had traveled from Rome, where the Pope had beatified Ceferino Giménez Malla, or El Pelé, a Spanish Romani killed in Spain's civil war, as a saint. We'd gone from there to Saintes-Maries-de-la-Mer for the reenactment of Saint Sara e Kali's welcome of the Saint Marys to France. We were in the crowd of Romanies carrying her statue to the sea to welcome Saints Mary Jacobe and Mary Salome that year. It was one of my few memories of living in France. When I lost the charm a couple of years ago, I was devastated.

Scooping the replica in my hands, I read the lettering through my tears. "Priez pour nous," it read next to Saint Sarah's name. Translated from French, it meant, "Pray for us." A silhouette of the saint was centered between the words.

Sara e Kali is the patron saint of the Romani people. Any religious practices for her are closed to outsiders.

I flipped the charm over to see the name of the commune we had traveled to, along with a carving of the two Marys in the boat on their arrival to France. It was the exact same charm I had once owned.

Mom had been so excited that month. First, with the beatification of a Catholic Spanish Calé—one of her own—and then with our last voyage to honor Saint Sarah before we left Europe. I wasn't sure I believed in God, but there was something about this saint that held a special place in my heart.

I unhooked my necklace so I could string the charm next to the bottle of ugly dried herbs and stones. Clipping the necklace back around my neck, I clutched the charm and whispered, "Pray for us." Because even if God didn't exist, I needed those prayers. I needed protection. I needed peace.

I looked to Ursula, still clutching the charm. "What made you think of this?"

She shrugged. "We were going over world religions in history class today. Rebecca said something about looking for the truth in parallels. She used Sara e Kali as an example. She's a folk saint in the Catholic church, but she's also believed to be a form of Kali, the Hindu goddess. It reminded me of your old necklace—the one with the charm just like that one. I remembered that you lost it."

I shook my head, rubbing my thumb across the engraving. "I never even thought to make my own."

"You shouldn't be giving her gifts," Dad snarled, pulling the car into the garage. He hit the button to close the garage door and cut the engine. "We're not rewarding her behavior."

My throat burned once again, my lips trembling. I closed my eyes. I was so tired of crying all the time. "I'm not giving it back."

I heard Dad shift in his seat. "Do not give your sister any gifts," he ordered Ursula. I shook my head, refusing to open my eyes to the reality of his attitude. Shoving my door open, I stumbled out of the car and felt my way into the house. It wasn't until I was inside that I opened my eyes. I found Mom in the living room, biting her nails in front of the television.

"Priori Labs laid off over three hundred employees this week," the reporter said as I ran to my mother, dipping behind her when I heard Dad and Ursula's footsteps.

"Don't let him take away my necklace," I begged, one hand clutching the charm and the other my mom's shoulder.

She twisted, my entrance distracting her from the news story. "Why would your father take away your necklace? He knows that's nonnegotiable."

Ursula beat Dad to the room, explaining, "I made her a new Sara e Kali charm."

Mom's eyes widened as she tried to take a look at the charm, but I refused to move my hand. When Dad made it inside, she instinctively stepped in front of me, facing him. "You are not taking that charm." I knew Mom would defend me. She loved it whenever I took an interest in her religion. With Dad being adamantly atheist, it wasn't common for us to have legitimate theological discussions.

Dad snorted with derision. "We've talked about this. We are not rewarding her with new things that aren't necessary."

I couldn't see Mom's face, but I could practically feel her anger seep from her pores. Her voice shook. "What did you just say to me?"

Dad took a step back, his mouth gaping for a second like he wasn't sure which of his words were being perceived as incorrect. When he closed his lips, his nostrils flared. "She does not need a silly charm—"

"A silly charm?" Mom's voice rose. "Do you have that much disrespect?"

Dad didn't answer. He fumed, his lips sealed shut.

When my parents decided to get married, it was quick. They hadn't dated for very long. Dad was aging out of the foster system and needed a home. Mom's parents wouldn't allow them to live together unless they were married. Other than them both being diviners, they didn't really have that much in common. So, when they got married, they'd laid down some ground rules. One of those rules was that they would respect each other's religious practices. For Dad, that usually meant keeping his mouth shut. He'd allowed my mother to baptize my sister and me in the Catholic church, and as far as our baptisms and their wedding went, those were the only days he stepped foot in any church. He'd gone with us when we traveled to Rome and Saintes-Maries-de-la-Mer, but he'd stayed in the background, avoiding the festivities. Not once since I could remember had he spoken ill of Mom's beliefs, but I guess he'd crossed a line with my charm. I hadn't meant to trigger a fight.

"Sara e Kali is the patron saint of the Romanies, Milo. Which *you* are! And to disrespect a symbol of protection for *your* people—for *our* people…" She shook her head, her words trailing off as she scrambled to gather her thoughts. "I don't care if you don't believe in God. This isn't a God issue, Milo. This is a cultural issue. This is you standing in the way of our daughter embracing who she is. She is allowed to wear that symbol around her neck because God knows we don't have a lot of people representing us. Not like the gaché do. I thought that was our goal, Milo—to make sure our children knew of our history and our culture so they could pass it to the next generation."

Dad couldn't keep his tongue bitten any longer. His hands shook, grasping at air. "What culture? What history? We're always struggling between two identities in this house. Are we diviners or are we Romanies? And whenever *you* say we're Romanies, the only culture our children get handed is yours! It's the Calé!"

For a while, the room was silent. I couldn't see Mom's face. Dad knew exactly why the only Romani customs we were taught were Calé in origin. Was he really expecting us to spell it out for him?

Mom bowed her head. "Girls, please go to your rooms."

Ursula and I shuffled to the stairs, eager to leave the argument, but I could still hear Mom's voice when we reached the top.

"I can't teach the girls a culture I don't know much about," Mom admitted, her voice low. I paused on the last step. "I know you don't feel very connected to your Romani origins, but—"

Dad's voice was gruff. "I don't see the point. It's those origins that get us killed. I don't want to be associated with my Polska Roma grandmother. Being associated with her was what got my parents killed. And you know what? It's what's gonna get Savanna killed."

My heart dropped at the realization that he wasn't entirely wrong. His grandmother was the reason we were on a Nazi hitlist to begin with. But I also hated the way he used it as an excuse to hate and dismiss the beauty of our ethnic heritage. She wasn't on a list for doing anything wrong. She was trying to save our people. And we were letting the neo-Nazis and white supremacists win by hiding behind their gaché ideals. Maybe I wanted to know more. Maybe I was hungry for it.

9 // SANDWICHES, KNIVES, AND THE OCCULT LIFE
BRADLEY

Pickles. That was the stench that wafted through the establishment on Friday afternoon, the vinegar so strong I questioned why some of the patrons stayed. All along the front wall were shelves lined with jarred edibles and ingredients—pickles, squash, ginger, onion, carrots, green beans, okra, figs, and more. They seemed to be multiplying by the day. I swear I spotted some watermelon rinds in a few of the jars. I was so distracted by the abundance of pickled foods that I nearly jumped out of my skin when Mr. Porter's excited voice seemed to come out of nowhere.

"Bradley!"

I whirled around to be greeted with a massive bear hug. When he pulled away, he kept his arms on my shoulders, holding me in place. "How are you doing?"

I scowled. Had word already gotten around about the incident at my locker? "Fine," I mumbled. I hadn't come here to relive it. That wasn't what work was for. It was to distract myself with the oddities of the Porters' witchy sandwich shop. And for the money. Yeah, I couldn't forget that too.

Mr. Porter's hand caught mine, his dark eyebrows burrowing close at the sight of the bruises on my knuckles. I yanked it back, stepping out of his reach. The man was too touchy-feely, more so than any psychic I had met. "It's nothing."

He frowned. "That's too bad. Say, are you a fan of tea?" His dark eager eyes bore into mine, pleading for me to say yes. I shrugged, knowing he had something up his sleeve. Mr. Porter had a way of examining a problem and finding some kind of edible or drinkable solution. He led me to the large beverage dispenser where four clear cylinders stuck out vertically, each containing different shades of a dark liquid that swirled gently in a circular motion. Without asking me which I preferred, he grabbed a biodegradable cup from a stack and filled it with the tea labeled Ginkgo.

"It'll be good for your hand." He smiled proudly, his white teeth bright against his dark skin. I couldn't help but notice a singular gold tooth in his smile. He scratched at the base of his locs, murmuring something under his breath as I took a sip. I forced myself to swallow the bitter, earthy liquid, despite my initial urge to spit it out. I don't know how they manage to keep customers when their food and drinks were subpar at best.

Mr. Porter rubbed his hands together. "I'll let you finish while I check on a few things in the back." He disappeared behind a swinging half door, leaving me standing by the teas. A couple was sitting at a small round table in the corner studying a laptop screen, earbuds dangling from their ears. Besides them, the place was devoid of customers. I sipped at the tea as I paced in front of the register, where a lit display case begged for attention. It wasn't filled with much at that time of day. Spice blends labeled as emotions lined the top shelf, stones and handmade jewelry on another. If it wasn't for the large chalkboard behind the counter, I wouldn't have guessed this was a sandwich shop.

They'd only been open for about a month. The display case had been empty for weeks, but like the jars, it seemed every time I came in for a shift lately, they had added a new section of items.

"The damn stove won't light," his wife complained from the kitchen.

I looked up to see Mr. Porter through the archway as he stuck his fingers into the invisible gas, snapping them to ignite the flames.

I only knew one other pyrokinetic, and that was Liam Brown. He and his older brother had tried to help us in our failed attempt to take down Priori Labs the first time. Even though we still attended the same school, I hardly saw Liam. He's a year older, so we didn't share any classes.

"You should probably finish that." Victoria's bored voice came out of nowhere. I almost dropped the cup.

Ignoring my near-heart attack, she tossed an apron in my direction. "We got work to do. Chop chop!" A butcher knife materialized in her hand, and she carelessly waved it in the air. Quickly, I swallowed the last of my tea, tossed the cup in a nearby bin, and tied the black apron on before she could accidentally chop me in half.

She cackled in amusement. "What's the matter? Afraid I'll carve you up and serve you to a customer?" She stepped back, addressing no one in particular as she held the knife in the air. "Welcome to Wich Wharf," she said sarcastically, "where we serve fresh, authentic human meat." The couple in the corner didn't flinch at the admission, too engrossed in whatever they were listening to. She lowered her arms, rolling her eyes. "Turkey and Swiss between two slices of Brad would satisfy my dad's ridiculous obsession with puns."

I followed her as she stalked to the backside of the counter, shoving the knife into a hidden bin underneath the registers. The label on the bin read For Use with Rude Customers. It had Victoria's dark sense of humor written all over it.

The shop was mostly dead for the three hours that Victoria spent training me on their new register. We'd been using a glitchy old machine until the new one had finally come in after months of it being back-ordered. It sucked that there weren't many customers to practice using it with.

"You'd think Fridays would be better," Victoria said at one point, leaning against the counter. She blew out a bored puff of air, picking at a dark spot in the wood. "They can't exactly ding us for child labor laws when there isn't any labor," she grumbled. "Which reminds me, you gotta be out of here by seven." Her finger tapped the digital screen of the register, waking it up. The clock on the screen showed it was a quarter till. She must have misread my equally bored expression for contempt because her next words were mildly defensive. "Hey, I'm sixteen and my parents own the place. You're not."

I think the suckiest part of this whole situation was that I was old enough to get someone pregnant but not old enough to work more than three hours per school day or after seven. How was I supposed to support anyone with that?

Victoria tapped her ID number on the screen, unlocking the computer. Then she tapped a button that released the drawer, nearly smacking me in the groin.

"Hey!" I tried to step out of the drawer's path, but I didn't clear it in time. Luckily, the drawer only lightly tapped my upper leg.

Victoria shrugged. "Should have stepped back first."

"I would have if you had warned me," I explained through gritted teeth.

Grabbing the drawer and a freshly printed receipt, she stalked back to the office. I begrudgingly followed her.

"As usual, you have to count this drawer at the end of each shift and pull out the profits, which should be easy since we only had five customers come in," Victoria said before I reached her as she pulled out a wad of twenties. She counted it so quickly I had barely enough time to process what she was doing. I'd counted out a drawer before, but for some reason, she felt the need to remind me how it was done. As she typed the amount into a calculator, I attempted to convince her to let me do it on my own. Huffing in annoyance, she rolled her dark brown eyes before fixing them on mine. "The last drawer came up short. You're fifteen, not five. I know you can count better than that, but I have to make sure this is done right." I wasn't sure how to argue with that. The drawer *had* come up short the day before, but only by a dollar, and I was pretty sure it had started out that way. She pulled about fifty dollars from the drawer before placing the stack of bills in a safe.

"Are you gonna tell me the code for that?" I asked, pointing at the flame-retardant box of steel. I'd worked here long enough that I should know it, but for some reason, it was kept secret from me.

"Not in your wildest dreams," Victoria said, grabbing the freshly balanced drawer and walking it back to the register. "You're free to go about your bus—" I couldn't hear what she said next.

After sliding off my apron, I made my way to the front of the store where my mom was standing in the center of the dining area, clutching her purse, her brown eyes nervously assessing her surroundings. I'll admit, this wasn't an average sandwich shop, but Mom's usually light brown face was almost as pale as mine as she took in some of the new decor. I turned to Victoria for a clue as to why my mom was acting the way she was, but Victoria had busied herself with unnecessary work—wiping down the already pristine counter space.

"Hey, Mom," I greeted her nervously, stepping out from behind the counter.

Mr. Porter popped his head up, appearing behind a small windowless area in the wall separating the registers from the food prep area. "Clarinda!" His face brightened at the sight of my mom, his wide toothy grin back. Mom managed a weak smile but didn't respond much more than that. Mr. Porter threw a dish towel over his shoulder as he stepped out into full view. "How is the rest of your family doing? My wife is always going on about how difficult it must be to have four teenagers under your roof—and six diviners. We could barely rein in the one."

Victoria scowled, rubbing a spot on the counter with excessive force.

Mr. Porter leaned down to grab something from the display case.

Mom let out an almost inaudible sigh, brushing a few strands of her brown hair from her face. "Blake's hit a bit of an adjustment period with his new powers and, uh…" Her eyes flickered to me, but she didn't say anything. She didn't have to. I was glad for her silence, tired of being unable to go a few hours without someone bringing up Savanna or the baby. "Paige is doing good. I think." She strained her smile, the skin at the corners of her eyes pulling into tight crinkles. I didn't know her expression. Mom was usually mellow with people, at least on the outside. Something about the Porters had her putting on a false facade—a poorly executed one.

Mr. Porter straightened, a necklace dangling from his fingers. The chain was gold in color. It displayed a gray crystal-like stone, black spots dotting the substance like mold. He leaned over the counter to show Mom, eager to make a sale. "The jasper dalmatian is a protective stone known as the supreme nurturer. I believe it will suit you."

Mom stiffened at the assumption. "I'm aware of the healing power of crystals, Markus," she said tersely, her fake smile dwindling slightly.

Mr. Porter didn't let his smile falter as he examined the crystal. "Magick is a spectacular phenomenon, don't you agree? There are so many different ways people go about practicing it. But I assure you, you'll find this crystal much more powerful than its typical intention. I blessed it myself. I mean no harm to you or your family. There are no tricks up my sleeve." His dark eyes tried to meet Mom's, but she was studying Victoria, who had frozen in place at Mom's silent judgment. Mr. Porter continued, "I apologize. I'd been told you were quite the source of supernatural energy earlier in your life. I didn't realize you had such a poor experience that you can no longer trust a čoxani." His tone turned bitter as he frowned, dropping his eyes back to the stone. Flames burst from his palm, licking at the jasper. I stepped back, startled by the sudden eruption of fire.

Mom gripped my arm tight enough that her nails dug into my skin. Her uneasiness around the Porters had always confused me. They had moved here to help. Nothing they had done in the last three months had caused anyone harm. In fact... I glanced at my knuckles, the bruises having disappeared—they were protectors as far as I was concerned. If it weren't for them, the captivators would be able to keep better tabs on Savanna.

"We have similar goals. We come from the same people," Mr. Porter explained, attempting to convince Mom to be on his side. "Our language and pronunciation are constantly affected by the surrounding languages of our home countries, and although my family has been in America for generations, the language and culture are not lost on us. We remember the old. My wife's family does too. She may not have the witch gene, but she is familiar with the traditions."

Victoria abandoned the rag, storming off to the back. I wondered if it bothered her that she hadn't inherited her father's magick. I knew she could perform traditional rituals, but she didn't have that added power.

Mr. Porter was rare—half witch, half diviner—but he hadn't passed the witch gene to his daughter. It worked differently than the diviner gene. The diviners always passed the gene to their children. The witches only passed the gene to the children the same gender as them. It was usually a hint that a witch might be trans if their magic didn't appear to align with their gender assigned at birth, although I bet it was always a tossup with intersex, gender-fluid, and non-binary people.

He must have decided he needed to re-explain his origins because he continued. "I like the Romani word because the stigma isn't like it is in English. It's better than witch doctor. People think that if a Black man practices magick, he should have a bone through his nose and wave around animal skulls, calling it voodoo. I was born of magick—with a *ck*. My father passed on what he called the root healer gene to me. My mother, a diviner, calls us čoxani. We use the natural elements to help heal the wounded and the hurting. We are not evil. We do not summon demons or malevolent spirits. When my wife and I received word of your son, we agreed with Maria that having a diviner around who is also a čoxani could be beneficial to your family."

His wife appeared behind the half door, biting at her lower lip. Her light brown skin was only a shade darker than Mom's. The two women had the same shoulder-length brown hair, styled the exact same way. Even their eyes were similar colors and shapes. I'd already accidentally called her "Mom" on several occasions.

My real mom frowned, slumping her shoulders and loosening her grip on me. "I didn't mean to insult you, Markus. As a parent, you must understand that my first instinct is to protect my children."

Mr. Porter nodded grimly. "If your first instinct when you see me is to mistrust, then perhaps it is you who needs to reevaluate why that is." He eyed my healed hand. "You'll see I mean no harm." His lip twitched into a small smile for a split second before returning to a frown. "I'll let you get home to your family."

Mom lightly shoved me toward the door, smiling her fake smile again as we left. Once we were outside, she muttered under her breath, "That man is out of his mind."

I admit, he was a little odd, but I didn't think she needed to be so harsh. "Why do you say that?" I asked, hoping she would explain her behavior.

She huffed, unlocking the van door. "His mission is supposed to be to protect you and Savanna, and yet, he refuses to keep a low profile." I joined her in the van's front seats as she continued to rant. "An occult shop? Really?" She stuck the keys in the ignition. "Does that not scream disaster?" The van didn't start on the first try, and she had to restart. The engine finally roared to life. "You know, he asked me the other day if I'd like to put in some fortune-telling hours, as if that wasn't going to invite trouble. I'm not putting myself back in the yellow pages. Not after you and Jesse."

At the mention of my dead brother, she sucked in a breath before yanking out the keys and burying her face in her hands. She breathed deeply for a moment before pulling herself together. "I'm not doing it anymore. And I hope he cuts it out before somebody gets killed."

10 // SEX EDUCATION IS THE NEW DETENTION
SERENA

"**D**o you mind if I carry those books for you?" Jay-Jay's voice was so close that, at first, I thought he was talking to me. I slammed my locker shut, ready to grill him for such a misogynistic line—I can carry my own books, thank you—when I saw Alyssa nodding, ducking her head so her straight brown hair covered half her face. She bent her knees as she heaved the pile into Jay-Jay's waiting arms.

Traitor.

When did they get so buddy-buddy anyway? Had they been assigned the same dispatch team over the weekend? The diviners had been wrapping up Dallas and San Jose. It was only a matter of time before Priori Labs announced the cure. They laid off three hundred employees last week. So why weren't they picking up the slack yet?

Jay-Jay and Alyssa disappeared around the corner where their chemistry class was. I'd have to wait to interrogate them about their relationship later.

Repositioning my bag on my shoulder, I waded through the crowd toward health class. This was, by far, my least favorite class of the day. To be honest, it probably would be slightly more enjoyable if Savanna and Victoria weren't also in it. And, okay, yeah, I get it. Savanna probably had a worse time than me in the class because every time Mrs. Traille had to talk about something related to sex education, her eyes always hesitated on Savanna. But ever since I said what I said to her after school on Friday, I knew I had stepped in it. How was I supposed to feel, though? She preached so much about her choices being taken away from her and completely forgot that mine were too. Like, you know what I think of birth control? If you don't want to get pregnant, have someone shove a bunch of magnetic rods through your insides while you're under the influence of some toxin from the Maria Project. Forced sterilization isn't a joke. She should count her blessings. She was lucky.

Savanna snorted in derision when I took the open seat next to her. "Still think my life's better than yours?" Her fingers played with a charm on her necklace as she stared straight ahead, refusing to make eye contact.

I scowled, dumping my textbooks on my desk. "Still comparing our traumas?"

"Still adding to it?" Victoria accused, eyeing me coolly as she took the seat on the other side of Savanna. Ugh. Ever since Victoria and Alyssa arrived, they'd been unapologetically attached to Savanna's side of every argument. It was annoying. Plus, Victoria had this holier-than-thou attitude, like everything she said was to be considered law or something.

"What's that?" she pointed to her own neck as she eyed the charm on Savanna's necklace.

Savanna's eyes fluttered as she briefly glanced in Victoria's direction. "Saint Sara e Kali." She bit her lip, her leg bouncing.

Victoria nodded, but I had a feeling she didn't know who that was. I smiled, crossing my arms. Glad to know she didn't know everything.

"It's not gonna interfere with the protection charm?" Savanna asked, this time turning her head to look at her.

Victoria shrugged. "It shouldn't."

Angela passed our desks, slowing to sneer at us. "What is this? The Romani Breakfast Club? The prep, the princess, and the emo?" Angela snickered, sliding past.

Victoria slumped in her seat, mumbling something unintelligible under her breath. Savanna scowled, continuing to play with her necklace. At least her drama had the cheerleaders forgetting about last year's incident. Not referring to me as the slut was a definite improvement. How kind.

I flipped my notebook open to the next blank page and glanced above the door just in time to see Bradley pass by, his head down as he swiftly moved through the crowd of procrastinators. Anger sparked through my veins. What was he doing? He was supposed to be in chemistry with Jay-Jay and Alyssa. Was he heading to chemistry class? Not in that direction, he wasn't. God, what kind of loser—

The bell rang, and Mrs. Traille cleared her throat. She pulled the door shut, raising an eyebrow at a straggler through the window as she locked it. The student pounded their fist against the glass, their shout muffled by the door. "It's only been two seconds!"

"You know the rules," Mrs. Traille shouted back. "After the bell rings, you need a late pass to get through this door."

I snorted as my classmate scowled, hitting the door one more time before disappearing. "You snooze, you lose," I muttered, jotting down the date in the corner of my note page.

Mrs. Traille smiled smugly, grabbing a marker to write today's topic on the board—goal setting. When she turned to face us, she sighed with her smile still plastered on her face. "Today, we're going to be discussing health-related goals. Let's brainstorm here. I want you to give me some goals you intend to reach or keep by the time you graduate." She paced in front of us in the resulting silence. "Anyone?" Her eyes flashed to someone sitting in the row behind me. "Angela?"

"Well, I don't know about the rest of this class, but I intend to not get pregnant."

I turned to see her dark eyes land on the back of Savanna's head as Savanna dropped her hand to her desk.

"Alright." Mrs. Traille nodded. "Well, that's a good goal." Her marker squeaked as she wrote it on the board. This class was complete and utter bullshit.

The girl next to Angela raised her hand, spewing her response before the teacher had a chance to call her name. "I intend not to get married. I want an education first. Besides"—she let out a short chuckle—"it wouldn't be very feminist of me to marry some loser I met in high school." Her eyes had also landed on the back of Savanna's head like she was also throwing shade. But who said anything about marriage? Had Bradley and Savanna gotten engaged without me knowing about it?

I narrowed my eyes as Angela and the other girl exchanged smug looks. No. Why did this feel like it was about to turn into a roast?

Someone near the front of the class piped up. "My goal is to never date anyone who experiments with drugs."

I turned toward the front to see Mrs. Traille stop writing. She glanced at the last girl who spoke. "Why do you say that? Shouldn't your goal be to never do drugs yourself?"

"Yes, well," the girl explained in an innocent tone, "I'm just thinking ahead. Everyone knows if you date a guy who does drugs, he inevitably gets you to do them too. And the next thing you know, you end up sixteen and pregnant with a loser fiancé."

Savanna flinched at the "sixteen and pregnant" bit, but my mind was already working overtime to connect their bullshit answers. Someone else started to speak, but I cut them off, half standing as I pointed at them. "If you're gonna perpetuate another shitty rumor, then you need to shut the fuck up!" I screamed.

The girl snapped her mouth shut as Mrs. Traille gasped in shock. "Serena!"

Savanna glanced among the four students, her mouth agape. "What rumor?"

Maybe I should have let them keep their subtlety. She gasped in recognition at the third girl. "Bradley does not do drugs. How many times do I have to tell people that?" The girl rolled her eyes but didn't say anything. Savanna spun to look at the second girl. "And marriage? What the heck are you talking about?"

"Forget it," I spat, sitting down. I was fairly certain that marriage crack was rooted in some kind of racist idea that all Romani women married as children, which wasn't true.

"No." Savanna shook her head, her jaw set. "I'm sick of this class encouraging marriage whenever someone gets pregnant like it's some kind of magical cure-all, and I'd appreciate it if people would stop assuming things about Bradley and me that aren't true. Not everyone should be getting married just because they're having a baby. Children don't need parents who are going to resent each other and get into arguments all the freaking time. Marriage doesn't automatically mean stability."

She turned back to the front. "Take my parents for example. They got married because my dad was aging out of the foster care system and needed a home. Mom's parents wouldn't let him live with them unless my parents were married—it wasn't because they were in love, and it didn't necessarily provide stability for me and my sister. In fact, maybe we would have been better off with one parent instead of being raised by two people with completely different parenting styles who felt trapped in a marriage they didn't even originally want."

The room was silent for a few seconds, shell-shocked, as her eyes scanned the sea of faces staring back at her. To be honest, I never really knew that much about Savanna's family, but still, she didn't have to air their dirty laundry to a bunch of tenth graders who were probably just going to use it as ammunition.

Angela broke the silence. "Guess we know how you got knocked up. Bad parents. Bad daughter."

"Ugh!" Savanna screeched, slamming a folder filled with notes against her desk before struggling out of her seat.

"Savanna, please sit down," Mrs. Traille demanded.

"No." Savanna's voice shook as she gathered her things. Not gonna lie, this was a total Bradley move. Storming out of class? Iconic. The only difference? I could see the tears coming from a mile away. I'm not saying that Bradley doesn't cry. I'm just saying he's good at waiting until he's alone to do it. Savanna, on the other hand, was more of an open book. Maybe it was the hormones, but I wasn't completely convinced. Honestly, it was kind of entertaining watching Miss Perfect become completely unhinged.

She sniffled. "Screw this class. Screw this school. Screw the fucking department of education." The tears glistened on her cheeks as she rushed to unlock the door, nearly running into the late kid. As she went around him, he gaped at the class, a late pass in hand. "What did I miss?"

"Angela being malicious," Victoria sneered.

"Everybody else spreading racist rumors," I muttered.

Angela got defensive, crossing her arms to glare at me. "What racist rumors? Nothing I said was racist."

"Like you don't know," I scoffed.

"Ladies," Mrs. Traille warned, "if I have to send you all to the principal's office, I will." She turned to the late kid. "Have a seat. We were just discussing goals."

Like hell we were.

"Perhaps yours will be to buy a watch."

11 // I SHOULD HAVE EXPECTED THE WORST-CASE SCENARIO
BRADLEY

"Something's wrong." My hand rubbed my chest, my heartbeat pounding wildly inside it. I'd been wrestling with the urge to puke since my first class. I probably should have gone straight to the nurse, but I had wrongly assumed I could power through it. I hadn't felt this sick since my last hospital stay. I'd taken the diabetes cure, so this couldn't be that. It had to be, like, the flu or something. I was about to lose my breakfast standing in Frank's office.

Frank took one look at me, dropped his pen, and urged me to sit. My breath hitched in my throat as I stumbled to the nearest chair. Closing my eyes, I tried to count to three, but my lungs distracted me as they struggled to keep a steady pace. I could hear Frank jiggle a drawer, slam it, and curse. "Damn it. I gave that emergency kit back to the nurse after you took the cure." I leaned forward, my head swimming violently. I didn't have the energy to remind him that there was no way this was diabetes related.

But yeah, my breakfast was definitely making its way up. I felt the rims of the trash can Frank quickly shoved between my legs as I heaved. His feet shuffled across the floor back toward his desk, his fingers violently punching buttons.

I gotta say, part of me was kinda hoping the nausea was just fate's payback for knocking Savanna up, but this was worse. And I hated how familiar it felt.

"The cure didn't work," Frank muttered as I gripped the edges of the trash can. Those four little words felt like absolute bs. There had literally never been a reported instance of the cure not working. So why would it have not worked on me?

Frank started to explain my symptoms to the nurse over the phone. Symptoms he'd noticed just from me being in the same room as him. "I don't know why he came to me. Maybe he's not thinking straight."

Yeah, I got that way whenever my sugar was low. Sometimes when it was extremely high too, but not as often. I should have gone to the nurse. He was right. But I didn't want to walk that far.

"He's throwing up, and I noticed for just a second that it kind of smells like..."

Like my mom's nail polish remover. I noticed just before he said something similar. And it made my stomach drop.

Acetone.

The cure hadn't worked. Grandpa had insisted the cure worked ninety-nine percent of the time. The only reason he wasn't allowed to say it was a one hundred percent guarantee was for legal reasons. We'd been distributing it for weeks, and not one person had complained about it not working. I'd been a little thirsty, but I hadn't noticed any other negative symptoms in almost a week.

I wanted to hit my fist against the trash can. Damn it. Why did I always have to be the one percent? I was supposed to be done with the needles and the carb counting and all the little tedious things that kept me alive. I was supposed to be like everybody else, for once in my life, and not have to worry about my blood sugar and whether it was too low or too high. I wasn't supposed to be nervous that my blood would turn acidic and kill me anymore. It had been nice to not have that all on my shoulders for a week.

But this? No. Finding out the cure didn't work was worse than never having taken it in the first place.

My chin trembled and I pulled my hand in front of my mouth to keep myself from vomiting the sobs that were sure to come. My throat ached, dry and burning from the bile. It didn't work. The one thing that wasn't supposed to let me down didn't work.

Frank hung up the phone. "The nurse is coming as quick as she can." His arm rested over my shoulders, gripping my arm as I tried my best not to panic. The sobs didn't stop. They matched my exerted breathing. I squeezed my eyes tighter, attempting to keep the tears locked inside.

I felt so… weak. And I hated it. I hated being the weak link. I was so tired…

Frank shook me, and I opened my eyes briefly. At least my vision was still intact. Last time I hit ketoacidosis, everything had gotten blurry. This wasn't like that. Not yet.

"Stay with me," Frank urged. "How many fingers am I holding up?"

My stomach lurched once again, but there was nothing left in my stomach to upchuck.

The door banged open. "I already have an ambulance on the way." The nurse's voice was controlled as her cool hands found my wrist and forehead. "I'm assuming this is ketoacidosis. Are you sure he took that cure?"

"I saw him inject it with my own eyes," Frank answered.

"Cure, schmure," I mumbled. It didn't have a right to be called a cure.

The nurse said something about a light but didn't wait for me to comprehend her words before shining one in my eyes. I shook my head, blinking rapidly, which turned out to be a bad idea since it incited another dry-heaving incident. I swiped the back of my hand against my mouth when I was done, catching snot and mucus where I expected none. Dad was gonna be pissed she'd called an ambulance. He chewed her out last time for the bills.

"Lisa," Frank called, letting go of me and pacing toward the door. I couldn't quite make out the front desk attendant's voice. His words became muffled as he instructed her on what to expect. His voice suddenly cut out, then quickly sputtered Savanna's name. I could only make out some of his next words. "You… wait, don't… you need… stay put."

Savanna shouted my name. Did she have to be so dramatic? Paper rustled along footsteps and hushed voices. If the rest of the office staff hadn't known what was happening in Frank's office, they did now. Something sharp pricked my finger and I winced but I was too tired to draw it back.

"Sorry about that," the nurse apologized. "The paramedics are gonna want to know your blood sugar levels when they get here."

I closed my eyes, wanting to escape from the drama of it all as Savanna shouted my name again. *No, please, no. Don't let her back here*, I begged, directing my inner thoughts toward Frank, wishing one of us were telepathic. He seemed to be holding her at bay. She hadn't rushed in with her tears and her panic yet. What was she doing in the office anyway?

The nurse took a sharp intake of breath. "Four hundred…" she didn't enunciate the last few numbers for me to hear correctly, but dammit, that was too high, and we both knew it. "You're gonna be okay," she attempted to reassure me, but she was no longer hiding her concern. I could vaguely hear sirens in the background as the ambulance grew near.

"I think…" I heard Savanna start to say, but the rest of her words were drowned out by the commotion.

"…need to lower your voice," Frank said.

"No," Savanna argued. She sounded closer. I squeezed my eyes tighter. "This happened one time." She was definitely right outside the door now. Damn it. How did she get past Frank? My head continued to swim, and I hunched farther forward, hugging my stomach. "Bradley." She let out a breath. I ignored her, hoping Frank would get her to go away.

"You need to keep back, Savanna," the nurse ordered.

"I just want to try something."

The nurse wasn't having it. "Darling, the paramedics are going to be here any second, and they're going to need space to work."

Savanna's hand ran down my right arm in protest, tangling her fingers in my gross snot-and-puke-covered hand without hesitation. She grunted as she got on the floor to lean against my leg and the chair, resting her chin on my knee. I refused to open my eyes, even if I couldn't see her well through my blurry vision. I tried to slip my hand from her grasp, but she held on tight, her warmth gathering at my fingertips. I felt myself slipping, my muscles relaxing, and then…

★

I woke to the rhythmic sound of a heart monitor. Blinking in the sight of the hospital overhead lights, I coughed, the sensation tearing at my parched throat.

"There's my favorite patient," my doctor said, the wheels of his chair rolling toward me. I turned my head slightly to see him smiling at me as he wrote something in my chart. Then he set the clipboard near my legs, nodding across the bed. "Got quite a girl over there." He pocketed his pen in his white coat, trading it for a flashlight. "Refused to leave your side."

Someone squeezed my hand. I didn't turn to confirm, but I didn't have to see her to know it was Savanna. I didn't want to accidentally meet her gaze. Her dad was gonna be furious when he realized where she was. And you know whose fault it would be? Mine. Everything was always my fault.

I swallowed, but there wasn't much saliva in my dry mouth to coat my throat. I coughed again.

"Human touch is known for accomplishing some miraculous work. Your school nurse said your blood sugar was in the high four hundreds, but by the time you made it here, it had dropped to three-fifty." He shined the light in my eyes, and I blinked, listening to his words in an attempt to ignore Savanna. "It's still dropping, but we seem to have gotten you awake in record time." He leaned in closer, winking as he lowered his voice conspiratorially. "I say let her keep holding your hand. There's nothing better than a magic touch." I wanted to roll my eyes. I liked this doctor. We'd switched to him after the incident with Dr. Sauer. He worked out of the hospital, so he was always on call when things like this happened. But sometimes he was a little too quick to accept the supernatural. Magical touch? Really?

He leaned back, slapping his knees. "Your parents should be here soon. I'll update them when they arrive. But for now, I'd say get some rest. You were close to a real bad spell there." He stood to leave, then stopped near the dividing curtain. "A nurse may be in here in a few to take some blood so we can run a few routine tests. I gotta say, Bradley, I was hoping I'd seen the last of you." *Yeah, me too.* "Guess we're stuck with each other for a little longer until we figure this out." He walked back to my bed, grabbed the chart, and slid it into a pouch at my feet. Disappearing behind the curtain, he left me alone with Savanna. We hadn't been alone in a room together since the week after she got pregnant.

It was silent for a few moments as I stared at the ceiling, contemplating my fate.

"I'm not letting go of you," Savanna said after a long moment, her thumb stroking a vein in my hand.

I kept staring at the lights. "Where's Frank?" My voice cracked, froggy.

"Signing some papers." I heard her shift her weight in her chair. "Here." She held a jug of water out to me, tilting it so the straw bent toward my mouth. "You should drink something."

I didn't move. She was still holding my hand. If she was in any way inclined to attempt to force me to drink it, she would have to let go.

After a few seconds of my nonresponsiveness, she set the jug back where she'd taken it. "Are you mad at me?"

I closed my eyes.

She slipped her free hand under mine, cupping my hand between both of hers, then lifted my hand so it was in front of her chin. "Come on, Bradley. We haven't had a real conversation since you went away for Christmas break." Her breath tickled my fingers before her lips pressed against them. She must've wiped the snot and puke off during the brief time I was unconscious, but still, she knew exactly what had covered that hand earlier. What was she doing kissing it?

"You're going to get sick," I managed to say. Seriously, didn't pregnant people have lower immune systems or something? I blinked open one eye then another as I finally took her into view. My heart fluttered at the sight of her blue eyes. It was always a traitor.

A small smile tugged at the corner of her lips as she held my hand against the skin of her cheek. "That's at least one thing you've said to me."

I glanced at our entwined hands—the source of a familiar warmth. We weren't glowing, but still, the warmth was there.

"I meant it when I said I wasn't letting go," she said, her eyes boring into mine. "If I let go, your stats skyrocket."

I grimaced. How long were we gonna have to stay like that? What if one of us had to pee? Savanna's bladder had seemed to be notoriously small lately.

"It's just until the meds kick in," Savanna said as if she'd read my mind, but then a funny expression flickered across her face as she pulled her head back, shifting her weight once again. She reflexively dropped her hands to the side of her stomach, tugging mine along with hers. My fingers brushed the fabric of her shirt and for a brief moment, I thought I felt movement as Savanna stilled. Her eyes glanced at me before pressing my hand flat against her stomach. "Can you feel that?"

I waited, staring intently at the spot where our hands met. There was nothing. I must have imagined it. As I started to pull away, Savanna gripped my wrist, guiding me back to a specific spot. "There."

To my embarrassment, a sudden movement below her navel caused me to flinch. She laughed as I tentatively placed my hand back at the spot. "It's strange, isn't it?" she asked. "There's a whole life in there." The fluttering beneath my palm continued. "I think that's her elbow. Her kicks are a little bit stronger."

"Her?" I croaked, my heartbeat stuttering. "It's a girl?" I had assumed it was gonna be a boy. The Chosen Ones alternated sex as they reincarnated, so I thought it was the same for Immortal Ones.

She shrugged. "I don't actually know, but I have a strong feeling. I can't explain it." The movement halted, but Savanna continued to press my hand against her stomach. It was amazing to me how another life could form and exist inside her. Even without her usual abilities, she couldn't possibly be as helpless as others treated her. At that moment, I couldn't help but think that there seemed to be nothing more powerful than a person with a human inside them. *We* had created a life, but it was *her* body that sustained it, and it was her body keeping me alive too.

"You're a life support machine," I said without thinking.

She snorted, almost like that statement was offensive to her somehow. "What?"

I bit my tongue, struggling to make it sound more romantic. "You're my life support," I whispered, flipping my hand so our fingers could once again intertwine.

She gripped my hand with both of hers, holding it up against her cheek as she leaned forward. Her smile faltered as she drew in a deep breath. "I'm only human." A tear slipped from her glistening eyes, splashing on my fingers. "I don't know how to explain this to you when you can't feel my feelings anymore, but I am so scared.

And I know I've said that before, but there's just no other way to say it."

She sniffled, and I squeezed her hand, unsure how to respond, because the truth was, I was scared too, but we couldn't both be scared. It was still her turn. She had more of a right.

"Remember when Jay-Jay thought I was going to die, and before we realized I wasn't, there was this awful suffocating sense of dread and panic?" she asked.

I nodded, bringing my free hand—IV and all—to rub a spot on the side of my nose, just below my eye, where I was sure I'd felt a tear slip.

She shook her head. "This feels worse, and I can't explain why. Nobody's had any horrible visions that foretell either of our deaths and yet this feels like the end. Bradley, you could have died today." She moved her hands to the bed, scooting closer.

"The paramedics would have—"

"You could have died today." Her tone was serious. She stared at me long and hard, the way Frank usually does when he's feeling particularly convincing. "Fate doesn't need you like it needs me. Our connection exists just enough so that I can heal you, but I'm starting to think you can really die. You're not as immortal as history has led us to believe. And I know we've gotten used to the idea that we would die someday together, but… what if this is a loophole? Bradley, I refuse to let you go first."

I averted my eyes, staring at the curtained wall instead. I was correct back in Frank's office. I would always be the weak link. This time, fate didn't need me to be a survivor. My life was no longer guaranteed.

I closed my eyes. "Why didn't it work?" I groaned. Why didn't the cure work on me? What did fate have to gain from this?

Savanna sighed. "I'm sorry about the cure. I didn't mean to get your hopes up."

I reopened my eyes, turning my head to gaze back at the ceiling. "It's not your fault," I muttered. "Nothing is ever your fault."

"Everything is falling apart around me—my family, my friends, my life as I knew it. I just... I know we kind of crashed and burned, and I don't really know where we stand anymore, but it would be nice if—"

I tugged her hand to my chest. "I don't want to promise never to leave you again," I said to the ceiling. "I always break that promise. With everything going on, I'd be surprised if we didn't have to split up for a while. It might be safer that way. But I'm gonna be really bummed in the afterlife if I can't see you every day. I don't want to leave you, but I'm afraid I will have to."

She nodded, sniffling. "Normally I'd object but"— she pulled one of her hands away to stroke her stomach— "it's not just us anymore. It's every diviner."

I peered at her stomach from the corner of my eyes, my shoulders never feeling heavier. I swallowed hard. "I overheard my parents talking." I turned my head to meet her gaze. "I heard my dad ask why we couldn't just be kids—why we weren't allowed. And it hit me—the reality of our family's curse. Alcoholics and Holocaust survivors and asylum seekers down to my mom and her engagements and to me and New Mexico and Jesse and all the funerals of friends and now Paige and her issues and us… we never stood a chance. And I don't want to scare you more, but I don't think she"—I moved our hands in her stomach's direction—"stands much of a chance either. She's never going to get to be just a kid."

Savanna bowed her head. "Bradley, I don't know if I can do this," she cried. "The closer we get to August, the closer it feels like we're getting to doomsday. I want her to be a kid, but I'm not sure how long we'll have with her. No offense but having Rebecca here and the Sullys and Porters isn't really giving me any confidence. I'm trying not to get too attached to her in case we have to leave her with someone, but it's getting impossible when she is literally attached to me, which makes thinking about the future really hard right now." She leaned over, resting her head next to my stomach. I wanted to stroke her hair, but she still had a hold of my hand.

It struck me how, even if we weren't allowed to be kids, the likelihood that we would really truly be parents was slim too. If history repeated itself, somebody else would be taking care of our kid, and we would be dead—

never having been kids, never having been adults. We were only humans coveting a life.

12 // I VISIT THE SPIRIT REALM
REBECCA

Slipping from my grasp, my math textbook slammed onto my foot. That wasn't the most pressing issue, though. A strange coldness swept over my body. Like, instead of standing in the school hallway, I was in an icebox. I crouched to grab my fallen book, trying to ignore the cold, but the sight of my breath stopped me in my tracks.

I had thought the feeling of cold was a warning sign. Someone—probably Bradley—was injured or sick. But feelings like that didn't usually come with something so visible.

I glanced around me to see if my schoolmates were cold as well, but as I turned, they disappeared in waves of colorful smoke. Soon, I was alone in a freezing school hallway. Stranger still, I could still hear the chatter of middle schoolers blurred into a mix of sounds. I couldn't make out specific words, but their bodiless voices floated in the air I breathed.

That's when the singing started—the singing that I always heard when Maria was nearby. I followed the beautiful notes as they appeared in physical form, floating in wispy spaces of air. They decorated the hallway, beckoning me with their graceful dance. I examined the notes as I passed, remembering how I had planned to learn violin last year. If only I had an instrument to play gently in the background, serenading alongside them.

Rounding the corner, I walked straight through a note, the singing halting as the note turned to fog—shapeless and unimportant. I watched it float unhappily, running my fingers through its broken form. The fog shifted, revealing slash lines where I had touched it. When I lifted my hand to slash it again, a form seemed to be protruding from the cloud. I reached to touch it and screamed.

Something had clamped its clawed hand around my wrist.

I tugged, trying to free my hand from the cloud monster, but it was no use. The cloud elongated, stretching to the floor at a height taller than me. I pulled harder to free my wrist, but as I pulled, the denser the cloud became, solidifying. It didn't take long for me to finally see the hand that was refusing to let go. I gasped. It wasn't clawed and monster-like at all. It appeared to belong to a human with smooth, fair skin.

I stopped moving, adjusting my gaze to take on the newly formed human figure. The creature standing before me was tall, blond, and pale. She smiled down at me, her teeth in perfect white rows. Her ocean-colored eyes swam in swirls as she beamed. Her golden hair shimmered, not yet as solid as the rest of her body. "Rebecca." As she said my name, she almost sounded like she was purring. I stared at the sound as it reverberated off the metal lockers. Still, she gripped my wrist, pulling me closer. "The spirit realm welcomes you." At her words, whisps of gray smoke dropped from the ceiling, immediately forming into more human-like figures, all staring at me with a look of determined expectation. I was used to that look by now. As the Chosen One, the diviners I encountered all seemed to expect great things from me.

The blond-haired girl's smile faltered. "We need your help."

The new arrivals nodded, not a single face familiar to me. Of course the ancestors needed my help. As long as everybody else did, why not?

"With what?" I asked, attempting to twist my arm free. When it looked like she wasn't going to let go, I gave up.

"The universal balance has been tipped. Spirits are unintentionally crossing the divide among the realms. It is wreaking havoc on the living." She held my arm up. "I am holding you—don't you see?" Her calm attitude quickly shifted to agitation as she scowled, dropping my wrist. She crossed her arms. "There are dark spirits we keep hidden in our realm. Many have escaped into yours—taking over bodies…" Her ocean eyes drifted off-center with her voice. A thought must have distracted her. I waited until her eyebrows drew closer, her skin puckering above her nose. "Have you noticed anything in the last few months? Murders?"

I shook my head. It wasn't like I kept up with the news.

"What about suicides?" She narrowed her eyes, puckering her lips. "Especially from people you wouldn't normally worry about?"

My brain flashed to my sister. She'd always been moody and dramatic, but depressed? There had to be a reason not even Mom had seen it coming. Could her attempt last December have been the result of an evil spirit gone wild? It would make sense for evil to go after our family. With a Fated One and a Chosen One under the same roof and an Immortal One on the way, we were targets, whether we wanted to be or not. Most of our enemies knew to keep their distance as long as I was around, but what would a spirit have to fear? I had no power over the dead.

I nodded to the spirit girl, gulping at the thought. "My sister tried to kill herself a few days before Christmas. Could a spirit have done that?"

The girl dropped her head, sighing. "One of our captives was a Bulgarian serial killer in the sixties. He poisoned teenage girls, first in their minds, then in their bodies. If he has targeted your sister, her only hope is for the balance to be restored. Think of the world as an old weighing scale. On one side, you have the spirit realm; on the other, you have the land of the living. If we can tilt the balance to its rightful place, all the escaped spirits will be forced back to our side. They will no longer have a foothold in your world. Your sister will be safe."

My heartbeat quickened. Could I really stop Paige from ever trying to kill herself again? Could I keep her safe from the dark spirits and their influence? Without much thought, I knew I had to try. Even if Paige seemed stable now, I knew she wouldn't stay that way.

"Please, how can I restore the balance?" I begged.

She was quiet for a moment as she chewed her lip. Finally, she sighed. "We heard a rumor that a new Immortal One is about to be born." The spirits around us nodded in agreement.

My heart sank. They were talking about my niece or nephew. There was never good news that came with that subject.

She blinked, her blue eyes disappearing for a moment. "You can sense it, can't you?"

I bit my lip, nodding.

She huffed. "This happens every time a new one is about to be born. The dark spirits escape, people die at higher rates. It only ever resolves when the immortal count is down to one. Immortality comes with a price. Think about it. The last time an Immortal One was born, the Holocaust was happening."

I shivered as new sets of goose bumps formed on my skin. She was right. Maria was born at an infamous death camp. The only thing that didn't make sense was the fact that Maria was—according to legend—about to lose her immortality. Once the baby is born, her immortality is supposed to disappear. "Won't this issue fix itself in a few months? Immortal Ones aren't truly immortal. The Fates made sure of it."

The girl shook her head. "The last Immortal One didn't die until twenty years after the current one's birth. We were chasing dark spirits into multiple wars when they suddenly bounced back to our realm in the 1960s. We can avoid that this time. Fates like you have the power to end any life, including an Immortal One. You can stop the murders. You can stop your sister's life from being taken."

"You…" I stopped, going over her words in my head to make sure I had heard her right. "You want me to kill Maria?"

She lifted her head, widening her eyes. "It's not about what I want. It's about what the world *needs*." She stepped closer, her footsteps soundless. "We're talking about the fate of the world versus the fate of one person. Surely, as a Fate, this would be of special interest to you."

I scowled. "You're talking about murder."

"I'm talking about saving millions of people. Don't tell me you're a pacifist. I've met spirits in my realm who have died at your hands."

The eyes of a dead neo-Nazi—pale and lifeless— stared back at me in my memory. He had been a victim of the blast I had caused in the bunker. I opened my mouth to argue that it was self-defense, then closed it when I realized it wasn't. I caused the wall to explode in *Savanna's* defense. And who knows who else died when I collapsed their hidden fortress. That was before I knew about my powers. I hadn't known I could materialize earthquakes—not until I did it. I wasn't supposed to be a Fate.

The girl lifted an eyebrow. "The fate of the world is in your hands."

In a puff of smoke, she was gone, the other spirits following her disappearance. My ears rang violently, and I screamed, covering them and squeezing my eyes shut. Somebody tugged on my left arm, removing it from my ear as the ringing began to fade.

"Are you okay?" I opened my eyes to my friend Jenna peering back at me, quizzical. Clamping my mouth shut, I took in the hallway packed with students. I was back to standing in front of my locker, my math textbook at my feet. Half my schoolmates had stopped to stare.

I managed a weak smile, waving at them. They continued on, some of them reluctantly.

Jenna let go of my arm, pointing to her ear. "Do you have an earache? My brother gets terrible ear infections all the time."

I nodded, then bent to grab my textbook. Hesitating, I flashbacked to the last time I had tried to pick it up. Was it going to trigger another visit to the spirit realm? I glanced at the feet around me. I had to have been in there for at least ten minutes and yet no time had seemed to pass in this realm. Holding my breath, I lifted the book and turned back to the crowd of feet. They were still there, walking across the tile. *Phew.*

Standing straight, I caught Jenna gawking at me.

"What?" I asked, hugging my textbook to my chest self-consciously.

She snorted, smiling. "You're so weird."

I rolled my eyes. As an undivine, she had no idea. "Class?" I suggested.

She shrugged, turning toward our math class. "Guess so."

As we passed through the crowd, I heard Sage arguing with Paige. "I'm so done with your bullcrap." I craned my neck as we passed them just in time to see Sage slam her locker. "I know you weren't sleeping over at Mya's this weekend."

"You think I'm lying?" Paige shouted, defensive.

"I think you went to that party after your mom said no. Snuck out with Seth. God knows where she goes every night."

We were walking too fast for me to catch the rest of their conversation. A lot had happened the day Paige tried to kill herself. I was in San Diego with Bradley, so I wasn't there when it occurred.

Sage told me she found Paige barely conscious in their shared bedroom. My sister wouldn't say what she took, so while Mom was on the phone with emergency services, Sage and Dad tore the room apart for the culprit, finding nothing. With all the commotion, they didn't notice Seth was gone until after the paramedics took Paige and Mom to the hospital. That was when Sage started to panic.

Seth finally climbed in through the window a few minutes later, and when she realized what had happened, she checked her bag for a bottle of pills she had taken from Serena, only to find it missing. Sage had lost it on her. Dad had to break up the fight. Seth ran off, took a bus to the Lindts, got into an argument with Serena, then disappeared.

Bradley and I had come home to help look for her, but our search was interrupted by the captivators. We eventually found her at the high school football field, but by then, bigger things were happening. Nobody ever found out why Seth wasn't at the house that night, but I had a feeling it had something to do with her crush on Serena. Seth had those pills for a reason, but I doubted it was because she was taking them. I guess Sage still hadn't figured out the truth.

But anyway, had I heard Sage, right? Had Paige gone to a party over the weekend? That didn't seem correct. I distinctly remembered Mom calling Mrs. Lindt. Plus, Serena had dropped off Paige at home after the fact. Seth—as far as I saw—was home all weekend, except for her brief trip to San Jose to help distribute the cure. But wait… Paige was supposed to be in that group too with Sage. Had something happened?

Somebody bumped into me as I neared my class. I stumbled, and Jenna grabbed my hand, pulling me to the side to keep my toes from being stepped on. The other person caught themselves against a locker. The school hallways were always too crowded. I had to dodge feet and elbows constantly.

Kevin regained his footing, hiding the left side of his face with his textbook as he pushed through the crowd around us. He must've been hiding from Sage because she started to chase after him. She managed to cut him off at the turn. "Why did you cover for Paige on Saturday?"

Kevin heaved in exasperation. "Look, I'm just trying to help her."

Jenna pulled me through the door to our class, disrupting my search for clues. "Come on, the bell's about to ring."

A few boys barreled into the room, throwing wads of paper at each other. One landed in my hair. Resigned, I joined Jenna at our table.

If Kevin thought he needed to help cover for Paige—whatever that meant—then something must be wrong again.

I glanced at the clock. Time was ticking. I needed to decide who was worth more—Maria or people like my sister.

13 // WE SPIT THEORIES LIKE DRAGON FIRE
SERENA

Jay-Jay set his lunch tray down, rapping his knuckles against the table as he scanned the cafeteria. "Have you seen Bradley?" he asked, refusing to sit.

I stopped peeling my orange. Come to think of it, I hadn't seen him since I caught him sneaking off right before health class. He was a no-show in English. I shrugged. "He's probably with Frank having a mental breakdown somewhere."

Jay-Jay didn't seem reassured. He continued to stand.

I placed my half-peeled orange on the table. "You didn't have a vision, did you?"

He scowled. "I don't need a vision to know we're in trouble."

Alyssa emerged from the lunch line, heading toward us with her tray. Savanna wasn't with her like she normally was around this time. She and Alyssa came from the same class. Though I wasn't surprised, her absence still reeked of suspicion. Savanna hadn't been in any of our shared classes since she stormed out of health. I didn't blame her. I knew firsthand how cruel high school could be. But when Bradley was also missing?

"Savanna's not with you," Jay-Jay noted as Alyssa sat next to him.

She bit her lip, looking around. Her voice was quiet, barely audible as it always was when she spoke. "She wasn't in any of our classes."

Jay-Jay looked to me again, expecting an answer, like I magically knew everything about everyone's whereabouts. "Geez, I'm not everyone's keeper. Savanna left health class all mad. She's probably in the library or at home. Besides"—I crossed my arms, eyeing Alyssa—"isn't it *your* job to watch her?" I narrowed my eyes as she pursed her lips. "Or were you too distracted by your new relationship"—I kicked Jay-Jay in the leg—"to track her down?"

Her face quickly reddened as Jay-Jay exclaimed his hurt, finally sitting so he could rub his leg. "What the hell?" he said.

Alyssa didn't look at him. Instead, she bowed her head, staring way too hard at her milk carton.

"You don't have to resort to violence," Jay-Jay said through clenched teeth.

A huge sigh came from behind me before Victoria took her usual seat on the end. "Wow. Have we massively failed or what?" she asked, sounding more bored than apprehensive. She pulled a dead flower from a pocket in her cargo pants and started to crumble it with her fingers.

As the remnants of the flower landed on an empty corner of her tray, Jay-Jay groaned. "Do any of you actually care about our missing friends?"

"Not to be technical here, but we're hardly friends," I said, turning my attention back to my half-peeled orange.

Jay-Jay blinked, staring at me like I'd just knocked over his newly constructed LEGO set. "Why do you sit with us, then?"

"Survival," I answered simply.

Victoria snickered, cupping her hands over the crumbled remains of her flower. Since I knew she couldn't do any real magick, I didn't wait for her to do whatever trick she was planning. I glanced over my orange at Alyssa, who was still avoiding eye contact with everyone at the table. I swear if she bowed any further, she'd get pudding on her nose. Alyssa was so easy to embarrass, it almost wasn't fun.

Clearing my throat, I waited for her to look at me, but she didn't. *Whatever.* "So she wasn't in French class?" I asked her.

It took her a minute to respond. Finally, she shook her head, still staring into her uneaten food.

I groaned out of impatience. "Look, I'm sorry. I didn't mean to embarrass you."

"Aha!" Victoria exclaimed proudly. I turned to see her holding a black metal flower in her hand. "So frickin' metal." She held it at an angle against the tabletop. It took me a second to realize it wasn't just decoration. It was a pen.

"Clever," I said, unimpressed. "What's it supposed to do? Draw a map to Bradley and Savanna?"

She scowled. "It's a pen. What do you think?"

Jay-Jay straightened at the sight of someone behind us. I turned to see Frank making his way through the lunch crowd. He rarely patrolled the cafeteria unless someone called him, like whenever a fight broke out. He was part of the reason I wasn't worried about Bradley and Savanna's whereabouts. Once last semester, Bradley was late to school. Frank pulled us all out of class to interrogate us. If Bradley—or Savanna, for that matter—were missing, he'd have found us a long time ago.

I studied his expression. It didn't seem like he was about to lose his shit, so that was another good sign. When he reached our table, his fingertips grazed the laminate as he puffed his cheeks. After letting out a breath of air, he finally gave us the announcement we'd been waiting for. "The cure didn't work on Bradley. He's in the hospital right now recovering. Savanna's with him. So are his parents."

I snorted. "And Savanna's parents?" Surely they'd have been called by now if she wasn't in school. Judging by the way her dad reacted to the whole pregnancy news, he wasn't going to be keen on Savanna being anywhere near Bradley.

Frank knew where I was headed with the question. I could see the guilty glint in his eyes. He nodded, sucking in a breath. "I called her mom." Safe bet.

"Wait." Jay-Jay furrowed his eyebrows. "The cure didn't work?" He glanced around the table. "Has that happened before?" Like we would know the answer.

Frank sighed, shaking his head. "No. I called Bradley's grandfather, and while we can't exactly track the data, there have been zero reports of the cure not working. Bradley's been living a week thinking it has. He's got two working theories right now. Bradley was either experiencing a placebo effect until reality caught up with him today, or the cure did *something* but ultimately fizzled out. For some reason, Savanna's touch was helping him stay conscious and alert until the proper medication kicked in, which is why she is with him. She doesn't seem to be fully healing him, but something about them having physical contact is acting as a medicine."

Alyssa finally lifted her head enough to glance at Victoria. Her eyes were wide as she met Victoria's gaze. They knew something. They had to.

I snapped my fingers in front of their faces to break the eye contact. "Okay, what do you know?"

Alyssa glanced at Frank, then pulled her arms tight against her chest, curling into herself. I looked to Victoria for an explanation, but she just shrugged, blinking rapidly. "I'm surprised. Their collective powers have been missing since Savanna got pregnant. At least, that's how I understood it. The fact that she can heal him is… interesting."

Jay-Jay shook his head. "She's done it before. It's not new. When Bradley broke up with her, he had a bad physical reaction that went away when she touched him. Savanna told me about it. And when Bradley went to San Diego, my mom said he had a really bad cough, but he didn't have one when he came back."

Alyssa nodded, probably remembering since that was when she had met him.

Victoria rubbed her nose, scrunching it in the process. "I think he's stuck, then. Think about it. Even without their powers, Bradley and Savanna are connected. Doesn't the lore say something about if one of them dies, so does the other? Savanna's immortal right now. As long as she's pregnant, she self-heals. She can't die. Bradley sort of self-heals, but not nearly at the same level. His healing seems to be connected to his proximity to Savanna. Every time he's self-healed in the past, he was either across the street from her or in the same room. But theoretically, he also can't die, because if he died, so would Savanna and so would the baby. I'm not one hundred percent sure how this ties in with the cure, but maybe it won't work on him for the same reason? His body is stuck in this state of 'I can't die, but I also can't get better.' It's like he's stuck or frozen as he is. Maybe if Savanna wasn't pregnant, the cure would have worked? I don't know. There's got to be a science-y reason for it.

Life is pretty wonky for both of them right now, so it just, I don't know, makes sense for something else to just not work."

We all stared at her. I'll admit, I wasn't exactly following her logic. If there was any.

"I think it's simpler than that," Alyssa whispered. When she saw us all staring at her, she ducked her head behind her hair. "They're connected," she said in such a low voice that I had to lean forward to catch a word of it. "Maybe the baby rejected it." She grabbed her spork, distracting herself by stirring her fruit.

Jay-Jay nodded, rubbing his hands together. I couldn't believe he was accepting her nonsensical logic. "What happens when you inject the cure into someone who doesn't need it?" He looked around the table, a knowing smile cropping on his face, challenging us for an answer he clearly already knew. He put his hand on the table, his finger drawing unintelligible shapes on the tabletop. "Bradley once told me if he injected more insulin than he needed, it would be lethal."

I waited for a better explanation, but he just held his hand, palm facing up, like he'd just handed us the answer on a silver platter. Moron. I was now seeing how he and Alyssa made a semiperfect couple. God, I hated that. "Go on," I urged.

He huffed, putting his hand back down. "So Savanna has to watch what she eats and take all these vitamins and what-not because I guess everything that goes into her body goes into the baby's. What if it's the same for Bradley?"

I snorted. I couldn't help it. They may be connected, but Bradley wasn't the pregnant one. "He's been taking glucose and insulin for months," I argued. "So what? You're saying all that has been affecting a baby who's not even in his body? Next theory, please."

Victoria shrugged. "Maybe the cure doesn't work on diviners?"

Frank frowned. "I don't think sitting around a table bouncing theories off each other is going to help either of them. With the last fated couple having been dead for the last sixty-four years, we have no one similar we can ask. I'm about to make a phone call to Maria to catch her up, but I don't expect to get real answers from her. She may be immortal, but she can't talk to the dead."

Victoria straightened, waving her newly created gothic flower pen. "The dead," she said, moving her pen to tap her chin as she narrowed her eyes in thought. Oh God. She was going to insist we hold a séance. I just knew it.

"O-okay," Frank said nervously, nodding. "I'll update you kids if anything changes." He tapped the table a couple more times for emphasis before walking away.

I glanced at Victoria, who seemed lost in thought. "Let me guess. You own a Ouija board."

She didn't answer right away. After several seconds, she said, "Meet me at the sandwich shop after school." Then she picked up her tray and left.

Gertrude wouldn't start. I jammed the key into her ignition and cranked it for the umpteenth time, cursing under my breath. Victoria had already left ten minutes ago. I saw her car speed out of the parking lot, gloating. Finally, I heard the sweet tune of Gertrude's engine sputtering to life. Oh, thank God.

"So, we're really going to be summoning some ghosts?" Jay-Jay asked from the back seat, rubbing his hands in anticipation.

I rolled my eyes as I cautiously pulled Gertrude out of her spot. "Do you even believe in ghosts, Mr. Atheist?"

"Let's just say that I believe in the existence of some sort of spiritual plane. And atheist? Really? It's kind of hard to be an atheist when you've seen the things we've seen." Wow. He'd done a complete one-eighty since last year. "Just because I don't believe in God, doesn't mean I don't believe in other things."

I scoffed, adjusting my rearview mirror so I could see his face. "So what are you? Buddhist? Hindu? Jain?"

He turned to Alyssa instead. I couldn't tell for sure, but I was fairly certain he had grabbed her hand and was now holding it between them. God, I should have made one of them sit shotgun. "You know my great-grandparents were raised Buddhist. They left China after converting to Christianity."

I hit the brake a little too hard at the stop sign, stretching to turn back to him. Forget the part where he didn't actually answer my first question. "You're Chinese?" My eyes dropped to his hand, which was most definitely holding Alyssa's. He looked startled, like he wasn't expecting such a big reaction from me. I guess maybe I could have held myself back a little. But seriously. I thought he was Filipino. Or at least, that's what I thought his mom was based on her looks.

"I'm a quarter Chinese. You didn't know that?"

A car behind us honked and I turned around, hitting the gas. "You celebrate the Day of the Dead."

"That's 'cause I'm also a quarter Mexican. Not all of us can be one race like you." I had to admit, that stung a little. Sinti was in my blood through and through and while I was proud of that, the way he said it was… kind of insulting. Because here's the deal. In gadje eyes—especially white gadje—he was at least interesting. I mean, he was a rainbow of mixed races. No one knew quite what stereotype to associate him with. Once I was clocked as Roma, I was immediately categorized as a scammer or a thief. There was no escaping that by claiming another race, although Mya certainly tried. But let me get this straight. I don't wish to be anything other than Sinti. That's my blood. That's my heritage. That's my history. And I didn't need Jay-Jay or anyone else acting like it was a sin.

"Spoken like a true gadjo," I muttered under my breath.

Pulling into the parking lot of Wich Wharf, I spotted Victoria's black sedan in the back row. The parking lot was mostly empty as it always seemed to be. I stopped the car, pulling the keys out of the ignition, and had this bad feeling I was going to be made to cover Bradley's shift. I mean, this had to be a trap. Right?

14 // NEVER BRING A HOLOCAUST VICTIM BACK FROM THE DEAD
ALYSSA

I'm not sure why I agreed to go along to the séance. Maybe it was because I have a hard time saying no. Or maybe it was because Jay-Jay was going, and I didn't want to leave him hanging. But also, I'm convinced Serena hates me. And I'd rather not be around her at all. Plus, ghosts freak me out. But how could I tell anybody else that without sounding like a scaredy-cat? Or possibly inviting Serena to find something else to make fun of?

So there I was, standing in a witchy sandwich shop with Jay-Jay's oddly damp hand gripping mine and wanting nothing more than to be dismissed to the safety of my family's ghost-free apartment. And all for what? So we could potentially find out why Bradley wasn't cured of diabetes? What was the point of that? It wasn't going to solve anything other than maybe fill a void with useless knowledge. Why do people always need an answer for everything anyway? Are other people that insecure in their beliefs? There aren't always clear answers to everything, and the closer people get to accepting that, the less distracted they'll be.

Jay-Jay squeezed my hand and a shock traveled through my system. It was so weird to hold a boy's hand. I felt like that Colbie Caillat song with the toes and the nose. I wasn't sure I liked it. On one hand, it was nice to know someone liked me and was willing to hold my hand in the presence of ghosts, but on the other, it made my nerves all the more racked. Like, they're always bouncing behind my skin at every given moment of the day. I didn't need it to be worse.

Also, everybody is a first-degree burn. I don't know how else to describe how I see people. Red hands and arms spotted with flecks of blue and purple have been the default since I turned ten, and I don't think anybody else truly understands it. I have to squint and refocus to see the true pigmentation of people's skin. Now that spring had hit, I miss winter and all the clothes that people bundled in to keep warm. The cold weather had been a nice change of pace in the move from California, and I can't help but wonder if maybe, just maybe, that was why Maria recruited my family.

Nobody knows why I'm different from the other molecular manipulators. Sure, many could see through walls if they focused hard enough. It was often important to know what or who was on the other side. But I can't turn it off like they can. I am always seeing through one layer of everything. That first layer is always translucent—barely there in the image my eyes show me. It's not even a helpful ability. I've always had horrible social anxiety and let me just say, actually being able to see the audience half-naked is not in any way a comfort.

I was glad when Victoria came in from the back with an unlabeled plastic bin. I tried to focus on her. She with her love for dark layers was always a comfort. Mr. Porter followed her with his big, wide toothy grin, clapping his hands together. "I hear you kids want to contact the spirit world."

Serena crossed her arms, scoffing. "I don't." I nodded along with her, but I don't think anybody noticed.

"Are you gonna help us?" Jay-Jay asked Mr. Porter as Victoria set the bin on a table in the corner.

Mr. Porter seemed to hesitate, his smile not completely gone but also not as full as it was. He stayed by the cash register. I kinda felt bad for him. He was the only real witch we knew in the area, so he was always carrying the burden of all the witchy tasks we needed help with. Savanna's necklace, for example, was blessed by him. Victoria didn't hold enough real power to cast the protection spell. Anything magical she gave to us came from him first. "My way requires a graveyard and a direct descendant of the spirit you're trying to contact."

"And my way," Victoria said, pulling a candle from the bin and setting it on the table, "is a little something I picked up from my Wiccan friend back in New Orleans."

Mr. Porter scanned the empty dining room before stepping out from behind the counter and briskly walking to the door, where he flipped the open sign to closed. "It's probably best that you not get interrupted by hungry customers." He tracked back to the counter, rounded it, and disappeared in the back for a moment before returning with a spray bottle that looked a little like unlabeled perfume. By then, Victoria had emptied the bin of its contents—various candles, a matchbox, and one of those toy Ouija boards people buy at the mall—and arranged them on the table. She then started to bring the blinds down to cover the sunlight streaming in through the large windows.

Something wet hit my face, and I nearly jumped out of my skin. Jay-Jay's grip was the only thing that kept me from sprinting to the door.

"Sorry, sorry," Mr. Porter said, shaking his head while appearing to hold back a chuckle.

The skin on my face burned as I refocused on the perfume bottle in his hand. I was sure the heat on my face would evaporate whatever he had sprayed me with. He held it up so I could see the bottle more closely, but there was nothing of significance to it. "Rue water." As if I would know what that is.

I shot him a quizzical look, but he missed it as he gasped, looking back at the bottle. "Oh." His head swiveled among us, his eyes choosing first to land on his daughter before quickly moving to Serena and then me.

"Nobody else here is with child, correct? I should have asked first instead of assuming since, you know." His eyes fell to the floor as Serena snorted. She hugged her arms to her chest before approaching the table, saying nothing. I shook my head as Mr. Porter lifted his sight to catch my movement. He sighed in relief. "Good. This stuff can be fatal to the unborn." I squinted at the bottle, suddenly doubting its safety. I must have unconsciously taken a step back because Mr. Porter expressed a sudden urge to keep me from fleeing. "Oh, no. It's perfectly safe for everyone else. It helps rid negative energies. Catholics used to use it next to holy water to rid sins."

Jay-Jay let go of my hand and reached for the bottle, which Mr. Porter let him take. He examined it as though the lack of a label would give him answers. "So it's like holy water but can cause miscarriages?" He let out a small derisive snort. "No wonder Catholics don't use it anymore." He handed the bottle back to Mr. Porter. "You know, Savanna could have used that four months ago."

"And it would not have worked." Mr. Porter sighed, clenching the bottle.

"How do you know?" Jay-Jay backed up so he was standing next to me again.

Mr. Porter pointed to a spot below his neck. "Because the same herb that is in this water is also in her necklace."

Victoria reached the last set of blinds, letting them close over the full length of the window, shrouding us in darkness. "Wearing it and ingesting it are two different things, Dad."

Mr. Porter shrugged. "That is true, but considering the Fates seem to have a different plan in mind for Savanna, I doubt it would cause her any more harm than it would any of us if we sat around sipping it in tea. A stomachache and some mild vomiting, sure, but—"

Serena cut him off, having already chosen a chair around the table. "Can you maybe cleanse the negative energies with a less problematic herb? I can smell that stuff from here, and it smells like wet dog."

I pulled a wad of my hair in front of my nose to sniff. Ugh. I wrinkled my nose. Serena was right. Also, I was pretty sure my skin was starting to itch.

"Yeah, don't you have regular holy water?" Jay-Jay asked.

Mr. Porter clutched the bottle to his chest like it had a soul and we had insulted it. He gazed at Victoria, who was making her way back to the table. When she sat down, she noticed we were all staring at her. Well, everybody except Serena. "What?" she asked defensively. "If it happens to rain here in May, then we'll have some."

"May?" Jay-Jay asked.

She shrugged, grabbing the matchbox. "Just let him spray you. Talking to spirits can be tricky, and we need to purify the space."

Jay-Jay held out his hands questioningly. "And you can't just ask my mom's priest for some holy water?"

Victoria groaned, setting the matchbox back on the table. "And wait for however long that takes? We have rue water. We can use rue water."

I tried not to roll my eyes. Communing with the spirits couldn't possibly be as urgent of a task as she was leading us to believe. Like I said, we didn't *need* answers.

Jay-Jay finally glanced at Mr. Porter, then nodded. "Fine." Soon, we'd all been sprayed head to toe with the wet dog perfume and were sitting around the table. Victoria had lit all the candles, the fire creating shadows all around us.

"Turn off your cell phones," Victoria instructed, holding up hers to show it was already off.

Serena scoffed, crossing her arms. "Because that sounds safe. What if somebody needs us?"

"Geez, you act like we're superheroes," Jay-Jay commented, powering down his phone. I had left mine in my backpack in the back of Serena's car. Whoops. Hopefully nobody needed me. Not that I could get anywhere until Serena drove me home where my parents' car was at my full disposal… as long as they weren't using it.

Serena grumbled something I didn't catch, slipped her phone out of her pocket, and started typing furiously before powering it off. She slammed it on the table. "There. Done."

Jay-Jay turned to Mr. Porter. "I don't think that spray rid her of her negativity."

"Shut up!" She waved her arm like she'd thrown something, but there was nothing around her that was appropriate to throw, and he was too far for her to hit him.

Mr. Porter's voice was calm, his hands lying flat on the table as he peered at her. "Serena, it is vital we remain calm and open-minded during the séance. We don't want to attract the wrong type of spirit, nor do we want to disrupt the power bringing them to us. Close your eyes, take a few deep breaths, and think about your earring." He lifted his hand to flick his earlobe. "There is Romani lore about that hoop."

I smiled at the familiarity of his words. Although Mr. Porter seemed well versed in Hoodoo magick, this was a piece of knowledge taken from our Romani roots. I'd heard it enough times from the diviners and witches in San Diego to know the story. "It enhances your hearing. The bigger the hoop, the louder the spirits are."

Serena's hoop earring was small. I didn't wear hoops because they would constantly get stuck in my hair and made it too easy to accidentally yank. After one sliced a line straight down my earlobe a few years back, I let my piercing close. But Serena seemed to have clung faithfully to hers.

To my surprise, instead of fighting with Mr. Porter, she closed her eyes and took a few breaths in through her nose, letting them out through her mouth. When she opened them again, she nodded for the séance to continue.

Victoria and her dad clutched hands but didn't motion for us to join. Instead, they both closed their eyes as Mr. Porter hummed a deep, throaty hum. Victoria spoke over the sound, lifting her voice in places where her dad had grown louder, chanting in English. I wasn't sure if I was supposed to close my eyes too or watch for a sign of a ghost. I kept moving in between the two options, blinking slowly. I noticed Serena staring at the Ouija board in the center, but Jay-Jay's eyes remained closed.

"Fated One, we call you to us. Mateusz Lewandowski, we call you near. Make your presence known to us. We seek your guidance."

Whenever Mr. Porter seemed to run out of air, he would pause for a brief second to catch his breath, then continue humming as his daughter chanted. They went on like this for several minutes until the temperature dropped, and I noticed breath clouds escaping our airways. Victoria specifically seemed to have a never-ending stream of clouds dancing alongside her words. We were getting closer. I could feel it. My nerves tingled with fearful anticipation.

The pointer moved. I cringed, watching with Serena as it inched toward the I. The candles blew out. It was hard to see, but I think I heard Serena shuffle to grab the matchbox, working to relight the candles as Victoria continued to chant and Mr. Porter continued to hum. She finally managed to strike a match, holding it to the nearest candle. Her eyes happened to glance straight ahead at Jay-

Jay as she did this, but whatever she saw spooked her. She immediately waved the match so it would go out, drawing in a breath and scooting her chair back. "Holy hell."

I froze, refusing to turn to see what she was seeing. I was sitting right next to Jay-Jay and the only light in the room was the one candle she had managed to light. Victoria and Mr. Porter's chanting and humming died down as they opened their eyes, first at the Ouija board, the pointer stuck on I, not moving, then at Serena, who couldn't seem to unfreeze her terrified expression as she continued to stare at Jay-Jay. Instead, I kept my eyes on her.

Mr. Porter and his daughter didn't react like Serena. Instead, they said nothing, merely glancing at Jay-Jay in interest, as if he didn't seem any different.

Slowly, I turned, my veins running cold. But I turned to nothing. Just an empty space where he was. I blinked, squinting, and realized if I focused hard enough as I did whenever I tried to see the outer features of a person, I could sort of see him, but it made my head hurt to look at him through that lens. So I blinked again, seeing nothing. Not even his dermis or second layer of skin. I wondered what the others saw and if it was more frightening.

"Guten Tag." The bored, almost menacing voice that came from Jay-Jay's invisible-to-me direction wasn't his own. And it definitely wasn't in a language he supposedly knew.

Slowly, Serena managed to get a grip, closing her mouth and swallowing visibly, before leaning ever so slightly forward to reply in the same language.

He grumbled back in the same language I couldn't comprehend, but something in his tone made me think he was annoyed, possibly angry for summoning him. After the sound of a fist banging on the table, which I definitely felt as the table shook, he slipped into a string of Romanes. I recognized the Sinti dialect.

"Selfish. Selfish all of you. You bring me here to the world that threw me and my family to the vipers—to the gadje—those who seek and destroy. I am nothing. I am ash in this world. Ugh, I can smell it. I can smell the ash of my ancestors—of my family. It rains down on us all." His anger turned to grief, heavy hysterical sobs, shaking his words, making them almost unrecognizable. I had to strain to listen, to translate. "They hunt us. They torture us. They kill us. Why? Why did you bring me here? Why must you remind me of the horrors? How can I cross over? How can I go back?"

The table shook more violently. Victoria and Mr. Porter were still holding hands, but their free hands worked to keep the table from tipping. Serena grabbed the candle to avoid a fire, the light illuminating her face. A tear slipped from her eye, streaming down her cheek. Her lips hadn't moved to a pout, staying in their normal position as if she weren't crying at all. It took a few moments for her to speak, this time in Romanes.

"You can go." She gently set the candle back on the table as it stopped shaking.

Victoria's head swung from Serena and then to Jay-Jay's invisible form, her mouth open in shock. "U-uh," she stuttered. "Thank you."

There was no response. I waited. It was another minute before Jay-Jay's color came back and I could see him in the way I had before. He was no longer near invisible. The rest of the candles lit by themselves, the temperature in the room warming. Jay-Jay blinked, which to me, just looked like a weird trick of the light. He let out a sigh. "So that was a bust, right?"

Victoria and Mr. Porter let go of each other's hands as Victoria looked at Serena. "I wasn't catching all that. His dialect was weird. Why did you let him go?"

Serena stared at the center of the table, not moving. I wanted to tell Victoria she hadn't understood because he was speaking in the Sinti dialect, but, like usual, I could never make my lips move when I wanted them to.

"Wait, you all heard something?" Jay-Jay asked. "There was a ghost, and I missed it?"

Victoria glanced at him. "You were the ghost. You were channeling him."

Jay-Jay slumped his shoulders. "Aw, man."

I continued to watch Serena, waiting for her to say something. Finally, she opened her mouth, her voice croaky. "I understood him. He wasn't going to help us." She stood and walked toward the door, unlocked it, and left. Somehow, I knew she didn't just mean the language. She understood his emotion too.

We shouldn't have summoned a ghost who died in the Holocaust. He clearly had some unresolved issues. From what I knew about Serena, so did she.

15 // OLGA COMPARES MY BABY TO JESUS CHRIST
SAVANNA

"I think my dad is the devil incarnate. Seriously. I mean, at this point, I don't care. He can either get a grip or get out, because at this point, he is actively working against us all," I grumbled into my phone.

Days had passed since Bradley was in the hospital, and I was still mad at my dad for making me leave. I mean, at least by the time he arrived, Bradley was starting to respond to the meds, so me letting go didn't immediately cause him to lose consciousness, but the sheer disrespect he had for Bradley's life…

Olga's voice came through my cell phone speaker, her unsurprise apparent in her tone. "Parents suck." When it came to complaining about family, I'd found Olga to be the best outlet. Marcie didn't understand. Jay-Jay's mom would do anything for him. And Bradley's and Serena's? They had their pros and cons, but they came through when it mattered most. I used to think my parents were the same way, but my dad especially had gone off the deep end lately. Olga, on the other hand, was the rebel daughter of strict religious parents. She got it.

I covered my forehead with my hand as I continued to pace the women's restroom. "It's gotten to the point that I don't even want to go home." My voice broke near the end of my sentence, my throat burning as I tried to swallow the resulting lump. I hated how close to the end of the school day it was. Just thinking about the fact that I had to go home soon made me anxious. I brushed my fingers over my hair, feeling several strands that had come loose from my ponytail. "I've heard of parents overreacting, but not like this. My dad is so suffocating."

Olga smacked her lips. "You can always crash at my place. It's a dump, but my parents stopped trying to check my room eons ago after I got a lock installed. Besides, my mom's afraid to go anywhere near the 'dark energy' she senses from it. Between you and me, I think it's the dragon's blood incense she doesn't like. Hey! I have an idea. Shapeshift into a dragon and scare the living shit out of your dad. It worked for me."

I rolled my eyes, biting back the bitter envy for her functional abilities. "Yeah, I'll make sure to do that."

Olga huffed. "Savanna, I'm serious. If home isn't safe for you anymore, get the fuck out. I'm tired of my friends living in homes where their feelings and safety don't matter. I've been going through it with Chad for years, but his asshole parents have him so conditioned he won't leave. You have a chance to change your future— or more accurately, your present. If there's somewhere better you can go, go there."

I closed my eyes. Something in my chest felt like it was swelling. My heart? My lungs? "I'm *fifteen*," I reminded her, the various voices from my recent memories chattering the same thing in my head. My age always seemed to be a big deal. To adults, being fifteen seemed to mean I didn't have the capacity or capability to handle my situation. And sometimes, I couldn't help but believe them.

Olga snorted. "So what? You're older than the Virgin Mary was. And you know what? She had to leave her family too. She had to travel and make sacrifices and deal with everyone—including Joseph at one point—painting her as a whore. Nobody would offer her a place to stay, she had to give birth in a barn, and then King Herod was so paranoid he'd be overthrown by a fetus that he ordered all children under two to be killed. You have to admit, the parallels alone—"

I cut her off. Was she kidding me right now? "My baby isn't Jesus Christ."

Olga groaned. "My point is my offer still stands. And I'm sure I'm not the only person who's willing to share a room with you. You have options. Just because you're fifteen doesn't mean you can't consider them."

I racked my brain for potential options. As much as getting away sounded nice, I didn't want to leave Bradley. For once, Bradley had some sense of stability—he had a job and all these ties to people here. He had convinced himself it was better to stay instead of plaguing another city with our chaos. He was biding his time, waiting for the last minute to run. It was easy for him to do that when we hadn't heard from the captivators since December. For once, I was the one ready to run. Was this what it had felt like for him? Instability equaled danger? Danger equaled running?

I thought about all the times he left me. First, when he thought he'd hurt my mom. Second, when Jay-Jay had reconvinced him he was the cause of all our problems. And third, the day he broke up with me, which I later learned was to avoid all of what was happening now. I still hated him for that last one, but I understood his logic. He knew this whole situation we were in would suck. Too bad he was too late.

"What are you thinking?" Olga asked after my long pause.

I chewed on my nails, removing them from between my teeth to speak. "I'm thinking I don't want to be Bradley."

I thought I heard Olga smirk. "What is with us and traumatized men?"

I wanted to laugh, but instead a sob slipped from my lips, my eyes and throat burning. Something about her joke wasn't sitting right with me, but who was I to know why? The hormones never told me anything.

There was some shuffling on the other line, then her words came out rushed. "Hey, I gotta go. Don't forget to name me godmother of that little tyke, capisce?"

I managed to stumble out a laugh before she hung up. Standing in the bathroom awhile longer, I waited for my emotions to regulate. I didn't want to be seen in public if it looked like I'd been crying.

I managed to slip out before the final bell rang. As I slowly walked to my locker, the bell dismissed everyone and the hallways suddenly crowded with students. Most people tried to keep their distance from me, shooting me nervous looks with judgmental eyes. Occasionally, the crowd would get so bad that someone would accidentally bump into me. It was one of those times—someone pushing through the crowd behind me, brushing roughly against my arm as they passed. I was shoved into a nearby group, the members cringing and gently trying to steer me away like my pregnancy was contagious or something. I blinked, squinting at the boy who had knocked me sideways as he rushed through the crowd. "Liam?" I shouted over the noise.

He hesitated, getting caught by a roadblock in the crowd, and stopped, twisting to see me. I rarely saw Liam. He wasn't as involved in the diviner chaos, plus he was in the grade above me. He was a heavyset guy with blond hair gelled into spikes. I silently questioned if he dyed it or if his hair was naturally blond. It didn't match his roots and eyebrows, but it could still be natural. He stared at my stomach as he approached me, waving his hand in its direction. "You know, I heard through the grapevine about all this." He bit his lip, clutching his backpack strap.

"Congratulations, I guess." He didn't meet my gaze. Instead, he kept staring at my stomach.

I wanted to tell him my eyes were on my face, but also what had he just said to me? I blinked. I had to have heard him wrong. "Con…gratulations?" I repeated questioningly. Nobody had said that to me. Not once in the past five months.

Finally, he looked up, blinking rapidly like he'd just woken from a daze. He nervously scratched the back of his scalp. "Well, yeah. I hope that's okay for me to say. You probably don't hear it enough." He stuffed his hands in his pockets, swaying a little.

"I've literally never heard it. From anyone."

He pulled his hands out, seemingly shocked. "Well, I think you deserve to hear it at least once. I know you probably didn't plan it, and I don't know. I guess at the very least you should be congratulated for your bravery."

My heart fluttered at his words. Bravery. Was I brave? I hadn't really felt like it lately. I was more a victim of circumstance. He stepped to move away, but I caught his arm. "Wait." He turned. I couldn't let the only person who'd given me a compliment walk away like that. "What makes you think that?"

He shrugged and sighed, like my interest was minorly inconvenient for him. What was he in such a hurry for? Nevertheless, he stayed. "Look, I'm pro-choice all the way. No matter what choice you made, I would still think you're brave for it. But I think you being here, not hiding or running despite whatever rumors I'm sure you're dealing with, shows exceptional strength and... what's the word?" He snapped his fingers. "Perseverance. And you know what? I guess I've known that about you from the moment we met. You don't give up. You stay. You fight. You find another way. And I think that's really brave." He started to back into the thinning crowd, seemingly eager to reach his destination. "Don't let other people's expectations set your goals. Especially if they expect you to fail."

He dipped past a group of juniors and disappeared down the hall, leaving me shaking a little. *I'm brave*, I thought. I let that sentiment warm me, even just for a second. And I was grateful. Grateful for Liam's kind words amid my despair.

My feet ached from all the standing I'd been doing, but there was nowhere nearby to sit. I grimaced, heading in the opposite direction toward my locker.

Unlike Liam, I didn't have to be in such a hurry to leave. My dad was showing a house, so it was my mom's day to pick me up. She always took a little longer to get across town from her work.

When I rounded the corner, Jay-Jay was standing at my locker with his cell phone in his hand, his jaw slack and his eyes wide. The second he saw me, he crossed the distance between us. I gritted my teeth. I didn't need an escort, but it seemed everywhere I went, a diviner was waiting.

"Have you checked your messages?" he asked, his eyes bouncing from my empty hands to my bag. Without asking, he dove for my bag, lifting the flap and rummaging through it as it dangled from my shoulder.

"What are you doing?" I asked. If any other guy had gone through my bag without permission, I would have kneed him in the groin.

He pulled my phone out, revealing the notification screen. A voice mail from my mom was waiting for me and it looked long. "My mom just called," he said, handing my phone to me. I didn't listen to the message, instead waiting for him to summarize his apparent anxiety. "You're coming home with me."

"What?" I shook my head, not understanding. "No, I'm not." I was barely allowed to leave the house for school. No way would I have permission to go to Jay-Jay's house. I glanced at the voice mail on my phone screen. I couldn't be in immediate danger. If I were, Jay-Jay's house would probably be the last place I'd be sent. His mom wasn't a diviner, and Jay-Jay wasn't much of a fighter.

"Just—" He stopped, visibly gulping. The tension around his eyes remained, but his dark irises glistened pleadingly. "Just listen to the voice mail. I don't wanna be the messenger."

I stepped back, dread passing through me. Something bad really *had* happened then. The baby practically did a somersault in my stomach. I was never going to get used to her movements. I gripped my phone in both hands, staring at the voice mail notification. It was exactly three minutes long, which meant she'd probably been cut off while leaving it. She'd hit the recording limit. I turned away from Jay-Jay so we couldn't see each other's faces and hit play, holding my phone to my ear. My mom spoke fast, sniffling between every other word, her voice straining to keep calm.

"Savanna, honey, I know this is last minute, but I couldn't risk your father finding out and stopping this. I've done all I can to keep you safe while still keeping you in this house." My blood ran cold, my panic blocking out her next few words. I gripped the phone tighter, struggling to keep myself together. This was it. She was kicking me out. *Me* instead of my dad. "I had a horrible day at work today," she continued. "We waited too long to pull a kid from their house and we lost them." She paused to take a deep, shaky breath. "I don't want to lose you too."

Okay, Dad was mad, but I didn't think he was murderous. Had he said something to her or was she overreacting? For a second, I forgot I was listening to a recording. "Mom, no." My voice shook with the order. She didn't hear me. "Kick *him* out," I begged in a tiny, strangled voice. Jay-Jay's hand touched my shoulder, and I shrugged him away. The hallway had cleared. Nobody but Jay-Jay could hear me cry.

"I can't have him antagonizing or emotionally and verbally abusing you anymore. I need to separate you for a while. I need to shock him into seeing what he is doing to our family. I need my husband back."

"You don't need your daughter?" I screamed, stomping my foot. "Screw him!"

"Ursula is helping me gather your things. We'll be dropping what we can off at Adalyn Jones's house before your father gets home. I don't want him to know where you are. He might try to bring you back before he's better and I can't risk that. He loves you, but he needs to work through some of his anger, and I think you leaving is going to be the catalyst he needs to change."

I gritted my teeth. She was practically putting me in witness protection. I could always show up at the house and ruin her stupid plan. I was already thinking about leaving, but not like this. Not because I was being forced against my will. This hurt worse. The problem wasn't me. It was my dad. Did she honestly think she could change his mind?

"He could always show up at school," I muttered, knowing this time that she couldn't hear me.

"Addie's going to take really good care of you. I'm not going to be able to answer your calls while your father's around, and I'm really sorry about that. But I need to establish these boundaries—"

I didn't want to listen anymore. I had thought my mom was on my side, but it was all a lie. What had I done to suddenly spur this on? Was she mad about me skipping classes? If that was it, I wouldn't do it anymore. I'd do anything. Yanking the cell phone from my ear, I pushed the pause button, closing the app. Taking a deep breath, I speed-dialed her, bringing my phone back up to my ear to listen to the dial tone. A robotic voice answered. "The person you are trying to reach is currently unavailable." My jaw dropped as I ended the call, all the air leaving my lungs at once. "She blocked me." I couldn't breathe. She. Blocked. Me. Her own daughter. The one she's been standing up for since New Year's.

I needed to sit down before I fell down. Everything hurt—my feet, my calves, my back. The baby pressed against my ribs, trying to nestle herself to safety. Could she feel my panic? The feeling of betrayal sinking in the pit of my stomach? This wasn't happening. I hadn't had time to prepare for the apparently very real possibility. I was out—too much for my parents to handle. I hugged my stomach, leaning my forehead on a nearby locker, struggling to keep myself upright.

"I didn't see this coming. I swear," Jay-Jay said.

I closed my eyes. Of course he didn't. The downside of my necklace kept psychics from seeing anything having to do with me. Mind readers and telepaths could forget digging through my thoughts. It didn't keep anyone from trying, though.

I ran my thumb across my stomach, knowing I wouldn't feel the baby from the outside. She'd officially nestled farther in, making it even harder to breathe. My heart ached, wanting to apologize to her, wanting to coax her out from under my ribs. I was sorry—sorry her grandpa was a shithead. Sorry her grandma couldn't keep her priorities straight. Sorry her dad wouldn't promise to stay. Sorry she had me as a mother.

Was this bravery? Or were Liam's words lies? A sob escaped my lips, my chin trembling. Liam's advice meant nothing when I had zero control.

"Come on," Jay-Jay said, his hand on my back. "Come home with me."

Home. I had no home.

16 // SHE IS EVERYTHING TO ME
BRADLEY

My phone buzzed on the nightstand, interrupting my restless sleep. I glanced at the clock as I groaned, reaching for the phone to read the caller ID. *Olga?* I blinked, trying to rid the sleep from my eyes. It was the middle of the night. Three in the morning to be exact. I almost didn't pick up, but it wasn't as if I could sleep either.

"What?" I groaned again as I sat up, attempting to stretch my stiff muscles.

"Don't *what* me!" Oh good. Angry Olga. The perfect wake-up call. "What the hell is wrong with you?" *A lot of things.* "You need to be with your baby mama right now."

I rubbed my eyes. "No offense, Olga, but you don't really know what's happening right now. I can't go over there without getting my head chopped off."

"No, *you* don't know what's happening right now. I've been on the phone with Savanna for two straight hours! I had to grab my charger and plug it into a stranger's wall in the middle of the call."

I glanced at the clock again, sure I had read it wrong the first time. Nope. Still three o'clock in the morning. "She called you in the middle of the night?"

She huffed. "It's party time, Brad. I'm wide awake. I missed a game of beer pong and ran out of cigarettes twenty minutes ago for that girl." She coughed, and I cringed. It sounded like she was hacking up a hairball.

"You should really stop smoking," I commented, despite knowing it would only fuel her anger. If she was at a party, she was likely drunk or high too.

"That's not the point! If you two had fixed your communication issues, I wouldn't be playing telephone with you."

I rolled my eyes. "You're drunk, and I'm hanging up."

"Do I sound like I'm slurring?" she screeched. I held the phone a few inches from my ear to avoid any hearing damage. "You do not knock a girl up and leave her like you did."

"I didn't leave her," I mumbled. It was way too early for this conversation. Sure, our relationship was complicated, but I didn't just up and ditch her. Being banned from seeing her outside of school and leaving her were two completely different things. And hey, I got a job. I did that for *her.*

"Maybe not physically and by choice, but emotionally you've been a rock, and that's not a compliment."

"I tried to support her, and she pushed me away. And now that I've done exactly what she asked, what? I'm still just as evil? I'm not the bad guy here. I care. I told her I care. She's just sick of our reality. I can't change that. In fact, I can't change anything." I could hear my voice rising and I struggled to keep it down. Someone was bound to hear me and come asking questions.

"Look, I don't know what you said to her, but Savanna thinks she's alone in this."

I gritted my teeth. "She made herself alone. That wasn't me."

"Would you shut up?" Olga growled. "She doesn't have any family right now. They kicked her out."

My heart stuttered. I was on my feet in a second. "What? Well, where is she?"

Olga groaned. "She's at her gay friend's house. I think I remember his name being Jay-Jay?"

I rolled my eyes. Jay-Jay wasn't gay. At least, I didn't think so. "But that's not why I called. I called to tell you off for being an asshole. I never thought you'd be like this—"

I hung up in the middle of her rant. Olga could vent to me some other time. I needed to see Savanna. I needed to make sure she was alright. Grabbing the nearest pair of pants, I stumbled into them, tripping once or twice as I shoved my legs in.

Jay-Jay lived on the other side of the neighborhood, making it an easy jog to his house. The problem was escaping my own house without being seen or heard. Savanna used to jump from my second-story window, but she was a gymnast. She knew how to land without injury.

I glanced out the window, the darkness making it nearly impossible to see the ground, but just as I looked away, I thought I saw movement. A passing headlight briefly shone through the fence, revealing Seth dragging something out from behind a bush. It looked suspiciously like a broken skateboard. Unlocking my window, I tried to move the frame as quietly as I could. If I scared her and she screamed, we were both dead meat.

The frame squealed, having not been opened in months. I cringed, peering through the darkness at Seth's temporarily frozen form. I couldn't see her expression, but luckily, she hadn't screamed like I thought she would. There was a long silent pause as I hung my head out the window trying to gauge the appropriate speaking volume that would allow her to hear me but not get us caught.

She broke the silence first, hissing her words in the quiet of the night. "Don't tell Mom." The word *Mom* sounded strange on her lips. When had she started calling my mom *Mom*?

I leaned farther out the window. "Just help me get out of here."

She bent, moving the skateboard-shaped object directly under my window, and stepped back. Holding her hand out, she aimed her palm at the object. The skateboard floated toward me. Once it was horizontal with my window ledge, it stopped, waiting.

"You want me to get on that?" It was narrow and wheel-less. Barely enough room for my feet. In fact, now that I had a better view of it, I recognized it as the one I broke when I was nine. I thought one of my parents had tossed it. Where had Seth found it?

"Hurry," Seth hissed.

With the added sense of urgency, I reached to grab the end, hoping my grip would keep me balanced as I lifted my foot over the sill. The skateboard shook a little under my weight, and I closed my eyes, pulling my other leg over until I was crouching on the board. I kept my eyes closed the entire way down, hoping my weight wasn't too much for Seth's telekinesis. Paige had always been the stronger telekinetic. When I felt the grass touch my knuckles, I opened my eyes and quickly moved my hands so my fingers wouldn't get crushed. I stood, stepping off. "Thanks."

She shrugged. "No problem."

I made a move to leave but stopped myself. "Should I ask what you're doing here?" She didn't smell like booze, but it was too dark to see her eyes. She grabbed the board, moving it back under her window. "I won't ask if you don't."

"Deal." Whatever it was wasn't nearly as important as Savanna. I moved to the gate, unlocked it, and slipped into the front yard. Hitting the sidewalk, I bolted toward Jay-Jay's.

★

"I saw you coming." Jay-Jay's voice broke the silence of the night as I reached his yard. He was sitting on the steps outside his front door, the porch light illuminating the darkness behind him. I stopped, pausing in the driveway to catch my breath. "I can see you. I just can't see *her*." He aimed his thumb over his shoulder toward the door. "It didn't make sense why you would be over here at half past three in the morning, but now I get it." He huffed, running his hand through his hair. "This whole thing is stupid."

Still breathing heavily, I made my way toward him. "Did they really kick her out?"

Jay-Jay nodded, rubbing the sleep from his eyes. My heart clenched, my eyes darting to the door. "She's asleep," he said. "Cried herself that way."

I fought the urge to go inside—to wake her up. She probably needed to sleep. I couldn't believe her parents had done that. They weren't so conservative that the thought of her living in her house would be... shameful. Besides her father being overbearing, Savanna's parents' style seemed fairly progressive. They weren't like my parents, but they also didn't seem like the type to do something like this. If anything, I thought her dad would've acted the opposite, keeping her locked in her proverbial tower like Rapunzel. What was the motive? It couldn't be cultural or religious. If it was, they wouldn't have waited so long to do it. Their motive had to be something else…

I sat on the steps next to Jay-Jay, trying to hold myself together. Savanna deserved better than this. We sat there in silence for a long time before Jay-Jay finally stood. "I'm gonna catch some sleep. If you want, you can sleep on my floor. Just don't let my mom see you."

I followed him inside and up the stairs, passing the open door to the guestroom. Savanna was sleeping soundly on the fully made bed, an afghan draped over her. Two suitcases and a moving box were sitting just inside the door, appearing full and unopened.

Jay-Jay cleared his throat, nodding toward his room, but I couldn't make my feet move. They seemed rooted to the spot. "You can't sleep in there. My mom will catch you." My feet ignored him, pulling me into the guestroom. Jay-Jay reached to grab my arm, but I jerked out of his way.

"I want to be here when she wakes up," I said, moving toward a lounge chair in the corner.

"You mean you want to watch her sleep like a creeper?" he whispered.

I nodded, not caring how that sounded as I took a seat in the chair. It rocked unexpectedly, and I quickly set my feet on the ground to keep it from moving. Finally, Jay-Jay shrugged, scratching his scalp. "Whatever." Then he disappeared to his room.

★

"Kiddo? Come on, wake up." Someone's hand shook my left shoulder, attempting to jostle me from sleep. I blinked in the unfamiliar room, forgetting for a moment where I was. Ms. Jones's dark curls tickled my arm. I nearly jumped at her unexpected proximity. "It's sweet of you to be here, but you need to go home." She smiled apologetically, moving away and setting a mug of coffee on a nearby table.

I glanced at the bed. Savanna was still sleeping, sunlight pouring in through the windows. The light danced through the curtains to create patterns on her blanket and skin. I shook my head, wincing at my stiff muscles. "She needs me here."

Ms. Jones pursed her lips and was quiet for a few seconds. "I'm going to at least call your mom to let her know where you are."

I nodded in agreement before she grabbed her mug and left the room. I didn't think Mom would care that I was here. She'd be a little upset that I left in the middle of the night, especially without diviner supervision. If she had caught me sneaking out last night, she would have made me wait until after the sun rose. But being here felt right. Since I was already here, I doubted she'd make me come home.

Savanna stirred, readjusting her sleeping position so she was facing my side of the room. This turned out to be a bigger ordeal than it seemed her dream state had anticipated. She groaned, her leg getting caught in the blanket, and her blue eyes fluttered open. I moved to help untangle her, and she startled, sitting bolt upright. "Bradley?" I pulled at the blanket, straightening it out over her feet and legs. She studied me, her eyes sweeping over my hair and my wrinkled clothes before darting to the chair. "Have you been in here all morning?"

I nodded sleepily, taking up space on the edge of the bed by her feet. My fingers played with the curled edges of the afghan as I yawned. "I felt like I needed to be here."

Savanna sighed. "Who was it? Jay-Jay or Olga? One of them had to have called you."

I smiled despite myself. It felt wrong to smile at a time like this, but her prediction was amusingly accurate. "Olga."

Savanna puffed her cheeks, slowly letting out the contained air. "So you came because Olga yelled at you?"

"I came because I wanted to. I hung up on Olga. She seems to have our narrative wrong, which makes me think somewhere along the line, we got our signals crossed."

Savanna pulled her feet away, tucking them underneath her. Her expression was somewhere between angry and confused, her forehead puckering. "Let's pretend for a second that our fate isn't to die trying to protect this baby." She pointed to her stomach, which I swear had gotten bigger since Monday.

I nodded, forcing myself to remain calm. "I'd like to pretend that too." *I'd like it to be reality,* I thought.

She sighed, her shoulders slumping. "I'm tired, Bradley. I'm tired of trying to decipher your intentions. You told me in the hospital that you weren't going to stay—that you weren't going to be in her life."

I shook my head violently, needing to correct her. "I said I couldn't *promise.*"

"Then that's as good as saying no," she snapped.

"I want to say yes."

"Then say it."

I hesitated, which she caught in a second, rolling her eyes and crossing her arms. "You have not been there when I've needed you the most."

Her words stung. I stood, needing her to stop misinterpreting me, but feeling helpless in doing so. One thing I did know—I wasn't leaving. It would only prove her fears. My feet paced the floor in front of the bed as I tried to think through her incoming rant.

"You were not there for me when I had to find out through a stranger and in front of a bunch of diviners that I was pregnant."

I gritted my teeth. What did she want me to do? Apologize for having a breakdown? Apologize for reacting to the fact that I screwed up so much that she and our child were suddenly tied to a destiny that most likely involved pain, suffering, and death? I was sorry for the way she found out, but I wasn't going to apologize for being upset about it.

She continued, "You weren't there for me when I had to tell Mom and later my dad—who *hit* me, by the way."

I flinched. He what?

"Did you know that? That day I called you when you were in Tennessee? Tennessee, Bradley!" Her hand hit the blanket with a slap. "You weren't even in the state for that!"

I rubbed my forehead, feeling a headache coming on. I couldn't help being out of state. The world hadn't stopped when we discovered she was pregnant. My sister had just been released from the hospital. My grandpa had news about the cure. My family needed to get out and breathe for a moment. And to be fair, when she had called, she hadn't mentioned her dad hitting her. She was mostly begging me to come home, which I had no control over.

"You weren't there when I tried to get an abortion. You weren't there when I found out it didn't work."

I stopped pacing. *What?* Seriously, it would have helped if she'd *told* me any of this.

"All you've cared about for the last five months is that stupid cure and your occult sandwich shop job. What are we, Bradley? 'Cause we're sure not boyfriend and girlfriend."

She posed a good question. My hands were held together in a prayerful position under my nose. I tugged absently at my lips, squeezing them between my fingers. *What are we?* I sat back down in the chair, forcing my thoughts to regroup. "You tried to get an abortion?" I wasn't upset, but I wish I had known.

"It's my right," she snapped.

I shook my head. "No, I know. I just don't remember us having a conversation about it." Dropping my hands, I tried to imagine what she must've gone through. Was there a lot of waiting involved? Had it been painful? I honestly didn't know much about how abortions worked. "That must've been scary for you."

She wiped her wet eyes, sniffling. "It was. It still is. I told you that."

I nodded slowly, processing. I didn't want to react too quickly and set yet another metaphorical fire. She *had* told me she was scared. Multiple times. My tongue felt heavy as I forced my next words. "I'm sorry I wasn't there." I paused, avoiding meeting her eyes. "Dr. Lamb says I spend too much time preoccupying myself with outside issues to distract myself. I know I need to work on that."

There was a pause as Savanna once again readjusted her legs. She sighed. "I remember that."

My head snapped up to meet her gaze. I missed our psychic connection. It had made everything easier to forgive. Now everything was hard. Uncertain. Renewing my promise wouldn't work its magic anymore. I had to come up with something new.

"You." I dropped my hands, smiling a little as I stood to walk toward the empty side of the queen-sized bed.

"Are epic." I kicked my shoes off. "You are brave and sweet and strong." I finished extracting my feet from my shoes, hopping onto the bed next to her. I reached my arm around her back, pulling myself in. I kissed her cheek. She managed a small smile as I continued, talking directly in her ear. "You are everything to me, and you know that. You've felt that. Just because you can't feel it anymore doesn't mean it went away. Everything I have done—get a job, take the cure—has been for us. Do you really think I could leave after all that? I see no life without you in it." Never mind that our life forces were connected.

She was quiet for a moment. For a second, my hopes dropped. I thought I was failing.

Finally, she reached for my hand, resting mine and hers on her belly. "That's nice." She smiled, but it was a droopy smile—refusing to stay in place. "But that doesn't explain why you've been shutting me out."

I frowned, staring at her stomach. I didn't want her to know what I'd been worried about because, suddenly, my fears didn't seem right. I was self-conscious of their validity. I didn't look at her, pausing for so long that she nudged me back to my senses. I rested my head on her shoulder. "It's stupid," I mumbled.

"Well, you've been stupid."

I let out a short laugh at my own expense. "Right." I paused again, recalling what Frank had told me not too long ago. Savanna and I needed this to heal. I took a deep breath and let it out. "I was worried when we, you know…" I lifted my head from her shoulder. "That maybe you didn't really want to—"

Her laugh interrupted my explanation. "What?" She pulled out of my grasp, beaming at me in astonishment. Her hands gripped my arm. "Bradley, the only thing you've done without my consent is leave me."

I couldn't help but laugh too, more in relief than anything. We were back to the topic of me leaving her, though, which wasn't exactly where I wanted to be. I lifted one of her hands and traced the lines in her open palm. "Your parents are assholes," I said. That stopped her short. "A parent's love is supposed to be unconditional. I don't understand why a lot of parents don't seem to get that. I get that, and I'm not even—" I glanced at her stomach. I was about to say I wasn't a parent, but… "Well, I guess that's not true anymore."

Savanna managed a weak smile. "I get it. It's weird."

I paused for a second before continuing. "My parents have never left me once. As much as I've tried to push them away, they have always refused to give up on me. And I want that. I want that for our kid. And I'm gonna be that for our kid as long as I get to be. And I'm gonna be that for you too."

Savanna closed her eyes, crying again, so I laced my fingers through hers and squeezed. "So many of my friends have had bad parents. Olga for one, and Chad. Jay-Jay with his dad. And now you. You deserve so much more."

It was Savanna's turn to lay her head on my shoulder. She curled into the space near my collar bone, balling up a chunk of my shirt in her fist as she shook. "I'm really sorry," I whispered, wishing they were magic, healing words. "You don't know how sorry."

17 // REBECCA HAS PURPOSEFULLY TERRIBLE AIM
BLAKE

Noise-canceling headphones are the best invention in the entire world, and no one can change my mind. The second-best invention is heavy metal. Avenged Sevenfold blared through my headset, drowning out all the voices inside and outside my brain. The sound was soothing, blasting away the chaos around me. I breathed a deep sigh, slumping deeper into the living room couch, closing my eyes to rest through the lullabies.

Someone poked me.

Squinting open one eye, I caught Rebecca staring at me, her expression blank. She'd been weirder than usual lately. Sometimes her shield slipped, and I could hear bits and pieces of nothing that made sense. For the most part, she was almost as big of a relief as my headphones, but not enough to make me remove them. Besides, she didn't really look like she wanted to talk, so I closed my eyes again to lose myself in the music.

She poked me again.

This time I ripped my headphones off. "What?"

Immediately, my hearing was flooded with the echoing voices of my family blending with the television. Mom was chopping something in the kitchen, out of rhythm with my music. Sage grabbed a chess piece from Tuesday to keep her from choking on it, which only made her screech.

Rebecca shrank back, her teeth hitting her bottom lip. "I need a favor," she said in a high-pitched voice.

I rolled my eyes, ready to slip my headphones back on. This wasn't worth it.

She grabbed my arm, stopping me. "Come with me."

I groaned, not looking forward to having to bear the noise much longer.

She tilted her head toward the back door. "Outside?"

I huffed, pushing myself off the couch as she stood to lead the way. At least the backyard was quieter. I followed her to the trampoline, hoisting myself on top of it and planting my butt in the middle, facing her crisscross applesauce. I still had my headphones in my hand in case it got noisy. The outside could be unpredictable when it came to hearing people's thoughts. Most of the time, it was quiet unless there were neighbors outside playing or mowing. Someone was gardening in the yard next door, but they were far enough to only have quiet thoughts.

Rebecca's fingers twiddled with a helicopter leaf, her gaze dropping to stare at it.

"What favor do you need?" I asked, impatient. What could I possibly do that she couldn't do herself? She was Wonder Woman or something like that.

A thought pushed past her shield. "This is the only way to help Paige."

"Paige?" I asked, confused.

Her head snapped up, her eyes wide. She parted her lips to speak. "What do you know about Paige?"

"That she's our sister," I said, stating the obvious.

Rebecca's shoulders dropped, her eyes returning to the leaf. Her lower lip jutted into a pout. "I thought you would know her secrets. You would know if she was getting bad again."

I don't think Rebecca understood that I spent most of my time *blocking* thoughts, not reading them. I didn't exactly enjoy being a witness to anyone's private thinking, especially Paige's. She thought in circles and loops, repeating the same thoughts over and over. Sometimes, a thought would come out of nowhere—large and in charge. It would leave me on the edge of my seat, but she usually managed to shake them. It was like a constant game of psych. "I'm going to do this. Haha, gotcha! No, I'm not."

The day before, Paige had taken one look at the candelabra on the dinner table and imagined throwing it across the room. *Would the candles blow out?* she had thought. *Or would they catch the house on fire?* I admit it would have been an interesting experiment if one of the options wouldn't have left us homeless.

I shrugged. "She hasn't burned the house down, as you can see." I pointed to our house, all two stories of it sitting behind her in one piece.

Rebecca didn't lift her head, but her forehead scrunched. "Was she going to?"

I shrugged again. "Maybe. I'm not psychic." If she wanted to know about anything Paige was *actually* going to do, she would have better luck talking to Mom, even if Mom hadn't seen Paige's suicide attempt coming. She'd been too busy with Bradley. Even as a mind reader, I didn't know why Paige had done it. I didn't know why she did *most* things.

Rebecca groaned, gripping her head. "I just need to know how bad she is. I need to know how bad *everything* is."

"Things are pretty bad," I said, thinking about the bigger picture. Forget Paige and her issues. There was Bradley and his, and now Savanna didn't live with her family. There was Sage and Seth and Tuesday living in our house, parentless. Jesse was gone. We weren't in Itasca anymore. The only good thing happening in our house was that I was living with a secret superhero, but she didn't want anyone to know.

Rebecca's face turned to stone again—bored and unreadable. Her eyes unfocused, and I knew she'd gone elsewhere, following a track in her mind I couldn't hear. I was okay with that. I was okay with the silence.

Sighing, I flopped onto my back, the trampoline bouncing at the thud. Staring at the clear blue sky, I watched clouds merging with each other to form shapes. I didn't need my music in my temporary bubble of thoughtless sound. The gardener next door had gone inside, their quiet thoughts leaving with them. A dog barked in the distance. A little kid screamed, but they were too far away for my brain's radar to catch their thoughts. I smiled, breathing in the scent of freshly mowed grass. Spring was my favorite season—not too hot and not too cold. It was perfect and peaceful until—

The trampoline moved under my body weight, Hanna appearing next to me as she fell. Her thoughts came with her, interrupting my peace. "Whoa." She caught herself with her wrists, pushing up on her hands and feet and flipping to see Rebecca. "You said you wanted to join our group today, but you didn't show."

I propped myself on my elbows so I could see my sister better. She had her lower lip between her teeth, chewing it until it bled. Hanna's thoughts were loud and full of concern. I found myself thinking about what she was thinking about—noticing the terror in my sister's wide eyes and the way the helicopter seed she had been playing with had snapped in her hands. Rebecca's eyes darted to me, her head tilting almost like she was trying to silently apologize for something. Then she released her bleeding lip, her eyes again on Hanna. "M-Maria's in trouble," she stuttered, licking her lips.

Liar, I thought. I didn't need to read her mind to know that. Rebecca only stuttered when she lied. I squinted, wishing for once that I knew what she was up to.

Hanna's mind raced, her thoughts blurring at a fast pace, worried about her leader.

"Can you take me to her?" Rebecca asked.

Hanna didn't hesitate, and as she reached for my sister's hand, I reached for Hanna's ankle. Something wasn't right.

The air threatened to blow out my eardrums as it whooshed past us. My hand clung tighter to Hanna's ankle as we traveled. For a second, I wondered where I would end up if I let go. I wouldn't want to end up in Timbuktu.

The second my body hit concrete, the voices came— tons of them pounding into my brain. The wind stopped, and I let go, curling into myself. Wherever Hanna had teleported us was a place full of people and their thoughts.

She looked down at me, standing from her crouch as she frowned. "You could have just asked to come with."

I scowled, unfurling myself, realizing I'd left my headphones on the trampoline. I had nothing to block the noise. I stood as Rebecca brushed herself off. Why were girls always doing that? What dirt could she have possibly picked up between the trampoline and the floor?

It took me a minute to realize most of the voices inside and outside my head weren't in English. Their sounds blended so much that it was hard to focus on one person. I turned to see the longest table I'd ever seen. Various diviners were gathering around it. One girl, who looked to be Muslim, was having her fortune read with tarot cards. A few more groups of people were playing card games. There were a couple of kids in the corner tossing a ball. I didn't recognize anyone.

"Where is Maria?" Rebecca asked, picking at a piece of imaginary lint on her sleeve.

Hanna opened her mouth to answer but a man in a turban answered first. "Maria is with Khayr. She isn't healing so well."

Neither is Bradley, I thought, remembering how the diabetes cure hadn't worked on him. Maybe Maria really *was* in trouble—sick kind of trouble. But why had Rebecca stuttered? What was she hiding?

Hanna sighed, kicking her foot against the floor. "Yeah." She swung her arms in a circular motion for no reason other than to move. "The closer we get to the baby coming, the slower Maria heals." She pulled a face, the right side of her lips lifting. "She's not used to having bruises." Hanna turned, skipping down a large hallway. I was eager to follow, needing to put distance between me and the room full of people. The hallway, which was lit more like a school with artwork displayed along the wall, was mostly empty of people. It was only Hanna's thoughts I was stuck with for a moment as Rebecca and I followed.

She turned left at a fork, guiding us to a door. Knocking, she waited patiently for an answer. The door opened, and a man with blond hair I'd only met once stepped out. I'd have forgotten his name if I hadn't heard Hanna thinking about him healing Maria the whole way there.

Khayr was surprised to see us, but he hid it well, distracted by Hanna bouncing on her toes. "Is Maria here?" she asked, somehow both excited to see Maria and scared to find out how hurt she was. I'd come to understand through her mind wanderings that Maria was like a second mom to her, when many of the others viewed Maria more like a god.

Khayr nodded and stepped back, leading the way inside the room. The room wasn't as lit as the hallways, but a bright light similar to what I'd seen at the dentist's office was shining on Maria in the corner. The rest of the room was filled with jars and plants, reminding me a little of Wich Wharf.

Hanna rushed to Maria, her fingers reaching to touch the yellowing bruises around her left eye and upper arm. "What happened?" I couldn't read Maria. I was fine with that, but Khayr's thoughts—although calm—had added to Hanna's inner chaos. He was thinking about the many herbal healing techniques, worried about one that wasn't working like it should.

Maria smiled, patting the space next to her, inviting Hanna to sit. "It's nothing, my child. Just a little bruise. It will be gone by dinner."

Hanna hopped on the bench, letting Maria pull her into a side hug. "But what happened?"

Maria patted her head. "I was showing the boys a few techniques upstairs. I bruise much easier now, but it is no big deal."

Khayr turned to his workstation, heating a teapot over a flame while Rebecca closed the door. My sister looked terrified at the sight of Maria. She quietly stood there, eyes wide and hands trembling. She took a deep breath, steadying herself. "Bradley isn't healing on his own either," she said in a slightly more even tone than I expected.

Maria looked over at her, her smile disappearing. "Yes, I would expect that." She rubbed Hanna's back as she sighed. "I heard the cure did not work."

Rebecca shook her head, eyes dropping to an herbal encyclopedia open on a nearby table. She flipped through it distractedly. "I don't understand. He used to self-heal."

Maria took a deep breath, letting it out slowly. "Perhaps it is proximity, or maybe it was fate trying to warn him. Some men need a little push to realize something is wrong." She almost smiled, her lips rising for a second before stopping. "Khayr is waiting to hear from a contact in Colorado who has the same condition as your brother. Perhaps the cure didn't work on her either.

Otherwise, it may just be something about him being fated to Savanna. Maybe if she wasn't with child…" Her voice drifted off, and I couldn't follow her thoughts to complete the sentence.

"What if she loses the baby?" Rebecca asked, stopping on a page about a plant called rue, which I'd never heard of. She'd asked it so plainly as if it were a fact that was already bound to happen.

"Bex?" I blurted one of her hated nicknames without thinking. As much as I hated that Bradley and Savanna had gotten us into this mess, I didn't want there to be any more loss in our family. Not after Jesse. Not after the Burnetts' parents.

Maria stood, unfurling herself from Hanna as she studied my sister. "What are you planning, my dear?" she asked, suspicion written all over her face.

Rebecca flipped the page, shrugging. "N-nothing." Her stutter put me on full alert as Maria came to stand beside her.

"You would feel that devastation. Your innate loyalty to that child will destroy you if it dies," Maria warned, one eyebrow cocked.

Rebecca winced, flipping to a page on red willow.

"But you know that," Maria said, tilting her head.

I saw the silver before Maria did, a knife glistening into existence in Rebecca's hand. I lunged forward as my sister lifted it, ready to plunge. She aimed it at Maria's stomach, but before she could hit her, Maria stepped out of reach. The knife sliced through the air as I knocked into my sister's outstretched arm. Rebecca's mouth was wide open, seemingly shocked that an old woman had caught on to her violent behavior in time.

Hanna shouted, leaping from the bench as Khayr turned in time to see Rebecca drop the knife. It clattered to the floor, her arm staying outstretched, her eyes unfocused. Hanna reached to pick it up as I snapped my fingers in front of my sister's eyes. She didn't blink, even as Khayr ran to stand between my sister and me and the others. Hanna aimed the knife at Rebecca, but her stance was uncertain, her eyes bouncing between Khayr and my sister.

"What is happening?" Khayr asked, gasping in breaths. Everyone breathed heavily except for Rebecca, who almost didn't sound like she was breathing at all. I resorted to shaking her until her eyes refocused. She gasped for air, blinking and stumbling, her outstretched hand pulling in to touch her head as if she had a headache.

I thought about the time she tried to spear Savanna with a knife. I hadn't seen it, but I'd heard the commotion. Savanna had been furious, but as I glanced at Maria now, I couldn't quite read her expression. She didn't seem angry, more like expectant, waiting for Rebecca to finish snapping out of whatever had caused her to try to gut her. When I looked back at my sister, *she* was the furious one, her nostrils flaring, her eyes glaring in Maria's direction.

"How dare you?!" she screamed. I cringed, trying to keep a hold on her. Rebecca hardly ever raised her voice, and the noise was a shock. "How dare you move out of my way? You know how much my sister means to me— how much the *world* means to me!"

Khayr had to help me push her back, although she didn't seem to be trying too hard to escape our hands.

I couldn't see Maria's face, but her voice stayed calm, as if my sister wasn't just trying to end her life. "You are confused, my dear. In no way does my existence harm your sister."

Rebecca stepped back, bringing both hands to her head.

"What's wrong with her?" Hanna asked in a shaky voice.

"I'm not certain," Maria answered. "But somehow, I am not surprised."

Khayr and I watched my sister, our hands at the ready to act as a shield between her and Maria. We didn't need them, though. Instead, Rebecca curled into herself, dropping to the floor as she sucked in a high-pitched squeal. If she wanted to kill Maria, she would've tried harder. She *could've* tried harder. But in this moment, she reminded me more of Paige, and I worried that whatever Paige had was genetic. Maybe that was why Rebecca had been asking about her.

"You should take her home," Maria said after some time. "Let her get some sleep."

Hanna sighed, setting the knife on the table. She held her hand out to me. "Promise you won't let her kill me?"

I couldn't promise anything, but I nodded, taking her hand before reaching for my sister's. Maybe Mom and Dad could snap her out of this.

18 // EVERYTHING BLOWS UP AT ONCE
BRADLEY

It was hard to leave Savanna—harder than when we had actual magic and fate holding us together before. In fact, I wouldn't have left at all if it wasn't for the fact that I needed to refill a cartridge on my pump.

"Well, there's *one* kid," Dad said pointedly from the front room as I entered the house. I stopped in the entryway. Ms. Jones had called them to say where I was, right?

Mom was sitting on the loveseat, biting her nails as Dad peered between the blinds, tapping the house phone against his chin. Had they been waiting all this time for me?

I shut the door behind me, listening for the usual chaotic noise of our house. I could hear Sage griping from the living room about trying to study. Someone cranked the volume on the television in response. One of Tuesday's toys jingled. "Who else is gone?"

Mom sighed, rubbing her forehead. "Paige was supposed to be back from a cure group two hours ago."

I walked farther into the room to read the city checklist on the wall. Paige's group would have gone to either Charlotte in North Carolina or… here. Diviners teleporting around Indy had to be careful to keep their distance from the lab.

"Rebecca had a group too," Dad said. "But we didn't see her leave. And now Blake's missing."

"Blake?" I asked, suddenly getting a bad feeling. Blake never left the house except for school. His new powers had made his hatred for socializing even worse than it already was. Mom and Dad had decided he was too new to his gifts to let him help with the distribution of the cure, so they'd been letting him stay in the house while everyone else traveled.

I went over the logistic plan for curing Indianapolis in my head. We were supposed to limit the number of new diviners coming into town and mainly rely on local diviners to distribute. We were also supposed to take it slower than other cities. We couldn't risk the captivators sensing the activity and retaliating. Serena's theory that Priori would take responsibility for the cure still hadn't played out.

As I thought that, the volume of the television was cranked up, Seth shouting for us to come see. I beat my parents, catching a news story midinterview. Mila Walker-Krause—the spokesperson for Priori Labs— stood at an official-looking podium with several microphones attached to it. "We have done our own research on this so-called cure for type on diabetes. This is the same cure that medical vigilantes have been distributing to hospitals and doctors throughout the United States in the last month. We at Priori Labs in Indianapolis were offered a sample that we then broke down to learn the components of this mysterious concoction. Unfortunately, we came to an important scientific conclusion that, ethically, we must share with you all today." She neatly flipped a page of her notes, her reading glasses balancing at the edge of her nose. I held my breath. This was it. This was the announcement we'd been waiting for.

She cleared her throat, gazing at the crowd of reporters before returning her attention to her notes. "We will not dismiss the many firsthand accounts of those who have accurately claimed the liquid has cured them. In follow-up visits with their physicians, many have been told their pancreas has repaired itself via a process called islet-cell regeneration. However, those who suffered subsequent damage to other organs did not see a regeneration in additional organs following serum injection. In the short term, the cure appears to work for type one diabetes only. It does not serve to repair collateral damages caused by the disease, nor has it been proven to cure other forms of diabetes.

"As the leading laboratory in diabetes research, we at Priori Labs are committed to forming a stronger serum that will tackle these additional concerns. We want to specifically focus on populations who may have a higher genetic risk for developing type *two* diabetes. Studying the habits of those populations will provide us with further insight into prevention, ultimately striving to produce a cure for type two and additional forms of the disease. As we do this, we are taking the cure for type one into our own hands, working vigorously with the anonymous vigilantes in continuing its distribution."

Sage and Seth leapt from their seats, cheering as Serena's plan made it into motion, but I just stood there slack-jawed. Mom and Dad, who were standing behind me, made no audible noise. Half of the "facts" coming out of Mila Walker-Krause's mouth were lies, and I had a feeling it was the same for the promises we couldn't verify. Priori had a history of promising to deliver a cure for diabetes and never following up.

She smiled from the screen. It almost looked like a smirk. "We are currently searching for research study candidates who come from populations that, according to the National Diabetes Society of America, are at a higher risk for developing type two diabetes. These populations include African Americans, Indigenous peoples, Hispanics and Latinos, and Romani Gypsies. Qualified candidates chosen for our study will be compensated for their time. Interested parties can contact the number on the screen for more information."

I felt like I'd been punched in the gut. There it was— the latest eugenics trap wrapped in a big bow for the country to see—and viewers probably wouldn't think twice about it. This had Dr. Sauer and his neo-Nazi friends written all over it. And it was our fault.

The twins high-fived. They didn't understand. We hadn't won. Not even close.

Seething, I stalked to the fridge to pull out a new vial of insulin. I needed it to be room temperature before filling a new cartridge; otherwise, it could cause air bubbles. Plus, injecting cold insulin wasn't exactly pleasant. After setting a vial on the counter away from the stove, I grabbed a magnetic timer from the side of the fridge, setting it for an hour. Checking my pump settings again, I tried to mentally calculate if I could wait that long. I hated having to switch between the rapid-acting insulin in my pump and the long-acting one I often injected myself whenever something prevented me from using my pump. A lot of people don't realize that not all insulin is the same, and whenever I had to switch types, I had to also change up my math. I glanced at the blood sugar level on the screen. It wasn't too high yet, but it was starting to climb. Disconnecting the pump, I started to mentally calculate how much of the long-acting insulin I needed to inject but was interrupted by the sudden appearance of Hanna and two of my siblings. The twelve-year-old teleporter quickly leapt away from them after she dumped them in the living room, not even bothering to greet us before popping to wherever she needed to be. Rebecca and Blake were both on the floor, Rebecca crying into her hands, and Blake blinking guiltily up at us.

Dad was on him in seconds, rounding us to get a better look at my brother as he stood. "What did you do? Where did you go?"

Blake's eyes widened, his shoulders up to his ears. He pointed at Rebecca. "Why are you asking me? She was the one who tried to stab Maria!"

"Maria?" Dad snorted like he didn't believe him.

Mom squeezed herself between the lounge chair and the couch, carefully traipsing over to Rebecca. "You said she stabbed her?" Mom was talking to Blake, but she had crouched next to my sister. Tuesday brought a toy over to them, frowning at Rebecca. "You sad? Here toy." She placed it on the floor, waiting for a response. Rebecca didn't give her one.

Blake spoke quickly, trying to tell his side of the story before Dad inevitably sent him to his room. "She was acting all weird—asking me questions about Paige and doing that stuttering thing she does—and when Hanna came to pick her up for the cure thing, Rebecca had wanted to go to San Diego instead, so I went with them. We found Maria in Khayr's apothecary and Rebecca tried to stab her. She was screaming about Paige. Maria didn't know what to do, so we came home."

Mom's voice was calm and sweet as she rubbed Rebecca's back, leaning to comfort her. "Sweetie, does Maria have something to do with where Paige is?"

Sage and Seth shared a look I couldn't decipher.

"Do *you* know where Paige is?" I asked them. Rebecca shook her head to Mom's question as the twins side-eyed me before having a silent conversation between each other full of lip-reading and headshakes.

Mom brushed a strand of hair from Rebecca's face, tucking it behind her ear. "I don't understand. Help me understand."

I crossed my arms, waiting for one of the twins to answer my question. Seth shook her head at her sister, clenching her jaw. Sage eyed me, formed her right hand into a Y-shape, holding her thumb close to her mouth, as if holding a small glass.

My jaw dropped, along with my arms. "She's drinking?"

Everybody but Rebecca turned to stare at us as Seth grabbed Sage's arm and yanked it to her side. "We don't *know* that," she hissed between clenched teeth.

I twisted to see the time on the clock. It was late in the three o'clock hour. Who threw parties this early in the afternoon?

Seth continued to argue with her sister, holding up an index finger as she emphasized her words. "We only saw her drink *one* time at *one* party."

"Yeah, but she was *splashed*," Sage emphasized.

"And? Tons of people were," Seth argued.

"*We* weren't," Sage pointed out.

Mom shook her head, her mouth open. "When was this?"

I tried to remember Paige and the twins being gone for a night, but everything had been so hectic lately. If they were saying this about Seth, I would understand. I caught her sneaking back in last night, and judging by the makeshift hoverboard hiding in the bushes, it didn't seem like the first time. But Paige wasn't exactly stealthy. She couldn't keep a secret to save her life. Well, except for the whole diviner thing.

Seth bit her lip, digging the tip of her socked foot into the carpet. Sage crossed her arms, suddenly clamming up.

"Oh, for Pete's sake," Dad grumbled impatiently, jabbing his finger in the twins' direction. "You two are grounded, and when I get my hands on Paige—"

Mom quickly finished his sentence as she stood. "We're having a long discussion about this."

Dad's nostrils flared.

Sage rolled her eyes, mumbling, "Not like we were going anywhere anyway."

Seth's eyes widened, looking from her sister to Dad, then to Blake. She looked like she wanted to protest.

Blake's eyes widened too, staring at Seth. "Oh, I thought drinking was just like… drinking." I rolled my eyes. Using euphemisms around Blake wasn't turning out to be helpful.

Dad turned to him, exasperated. "Do you know where your sister is?"

Blake started to answer, then hesitated, still looking at Seth. "Uh, try the Lindts?" He didn't sound so sure of his answer.

"Try the Lindts," Dad repeated, mumbling. He still had the phone in his hand and lifted it, jabbing the speed dial with an angry finger.

As he waited, Rebecca stood, rubbing at her red eyes. Mom put her arm around her shoulder, holding her up. "You want to tell me what's happening?" she asked softly. Rebecca shook her head, her snot-covered hands still hiding half her face. Mom glanced at Blake, and he sighed, reaching for the Kleenex box to hand to her.

Someone must've picked up on the other end of the line because suddenly Dad was talking on the phone, running his free hand through his thinning hair. "You haven't happened to see Paige over there by chance, have you?" There was a long pause, and Dad paced toward the kitchen. Leaning with his back against the counter, he gripped the edge behind him. His voice was curt, his eyes narrowed. "Frank."

I straightened. Even though Frank lived in the guesthouse on the same vineyard property as the Lindts, he usually didn't answer their phone. He had a separate line.

Dad's face grew redder with each passing second, his teeth clenched so tight, I half expected them to chip.

Rebecca buried her face in Mom's shirt. It was silent except for her cries. Even Tuesday seemed to understand something serious was happening. She was quiet as she sat on the carpet by the coffee table, watching them. Blake jumped as if someone had suddenly shouted, twisting to peer at Rebecca. He stayed that way for a while, his eyebrows scrunched, even when Dad's fist hit the countertop.

Dad turned away from us so we couldn't read his expression, though we didn't need to. "What?!" There was another pause.

Sage took the opportunity to step out of the room. "I'm going to go move my stuff into Tuesday's room now."

"Uh, Sage?" Mom called after her, but Sage was already making her way up the stairs. Mom glanced at Rebecca, who was anchoring her to the room.

Dad shook his head. "I'd like to think you're helping my kids, Frank, but I got to be honest—" Frank must've cut him off, 'cause he never finished his sentence, restarting again after whatever Frank had said to defend himself. "If you're tired of dealing with angry parents, get a different job!"

I flinched. I knew Frank had been fending off Savanna's dad for over a year, but I never thought my dad would become a similar problem. Frank loved his job, but I was suddenly worried my dad was about to bully him into quitting. Geez, what had Paige *done*?

Dad didn't let up. "All I know is if you'd been doing your job, I wouldn't have an almost sixteen-year-old son about to become a father, a daughter out drinking with boys in the middle of the day, and another going around stabbing people."

I stepped back, torn between escaping Dad's list of complaints and wanting to know what was happening with my sister. Had she really been out drinking? And with boys? She was only thirteen.

"That's how old *you* were," Blake muttered quietly. I jumped, not expecting him to be standing so close. When had he moved to stand beside me? He squinted one eye shut. "Actually, I was six, so you were more like twelve." *Twelve?*

I glanced at Rebecca, who would be turning twelve in a couple of months. She didn't look nearly old enough to drink. Even at her age, I wasn't quite drinking. Sneaking out with friends who did drink, sure.

It had only been a couple of years since our life in Itasca, but it felt like longer. I'd always felt older than I was, but I guess trauma would do that.

Blake lowered his voice. "I think something's wrong with Rebecca."

Dad's shouts distracted me from responding for a second. "*My* parenting?" Dad yelled. It took me a minute to redirect my thinking.

I pulled Blake into the front room away from the drama, keeping my voice low. "Did you hear something?"

He scratched his head. "I only hear bits and pieces from her, but, I mean, she tried to *stab* Maria. I couldn't figure out why—something about Paige. But that didn't make sense either. And then… it's like her wall came down. I could hear so much happening in her mind."

I cocked my head to the side. "What did it sound like?" With Rebecca's abilities, I had been wondering how her mind worked. Was it chaotic? Stable? A collection of different voices? Or did she sound… normal?

He took a quick deep breath, shaking his head like he didn't believe what he was about to say. "Someone has convinced her that having two Immortal Ones alive at the same time causes evil spirits to go after people. She thinks Paige is being told what to do by an evil spirit, which I know isn't true because I can hear her thoughts."

"Why don't you just tell Rebecca that?" I asked, trying to keep my heart rate even. This was a fixable issue.

"I will when I get the chance, but I wanted to warn you in case she doesn't believe me. Just because I can hear thoughts doesn't mean I can change people's minds. I'm guessing she thinks whoever told her this is more knowing than me. So, if she doesn't believe me, she could go after your baby. She was asking Maria questions about it before she tried to stab her."

My mind raced. I didn't need yet another thing to worry about. The captivators going after my child in the future was scary enough, but my own sister? I didn't know which was worse.

I was back in the living room before I could think any further, desperate to convince my sister she was wrong about the spirits. Blake was right on my heels as I called to my sister. "Rebecca."

She barely pulled herself away from Mom's shirt enough for me to see half her face.

"You gotta listen to me," I said. "There are no spirits after Paige."

Rebecca nodded glumly, seeming to accept what I had said. Well, that was easy. Maybe her experience with Maria had already convinced her she was wrong. I turned to Blake, waiting for confirmation. He squinted at Rebecca, then shook his head, shrugging. "I guess we have to take her word for it."

Damn Rebecca and her shield.

19 // I TAUNT MATA HARI FOR INFORMATION
SERENA

I yawned, my algebra homework blurring as I temporarily closed my eyes. I shouldn't have pulled all those all-nighters, but with Mrs. Chambers constantly checking rooms in the middle of the night, I didn't have Seth to help me sleep in shifts. Now that Priori had taken the bait adopting distribution and getting the FDA to approve the cure, we didn't need to dispatch diviners to random cities anymore. What we had failed to account for was their connection to the neo-Nazis and their drive for eugenics. They couldn't commandeer the cure for type one anymore, but what about type two?

I should have seen it coming. Type two was different. It had risk factors associated with the lifestyles of the lower socioeconomic class. Who disproportionately dominated the lower class? People of color.

Those sneaky bastards.

I'd managed to stop a few people on the street who were heading to the research study and convinced them to turn around, but most people who participated in studies were desperate for money. Some of them were unhoused. Some of them would do anything for a hot meal and a place to stay. Some of them just needed to pay their college tuition. God, I wished I had a bucket of persuasion dust handy. I wished I could save everyone from turning themselves in to that God-forsaken place. But I had to keep my distance. I couldn't break the treaty. I couldn't get more involved than staking out the place from a block away. Three hundred feet at all times. If Priori didn't need Bradley and Savanna alive, I'm sure they'd have been dead already.

I glanced at Savanna, who was sitting near the classroom's front door with her face buried in a copy of *Frankenstein*. At least she bothered to show up today, even if it was for study hall. Not that it was any of my business, but I didn't think she skipped class all morning except for the occasional bathroom break. Did I feel bad for her? Kind of. But what could *I* do?

Alyssa was sitting behind her, chewing on the end of her pencil and staring at a notebook. I didn't understand what Jay-Jay saw in her. She hardly ever spoke or looked anyone in the eye. The only facts I knew about her were that she was an only child, a dancer, and a molecular manipulator—and her family were transplants from the San Diego safe house. There was nothing interesting about her, so I didn't see why Maria of all people thought her family would be useful to us. Maybe there was something, but why did it have to be such a secret?

I found myself at the empty desk next to her, unsure how I got there, but not really caring. She had to have lots of secrets—the quiet girl—and I had to know them. It was only fair that we knew the real reason for her being here.

"So what are you, like a spy?" I asked, trying to keep my voice down. Mom would have my hide if she thought I was causing any kind of trouble.

Savanna lowered her book, her thumb keeping track of the page she was on, and twisted to shoot me a judgmental glare.

Alyssa tipped her pencil upside down so the eraser was touching the page. I leaned to get a better look at what she'd been writing before realizing it was a handwritten sheet of music. "Writing a love song to Jay-Jay?"

"Serena," Savanna hissed as Alyssa's light brown face reddened.

I ignored her. I knew Alyssa wasn't in any music class. She was too busy following us around. I squinted at the notes, wishing I could read them. I wasn't much of a musician. There were a few words scrawled under some of the notes, but they were hardly readable, written in tiny letters. I snorted, trying to imagine this shy, demure girl performing her song in front of a crowd. It was laughable, really. But then, maybe that was all an act. Maybe that was her specialty—hustling everyone into thinking she was meek and cowardly, only to come in at the last second and smash people's skulls in. People underestimated Rebecca all the time. It wasn't a huge stretch to think

Alyssa could pull off the innocent look just as well. But how could I prove it?

I leaned slightly closer, trying to act intimidating. "You're good, you know. Like Mata Hari—a dancer, a spy, pretending to be someone she is not."

That finally caused Alyssa to lift her head, imitating the glare Savanna was giving me, her jaw set. She still didn't speak, though.

"Serena, come on," Savanna begged, loud enough that I was sure my mom could hear. I glanced at her desk on the other side of the room. Mom was too engrossed in grading papers to pay attention to us.

The loudspeaker crackled, interrupting our conversation for the daily announcements. "Hello, Warriors!" the senior class president cheerily proclaimed. "Today is Monday, April 21st, and I'm here to remind you that prom is only five days away, so to the procrastinators who haven't yet bought their tickets, I am proud to announce that they are still being sold at lunch in the cafeteria. Please remember, juniors and seniors, if you have a younger date or are bringing a date from a different school, you will also need to fill out a slip with your date's information or they will not be permitted to attend."

I scowled. In all the drama, I'd forgotten my plan to get myself on an older guy's radar. I licked my lips, wondering if Liam had a date yet. I hated how the school administrators only let the upperclassmen attend such a momentous event. I mean, I didn't even know if I was gonna be here next year to participate. For all I knew, Savanna and Bradley were gonna get us all blown up.

The announcements droned on as I tuned them out, returning my attention to Alyssa, who was staring at the loudspeaker as if it had a face. "So what are you doing with Jay-Jay anyway?" She glanced at me from the corner of her eye. "I mean, obviously you're not going to prom, so what? You got plans?"

Alyssa looked back down at her sheet music, dipping her shoulder so her long brown hair partially hid her face.

Savanna finally stuck a sticky note between the pages of her book before setting it down. She glanced at Alyssa and back at me. "Stop trying to force her into girl talk when she clearly doesn't want to join in."

Alyssa lifted her head again, shaking her hair back behind her shoulder. She opened her mouth just enough that I could see her clenched teeth. "Ice… s-skating," she finally stuttered out, her voice barely audible.

I raised an eyebrow, shocked that Savanna's comment had somehow convinced her to finally answer me. "Ice skating? In April?"

Alyssa's eyes darted to the side, then back in my general direction. She rarely seemed to be looking straight at me. It was unsettling. "Is that weird?" she whispered.

I shrugged. "If he was straight."

Savanna's eyes widened, her mouth hanging open. "Serena," she hissed again.

Something about what I had insinuated seemed to spark this strange pit of energy within me, and honestly, I needed the metaphorical coffee. I couldn't help myself from drawing the energy, blasphemous words rushing out of my mouth. I'll admit, it was a little fun to see the color drain from both their faces from pure, unadulterated shock. "That's what Jay-Jay does," I said, my words firing in rapid succession. "He convinces girls he's straight, lets them be his beard, waits for the moment when they've fallen madly in love with him, and then he turns around and crushes their little hearts in the palms of his hands. How do you think he knows all the right words to say? Why do you think he comes off so soft? He's unlike most of the other boys because he *is* unlike most of the other boys." I jerked my chin toward Savanna, whose jaw looked like it was going to come loose from her skull. "Why do you think he hangs out with Savanna and her friends all the time? Why do you think Bradley is the only guy he bothers to talk to?" I leaned closer to Alyssa, emphasizing each of my words. "He's. Not. Straight."

She stared at me, this time in the eyes, unblinking.

"Don't listen to her," Savanna advised. "He's literally never dated anyone before. I would know. I've known him since kindergarten."

Alyssa blinked, dropping her gaze, but didn't say anything. Savanna's concerned eyes lit with fury as she glared back at me.

I lifted an eyebrow. This was a challenge, and I wasn't going to back down. "Maybe. But why do you think that is? A sixteen-year-old guy who's never been on a date? Not even a group one?" I paused for dramatic effect, licking my lips in anticipation of the biggest bluff I'd ever performed. "I'm a hacker, Savanna. You know that. Why would I be lying if I've literally seen his internet search history?"

"You're disgusting," she scowled.

"I'm a truth seeker. Can't be too careful who to trust." I made a mental note to look into Jay-Jay's search history when I had the chance. I don't know why I hadn't thought of it before. If Alyssa was trying to get close to Jay-Jay, maybe there was something worth knowing.

Savanna wouldn't break our staring contest even as the bell rang to dismiss us. I blinked, then stood. "Now if you'll excuse me, I gotta see a man about a prom date."

I left my backpack in the classroom, grabbing my water bottle before ducking into the halls. I had my mom's English class next, so I had no acceptable reason to leave during passing period except to use the bathroom or get a refill. I tried to remember Liam's schedule. He was the only diviner in the eleventh grade, so Frank couldn't easily slip him into any of our classes except for success time, but I seemed to remember that he'd been assigned my dad's classroom. Lucky for me, Dad conveniently had a cooler of water in his classroom because he hated how completely unsanitary the fountains by the restrooms were. I darted through the crowded hallway of students, searching every passing face for Liam's. *Please don't let him have a date already,* I pleaded to whatever god could hear me. Finally, I caught him talking to a buddy at an open locker around the corner from my dad's classroom.

"Liam!" I practically shouted, speeding straight for him. I skidded to a stop in front of him, interrupting the conversation. "Can I talk to you?"

"Uh," Liam hesitated, glancing between me and his friend. He gestured between them. "We're kind of in the middle of something."

His friend raised his eyebrows, his mouth forming into an O shape as he closed his locker door. "Good luck man," he said, patting Liam on his shoulder before walking away. I swear he was laughing as he disappeared into the crowd. Jerk.

Liam rolled his eyes, letting out a sigh of exasperation. "What?"

"Please tell me you don't have a date to the prom."

The corner of his lips tugged up into a smirk as he folded his arms in front of his chest. "Why? You gonna con me into taking you? Do I look like I want to go to some stupid dance?"

"So you *don't* have a date," I deduced.

"It's Passover."

I paused, his response admittedly tripping me up. I wasn't expecting it, but then again, I wasn't Jewish. I didn't have their holy calendar memorized. "They scheduled prom on Passover?"

"Don't look so shocked."

"I..." I really didn't know what to say. "I heard there's going to be strobe lights."

Liam shook his head, unraveling his crossed arms, and began heading in the opposite direction I needed to go. I followed him anyway, trying to explain myself. "People with epilepsy can't go too." I realized how stupid that sounded after it fell out of my mouth. All that said about the student council was that they were antisemitic *and* ableist.

Liam stopped short in front of a classroom, turning to me. "You know, even if I *could* go, even if I *wanted* to go, I still wouldn't take you. No offense, but you're not really my type."

I have to admit, even though I wasn't interested in him like that, it still stung a little. "Well, you're not my type either."

"Then why do you want me to take you so bad?"

"Honestly? Because I need a date, and you're the only upperclassman I have a shot with at the moment."

He leaned against the wall as someone tried to get around us. "I'm surprised to hear you say that. Don't you have kind of a rep?"

I narrowed my eyes, my throat constricting. "What's that supposed to mean?" I knew exactly what that was supposed to mean, but if he was going to be a coward and not say the words he really meant to say, I was going to pretend otherwise. Ever since Aaron and that stupid photo leak last year, I'd been branded as some kind of man-eating slut. And sure, while I'd had a few occasional hookups here and there since, it wasn't with anyone I cared to be seen with in public.

Liam didn't say anything for a few seconds, his tongue tracing his teeth. "Never mind." He turned to enter his class but stopped, facing me again. "I didn't tell you this, but I'm sure you already know that my brother has a bit of a crush on you. It would be kind of a douchebag move for me to take you to a dance."

Calvin's crush on me wasn't a secret, but we had mutually decided a long time ago never to date. He was three years older than me and honestly, we were better off as friends. Seth and I were better off too that way. *Everybody* who liked me was better off not dating me.

I just wanted to have fun—dance with someone without feeling like they had any other expectations for me. And Liam fit that bill.

The bell rang, and he slipped into his classroom. Crap. I was going to be late. I dashed back to my mom's class. I didn't dare entertain any further thoughts about Liam's brother.

20 // THIS IS WHY I DON'T HAVE NICE THINGS
JAY-JAY

The skating rink was closed for the season. I have so many memories of this place from when I was younger. Mom would take me here to skate after my dad left. She'd guide me around the rink, catching me every time I slipped or fell. It was fun, mostly because the amount of focus it took to balance myself distracted me from the fact that I no longer had a dad. It was a safe space for me and Mom.

Maybe that was why I brought Alyssa here. There was something about finally dating someone that reminded me of trying new things. I hadn't been to the rink since I was a kid, and knowing Alyssa's shyness, I figured I had a better chance of getting her on the ice if there was no one around. It was convincing her to walk us through the door—and I mean, literally through the door—that was the tricky part.

Pulling into the back of the pavilion's parking lot, I tried to avoid the security cameras. Mom wouldn't be happy if my license plate was caught on camera. As long as I could convince Alyssa to use her powers to get us in, we wouldn't trip any of the alarms.

Putting the car in park and removing the keys from the ignition, I chanced a glance at her.

Shrinking in her chair, her teeth clenched, her eyes wide, I quickly realized I should have explained what we were doing beforehand. I was beginning to learn that Alyssa wasn't much for surprises. She was one of those people who were always on edge. I related to that, I guess. When you possess the ability to see into the future, the anxiety that comes with the anticipation gets a little ridiculous.

I tapped my key against the steering wheel. "I kinda need your help to break in."

Her brown eyes grew even wider. "W-what?" I could see the gears turning in her head as she tried to decipher why I would ask such a thing.

I pointed at the large pavilion. "I thought we'd go skating." Of course, I'd already communicated that much to her.

She opened her mouth to say something but shut it before she could get the words out. Her crossed arms tightened against her chest.

"I know Serena's been giving you a hard time," I said. Alyssa shrank deeper in her seat, her eyes wandering. She hadn't actually told me that. Savanna had hinted at something, but she hadn't been specific. "I thought maybe if we did something together—you know, like, actually go out on a date—then maybe whatever she's said to you would stop going to your head. And I thought, what's a place that's not gonna be crowded—"

She cut me off—not with words, but with a hard slap of her hand against the seat. Her eyes flashed with anger, so briefly that I thought I'd imagined it.

I was starting to think this had been a terrible idea. "Are you mad? Did I assume something I shouldn't have?"

She scrunched up her nose, her lips twisting as she did so. Finally, she pushed a few words out, her voice barely above a whisper. "I'll go." Her hands fumbled with the handle, and I quickly jumped out of the car to help her with it. By the time I reached her side, she was already out and shutting the door. Her arms returned to her chest, crossed as always. I walked with her to the large double doors, the chain around the handles shining, warning us of the pavilion's closure.

She squinted at them, then turned her head to scan for cameras. There didn't seem to be any at the entrance, just a few scattered around the edges of the buildings. I held out my hand for her to take, having learned from past experience to always meet her halfway when it came to physical touch. She was as bad as Bradley when it came to flinching. She hesitated for a few seconds, then took my hand in hers, leading me through the double doors as if they weren't there to begin with.

The inside of the pavilion was dark. I removed my cell phone from my back pocket, using the dimly lit screen to find my way to a light switch. Instead, I found a huge lever. Shoving it into the on position, the arena lights brightened in chunks until every one of them was lit. Alyssa gripped a nearby pole, shaking a little as she stared at the windows on the upper deck. I knew why it worried her. Anyone who drove by the arena would be able to see the lights. I just hoped no one questioned it.

"Come on," I said, holding my hand for her to take. It took some coaxing before she finally gripped it. Leading her to the gated rental booth, I could already tell by her face that she didn't want to be breaking through any more gates or doors. I took both her hands, looking down at the floor as I tried to think of what I could say to convince her to help free a couple pairs of skates from behind the gate. Lifting my head, I tried to meet her wandering eyes. "Hey. I'm not going to make you walk through the gate, but if you could just get *me* through…" That way, maybe she could rid herself of a little bit of the anxiety that came with breaking rules. Too bad I couldn't do all this by myself.

She eyed the gate warily.

"I promise, if you want, you can lock me in there." I chuckled, imagining her running off the second she got me through the gate. I didn't doubt the possibility. I was so screwed if she did, though. "I'm putting my trust in your hands."

Something about the idea made her laugh too. She smiled, nodding, as she squeezed one of my hands tight, letting go with the other. I felt a strange weightlessness and joined her in her smile. Reaching for the gate, I easily slipped through the bars, letting go of her hand as soon as I was in. "What shoe size are you?" I gazed at the cubbies behind the counter. I hopped over it searching for my own size as I waited for her to answer.

"Seven," she said, and I was shocked to hear her speak at a normal volume.

I popped my head over the counter to grin back at her. "Seven it is." I grabbed both our pairs and hopped back over the counter, sliding them through the bars. When I reached a free hand through the bars, she grabbed it, pulling me through with ease. Tripping over one of the skates, I struggled to regain footing as we both crashed to the floor. "Oh geez, I'm so sorry," I apologized, scrambling to my feet. I stared at her silent, frozen form for a second, waiting for her to thaw. She surprised me with a fit of giggles, and I couldn't help but laugh with her. "Come on." I held my hand out to her again. "I'll help you up."

We carried our skates to the edge of the rink, taking a seat on the bench and removing our shoes. She hesitated before pulling hers on, wrinkling her nose. "Haven't other people's feet been in these?"

"Not barefoot," I said, hoping that would convince her to put them on. I really hoped I hadn't just lied to her.

It was too cold in the pavilion to do anything without socks.

She continued to scrunch up her nose as she slid them on. Even though she didn't say anything, I wouldn't have been surprised if she rushed home to wash her feet later.

When we were both in our skates, I led her to the rink's entrance, balancing on the edge of the ice. "You ever skated before?"

She nodded, biting her lip. I stepped onto the ice, still holding her hand, and watched her precariously slide onto it with me. She wobbled for a sec as I gripped her arm to try to keep her from falling, but she quickly regained balance. "I just have to think of it like dancing." She chuckled nervously. "But on ice." Her breath showed in the cold air.

"That's one way to look at it, I guess."

She slid away from me, tugging me with her. After her initial unbalance, I thought I'd have to hold her hand through it all, but she glided with ease toward the center, almost fearless. I wasn't expecting that, not from the girl who always seemed to look like something terrifying was about to happen. I let go so she could skate freely, watching her drift and twirl. Soon I skated around her, and she giggled every time our eyes met. Too often I'd catch myself freezing in place to stare at her amazing transformation. Little had I known that bringing her here was going to loosen her up.

"You could be a figure skater," I told her in awe.

She laughed. "And wear those skimpy outfits?"

I shrugged. "Maybe."

She twisted her mouth like she'd tasted something sour. "No way."

I pocketed my cold hands in my jacket, skating in a relatively straight line as she practically floated around me.

"Here," she smiled as she was passing by, holding out both her hands. I grabbed them, and we spun as she guided us across the ice. After a few seconds, she asked, "Do you have any music?"

I nodded. "I guess. On my phone." I reached for my back pocket, fumbling with my phone. I kept pressing the wrong buttons with my nearly numb hands. Finally, I opened the music app and set it to shuffle, pocketing it so I could hold her hand again.

She closed her eyes, listening to the opening tune. Soon, she was swaying her head to the melody. It was a slower song, the lyrics telling some kind of sad story. My heart pounded for a second, panicking that the song was going to bring her down from her happy place, but before I had a chance to switch the song, she began to guide me slowly across the ice, losing herself in the moment. I tried to lose myself too. I even tried to take over the lead at one point. I mean, if we were dancing, wasn't the guy supposed to lead? But she improvised better than I did, her choreography matching almost perfectly with the song.

I watched her closed eyelids as we glided in sync. If she got too close to the walls, I'd guide her away, and it seemed she trusted me to do that, continuing her carefree movements. When the song ended, we were near a gate, her eyes fluttering open to peer into mine. I thought it was the perfect moment to try to snag a kiss, but as I leaned in, the moment shattered with her pull. She let go, her hands reaching for the wall. Her eyes were wide and terrified again, and my heart sank. We were so close. What did I do wrong? A new song played—something classic rock— and I reached for my phone to stop the music.

"I'm sorry," I apologized as she made her way off the ice. "I didn't mean to scare you."

She shook her head as I followed her to the bench. She started undoing the laces as I tried desperately to talk her back into the moment. "No, wait. We don't have to be done. We can go back out there, and I promise I won't try to kiss you. I just thought, maybe, I don't know," I said, grappling with explaining myself. "I just thought maybe there was a moment."

The second Alyssa yanked the skates off I knew the magic was gone. There was no getting it back. Geez, what had I done? I'd moved too quickly. I'd forgotten in that brief moment of joy how careful I had to be with her.

"Please." I reached for her hand, but she snatched it away, refusing to look at me.

She stood, gathering her skates and shoes, and made her way to the rental counter as I scrambled to get my skates off. "Wait, Alyssa." When I made it to the counter, she was already behind the gate, placing the skates neatly in their cubby. "We can talk about this."

She leaned over the counter, running her hand across the smooth surface. I stared at her in desperation, my heart pounding against my chest, waiting for her to say something. Anything. Her mouth moved, but I couldn't hear what she said.

I tilted my head. "What?"

She cleared her throat, still not looking at me. "Serena said you were gay."

When I say my whole insides felt like they had crashed, I mean it. My pounding heart stuttered to a stop, the shock hitting me like a stray dodgeball from gym class. I couldn't speak. Instead, I just stood there, frozen like she usually was. My thoughts clambered in a million directions, piling onto each other until it felt like there was no space in my brain for any more originality.

"She said I was your beard—whatever that means," Alyssa said.

I couldn't even gather enough strength to roll my eyes. Was this what Savanna had neglected to tell me? And why? Why would she not have mentioned this to me before I went on this stupid date? And again, why would Alyssa even agree to go out with me if she thought… if she thought…

My lungs struggled to breathe, and I backed away from the gate as I pounded my chest, trying to clear whatever gunk had made its way inside. Alyssa finally looked at me, her forehead creasing with concern as my eyes watered from the lack of oxygen. She made her way back through the gate. "Are you okay?"

I nodded, choking on air for a second, before my breathing returned to normal. "Yeah, just…" I cleared my throat, continuing to put some distance between me and her. "I'm not…" I shook my head. "Geez, where did she hear that?"

Alyssa bit her lip, hesitating to answer for a moment. "S-she said she hacked your internet history." Her cheeks reddened at the insinuation.

I stared at her for a long time as she looked away, her arms crossed in front of her stomach like she was holding all her nerves inside. I thought I had enough code on my laptop to keep Serena out of it, but then again, she was the better hacker.

"Alyssa," I finally said, "I like you. I…" My throat constricted, trying to keep me from shoving the words out. I rubbed at my nose. I hated how she was practically forcing me to say this. I hadn't had to before. It wasn't relevant before. "I like girls. Actually, I"—I swallowed hard—"I like *every*one." I stuttered out the label I had only reserved for myself to know before now. "I-I'm pan."

21 // I SPY A FORTUNE TELLER AND A STOCK MARKET CRASH
SAVANNA

"Savanna." Ursula saw me before I saw her, her hands wrapping partially around me. I tugged too hard on my necklace from the shock, breaking the clasp. My Sara e Kali charm stayed in my hand, but the tiny potion bottle slipped from the chain, bouncing from my chest to my arm, to Ursula's shoulder, before shattering on the marble floor. I grabbed my sister's shoulders, steering her at arm's length. We both stared at the spilled contents as patrons meandered warily around us toward the pews.

I had decided to attend Mass with Ms. Jones, partly in an attempt to see my mother and partly because... I don't know. I just felt like I needed to be somewhere that held a semblance of spirit. Somewhere where a god who could potentially have more power than the Fates would be. Somewhere I could pray, even though I didn't do it often. I wasn't even sure I believed in the God my mother and Ms. Jones believed in. But I knew something besides my mother brought me to the church... a church I'd hardly been to in years.

Ursula looked at me, her mouth wide open. My heart leapt into my throat. The potion bottle had been the only thing that kept me off the captivators' radar. Without it, they could find me. I was no longer theoretically invisible to them. My sister's brown eyes widened. "Oh my God." A few passing patrons shot her stern looks as she bent to the floor, attempting to sweep up the contents with her bare hands. "I'm so sorry. Maybe I can put it back together."

My vision blurred as I struggled to keep my breathing steady. Someone's hand was on my shoulder, and when I turned, I saw it was Ms. Jones appearing from the quickest bathroom break in history. She'd been gone less than a minute.

"What happened?" she asked as Ursula bit her lip, meeting curious eyes as she searched the crowd of passersby.

She motioned us forward as I attempted to choke down the stupid tears trying to well their way out of me. Ms. Jones seemed to pick up on my sister's intention before I did, putting her arm around my shoulders and shuffling forward in an attempt to fill the gap between her and Ursula. She bowed her head and closed her eyes, murmuring a prayer under her breath. I stood shakily, unable to focus enough to pray. This wasn't what I had come here to pray about. Prayer wasn't going to solve this predicament.

It took me a moment to realize she was doing it mainly for looks so people wouldn't bother us as Ursula worked her magic. My sister clasped her hands like she had captured a bug, pulling them apart as an object formed in her palm. It appeared identical to the potion bottle predestruction. She waved her hand over the pile of broken glass, herbs, water, and rocks, willing them away. Then she stood, reaching for the chain on my neck and looping it through the little hole on the top of the bottle. I was still shaking in my attempt to bend to her height as she clasped the necklace back together.

Ms. Jones stopped praying, opening her eyes as I let go of the charm, letting the necklace dangle over my chest. "Will that work?" she asked.

I couldn't make myself answer. I was pretty sure it had to be blessed by a witch. Despite the intersectionality of witchcraft, I didn't know any legitimate witches in the Catholic church. Mr. Porter's main form of magick—Hoodoo—had a semblance of Catholic roots, but he didn't seem like the churchgoing type.

I turned to glance back at the door, wishing Jay-Jay had decided to come with us. Without the magical barrier protecting me, he could induce a vision to check if I was safe.

"Do you want to go, honey?" Ms. Jones asked softly. I swiveled my head back toward the pews, angling my neck in search of my mom. If Ursula was here, she had to be around somewhere. Ursula followed my gaze as I spotted the back of Mom's bowed head a few rows from the front.

"I can't believe she didn't follow me," my sister said, her disappointed voice falling with her shoulders. My throat burned. Mom knew I was here, and she hadn't tried to even look at me. She'd clearly not wondered what was taking so long for us to find our seats.

I nodded my head to Ms. Jones's question, quickly turning back to the door. "I need Mr. Porter to rework his magic."

Ms. Jones nodded solemnly. "Okay."

As we started to leave, my sister followed us. "Wait, can I come?"

We both paused, and I closed my eyes, taking a deep breath as Ms. Jones answered, "If your mom says it's okay."

I opened my eyes, spinning to look at my sister. "Mom's not gonna let you. She won't be able to explain to Dad why you're gone."

"She can pick me up from Wich Wharf after Mass. That gives us almost an hour." Ursula bolted down the aisle as the service began, receiving several dirty looks as she slid into the pew next to Mom. I saw Mom nod, but she still didn't look up before Ursula dashed back to us. "She said I can go."

I was surprised, but Ursula was shoving us out the door so fast, I didn't have time to question it.

"I missed you," she said as she skipped along the pavement. My throat still burned as I put my arm around her, drawing her to my side. At least somebody missed me.

I drew in a deep straggled breath before letting it out in a frustrated huff. "How's home?" She didn't answer, and I didn't really want to know. I knew it was bad. I had a feeling Mom kicking me out hadn't solved a thing. Dad was still mad because I was still pregnant. Kicking me out didn't erase history.

I let go of my sister to open the car door, letting her slide in first. When we were both situated in the back seat, our seatbelts buckled, she materialized a Slinky in her hands, juggling it as she finally answered. "Dad tried to leave." She chuckled a little like she hadn't said anything shocking, watching the Slinky shuffle its weight back and forth.

My jaw dropped, my hands clutching her arm. Ms. Jones briefly glanced at me through the rearview mirror before starting her car and backing out of her parking space. "Wait, that means I can come home, right?" If Dad was gone, that was good news as far as I was concerned. He was the reason I couldn't live in my own house.

Ursula pursed her lips, and I let go as she continued to play with the Slinky. She was quiet, her expression focused, determined as Ms. Jones pulled onto the street. We'd driven several blocks before my sister finally dematerialized the Slinky and dropped her hands onto her lap. "I couldn't let him leave."

A small pathetic sound erupted from me. I reached for my throat like that would somehow keep me from being a total baby. Part of me wanted to hate her for standing in the way of my return, but there was something in her tone that seemed so familiar… I couldn't put my finger on what it was.

She twisted in her seat, holding her hands up in an X shape, like she thought I would hit her. She cringed, waiting for the impact as I stared at her. I huffed, my nostrils flaring. My question came out all high-pitched and strange. "Why would you do that?"

Ursula opened one eye, then the other, lowering her hands as she registered the lack of physical contact. "Because he's my dad. He's *our* dad. He was there when we were born. He was there on our first day of school. He was there when I had chicken pox in first grade and when you caught strep in sixth. He's driven us to almost every karate class. He remodeled the entire basement so he could teach us how to kickbox. He was there when you tried out for cheerleading. He even went with us to that Nazi bunker to help keep us safe. He works so hard to give us the childhood he didn't have himself. And I'm not trying to defend him because he is being a total jerk right now, but there's just something about him leaving that I can't handle. Not after everything that we've been through." She huffed, taking a quick breath before continuing. "I don't want divorced parents. Everybody has those. I want Dad to go back to who he was before he found out you were having a baby. I wish there was some kind of spell to make him stop treating you so badly."

"And have everything be fake?" I shook my head. I didn't want Dad to be less of an asshole because of some spell. I wanted him to be less of an asshole because he *wanted* to or because he cared. I crossed my arms, scoffing at Ursula's plan to keep Dad in the picture. "You're as bad as Mom."

"How am I bad?" she shouted. "It's not bad to want my family together. You want the same thing!"

I couldn't look at her, anger boiling under my skin. I stared at the headrest in front of me, grinding my teeth once before their increased sensitivity caused me to shudder. I held my hand to my jaw, stretching it. "I couldn't care less if Dad stayed. I just want to be able to come home without feeling like I'm under attack."

It was Ursula's turn to cross her arms, turning to gaze out the window. "Again, I wish there was a spell for that."

"Spell?" I turned my head to look at her, an idea forming in my mind. Ms. Jones turned onto the street where Wich Wharf was located. This was excellent timing. "Haven't the other diviners been using some kind of persuasion dust to convince doctors that the diabetes cure works?"

Ursula nodded, her gaze dropping. "How do you think I convinced Dad to stay?" she murmured, frowning.

"You what?" I asked, still sure this meant we could still use it. If it worked on keeping Dad from leaving, surely it would work if we used it to convince him he was wrong. At that thought, I couldn't help but wince. As much as I wanted Dad to change his mind, was I willing to have it be fake? Was I willing to take away his autonomy like mine had been taken?

"It only works on the same person once," Ursula stated glumly.

"Oh." My hopes melted, leaving a small trickle of guilt behind. "I didn't want to use magic anyway."

Ms. Jones pulled into the sandwich shop parking lot as Ursula snorted. "You could've fooled me." Her hand hung from the door handle, waiting for Ms. Jones to put the car in park. "He'll come around," she tried to reassure me.

"Not in time." I was sure of that.

We followed Ms. Jones to the front door, peering at the Closed sign in the window. Ursula put her face up to the glass, shielding her eyes to peer through the tint. "I can't tell if anyone's here."

There were a few vehicles in the parking lot—one I recognized as Bradley's parents' ten-passenger van—so I knew the place wasn't deserted. Before I could tap on the window, the door opened, witch bells jingling at the movement. Mr. Porter beamed at our presence. "How delightfully unexpected," he said, moving to allow us through the door. He locked it as soon as we were all inside, but the rancid smell of pickles and cold cuts had me regretting the decision to come here. I closed my eyes as if not seeing would somehow remove the stench, but it was no use. "Sit, sit." Mr. Porter waved to a nearby table. "Can I get you ladies anything to eat?"

"No, thank you," I replied, pinching the bridge of my nose. I squinted at the centerpiece of unlit yellow candles. A few flower petals had been carefully placed around them, matching some of the flowers from the small garden bed out front.

Ursula ordered a Reuben on rye. Ms. Jones inquired about the assortment of teas.

I suddenly remembered the van I had spotted outside and snapped my head up in search of Bradley. Instead, I found Rebecca and Mrs. Chambers decorating a table in the corner. They had layered several red, purple, and gold fabrics over the tabletop. Sifting through a dusty box, they pulled out a deck of tarot cards and a small crystal ball. As I watched them continue to decorate, I realized that I'd never actually seen a fortune teller practice their craft in person. It wasn't a practice passed down in my family like it was in other families. From the little I knew about my ancestors, they were horse traders and blacksmiths. Despite this, I'd seen some Roma with cards on our travels in Europe. I didn't remember watching them perform readings, though, because it was an entirely illegal practice in Paris.

"You don't need all those gimmicks, Clarinda. You are the real deal, after all." Mr. Porter chuckled as he passed them on his way to the kitchen.

Mrs. Chambers raised an eyebrow, a hand on her hip. "Indianapolis isn't New Orleans. They may both be religious epicenters, but for entirely different reasons. Gadje look for witches with natural talent in New Orleans. In Indianapolis, they look for gifts from God. The gimmicks tell them what to expect, and they certainly are more likely to see the gadje down the street—the ones who claim to be prophets. I'll probably make no more than a dollar here in your little shop."

Mr. Porter notched an eyebrow, a sly curl on his lips. "Wasn't it you who told me only a few weeks ago that you didn't want anyone taking notice of us?"

Mrs. Chambers frowned, her brown eyes dropping to the box. "You may have noticed businesses are going bankrupt." Mrs. Chambers's eyes flickered to Mr. Porter's for just a moment. "Stocks are crashing."

Seeming uninterested in the conversation, Rebecca sidestepped out of the corner, heading to the kitchen.

Mr. Porter didn't seem perturbed by the ominous tone. "Businesses like Priori Labs going under wouldn't be such a bad thing."

Mrs. Chambers shook her head. "Priori Labs is struggling, but they're getting back on their feet. Meanwhile, Chastain's work has been close to announcing bankruptcy for months. They've been cutting spending, laying off workers… It's a mess. The higher-ups are threatening to close the Indianapolis branch if Chastain and his team can't get it under control, but he's been cutting his own hours just to make ends meet at the company. I can't say how long he'll have his job. All I know is his company isn't the only one. We've seen it in the news, in the papers… If I can just get my hands on a financial executive, maybe then I'll see what we're all fearing."

Finally, Mr. Porter's smile subsided. "You think you'll see a stock market crash? Another Great Depression?"

Mrs. Chambers didn't answer, her lips pressed grimly together as she continued to take things out of her box.

Ursula snapped her fingers in front of my face, drawing my attention. "Hey, Dad said fewer people are buying homes. Do you think that has anything to do with what Mrs. Chambers is saying?"

I shrugged. I was surprised Dad had time to gripe about anything other than me or Bradley, and honestly, what was it to me if Dad lost a few prospective buyers? He wasn't paying to keep me alive. Mom would probably be busier than ever with the unhoused population, and unless she started doing too much charity work, she could certainly sustain Ursula on her income. Call it something like karma or prikaza, but if Dad's business went under, it was well deserved.

As for the Chamberses, the way Bradley's mom talked made my stomach tighten more than it already was. When Bradley's family moved here, Mr. Chambers's position at the broadcasting company became their sole source of income, and while Bradley never said anything that suggested they were struggling financially, it made sense that they were. Their family had practically doubled when they took on the Burnetts over a year ago. Add that to the changes in their health insurance last year—which I only knew because Bradley's access to insulin had changed—that probably made their out-of-pocket medical expenses rise. And let's not forget the mounting hospital bills I was sure they had. With the cure having not worked for Bradley, future expenses were only going to get worse.

What if they lost their home?

What if they couldn't stay?

I knew Bradley and I would probably have to live on the run soon anyway, but I hadn't thought about what that meant for our families. Would we all be running together? And could any of us afford to do so? Living on the road was expensive—something I don't think a lot of gaché understand. In fact, many of them are praised for buying vans and traveling around the country, but what is traveling but poverty? Especially for Roma?

Rebecca approached our table, interrupting my slight panic. Handing me a glass of water, she said, "You look like you could use this."

I gripped the cup, sliding it toward me, thanking her for her thoughtfulness. I tried to breathe in the scent to distract me from the stench of pickles, but quickly realized that was a dumb idea. Water didn't have a scent, and this one smelled just as bad as the air. I took a sip and was surprised by a strange, bittersweet taste. My tongue started to tingle as I set the glass down. Water dribbled out the corners of my mouth as I struggled to swallow. I grabbed a napkin to dab at it, shooting a glance at my boyfriend's sister. "Did you put something in this?"

For a split second, I thought I saw disappointment flash across her face, her eyebrows drawing in. "Something that should help you."

22 // FATES, FAIRY TALES, AND ATTEMPTED MURDER
BRADLEY

Victoria groaned, probably from boredom, as she laid a piece of old parchment on her family's dining room table. "Please tell me you found something."

I flipped a page of an old grimoire that belonged to her great-great-grandfather. Half the scribbles were illegible, and from what I could read, I'd found nothing explaining what could be happening to Rebecca—*if* something was happening to Rebecca. "Don't you think I would have said something if I found anything?"

Victoria's hand landed on another old book, pulling it toward her. "I don't know you well enough. You could keep secrets close to your chest like Serena for all I know."

I looked up at her, blinking through the dusty air as my eyes adjusted to something other than paper and ink. "You still think she's keeping secrets?" Maybe we should have started our search for answers with her.

Victoria shook her head, flipping to the first page. "About this? No. But she's got this smug little attitude like she knows facts we don't."

I cocked an eyebrow. That was Serena, alright. But I was also pretty sure she'd learned her lesson about solo missions. If she'd discovered anything that could help us, she'd ask someone to spot her. I looked back at the grimoire, studying a bad art sketch that I couldn't quite decipher. "So your great-great-grandfather was a Chosen One?"

Victoria rolled her eyes. "Not that one. You gotta go about eight generations back, give or take." She reached for a scroll sitting at the edge of the table, unraveling it to reveal a family tree. "Most of this is just guesswork, but based on family stories…" Her voice trailed off as she searched for the name she was looking for, pointing at it when she found it. "Caleb lived during the Salem witch trials. I mean, he wasn't there at that time, but his mother-in-law was accused of witchcraft in their town. He and his wife, Judith"—she slid her finger to Judith's name—"helped her escape before she was executed." She eyed the grimoire in front of me. "That grimoire you're looking through belonged to my dad's granddad, who is a direct descendant of Caleb." She slid her finger several generations down the tree to land on some guy named Charles.

I closed the grimoire. "Okay, then shouldn't we be looking through a grimoire of Caleb's?"

She looked at me, dumbfounded. "You think we got all the family grimoires stashed away up here? You know how many aunts and uncles and cousins and all the greats could have Caleb's grimoire—if he kept one at all? We gotta hope some of the family legends were passed down in one of these; otherwise, we're screwed."

I flipped to the next page of Charles's grimoire, spotting nothing relevant. I huffed in frustration. "Maybe your dad's remembering wrong." After Mr. Porter heard what Rebecca had tried to do to Maria, he had been struck with a vague memory, like he had once heard the story of a Chosen One going rogue and murdering people, which was why I was helping Victoria dig through old books for a source. I flipped to another page. "According to my brother, Rebecca thinks something is wrong with Paige, which isn't exactly unreasonable given her history."

"It is when Rebecca's trying to kill people because of it," Victoria reminded me.

I groaned, closing Charles's grimoire. "I don't get it. Rebecca has always been a sweet kid. I mean, she freaked when she got her powers. She didn't want to use them. She wanted to stay sweet and innocent, I guess. I don't know. But I pushed her. I placed her in situations where she *had* to use her powers."

Victoria smirked. "You mean she hasn't always been Scary Mary?" I glared at her, which sent her into a fit of cackles. "Relax. I've only known the both of you for a few months, and the only thing about your sister that is remotely scary is the fact that she could end me if she really wanted to. She's sweet and still has that innocent little girl look. Her trying to kill Maria?" She shook her head at the ridiculousness. "That can't be her."

"What? So you think she's possessed?" I turned to look at one of the many shelves lining their living room walls. One of them was full of paranormal books.

Something about my question made Victoria's face straighten as she stood. I followed her to a shelf hosting books on mythology. She pulled one out with a symbol that looked much like one that I'd seen at Chad's church, the title reading, *The Cross-Cultural Phenomenon of the Triple Deity*.

"Triple? Like the Father, the Son, and the Holy Spirit?" I asked.

"Or triple like the Fates. If she *is* a Fate," she snorted, plopping on the couch and opening to the table of contents. I sat next to her, leaning in to see what she was seeing as her finger dragged along the paper. She tapped on the chapter that discussed the Greek Fates or Moirai before flipping to the correct page. I waited as she skimmed, finally landing on what she was looking for. "The Greek tradition is the best known here. Did you know there are names and different jobs for the Fates? Clotho spins the thread of fate. She's the one who is present at the time of a child's birth to protect them. Lachesis measures the thread. She decides a person's destiny. Then there's Atropos, who cuts the thread, determining a person's date of death." She closed the book. "What if the Fates aren't really separated like that? At least, not the three that we consider chosen?"

"I'm not following."

She shifted on the couch to face me. "Think about it. The Chosen One is supposed to protect the Immortal One. They feel drawn to them. That's how Liesel found Maria. Supposedly before Maria was born, Liesel innately knew where to be so she would cross her path. But what if instead of Maria being the beacon, Liesel was? What if Liesel somehow shaped Magdalena and Mateusz's destiny? Her capture somehow activated those two to come together because she was desperate for some sort of savior. I mean, she was seeing the destruction of her people in real time. Even if it wasn't conscious, something brought the Lewandowskis together."

Victoria's epiphany struck a memory. The night Savanna and I learned we were fated, Rebecca had claimed to have triggered a series of events, perhaps too early. My heart stuttered at the correlation between that moment and what Victoria was saying. I closed my eyes, groaning in frustration. Rebecca had started the chain reaction a year and a half ago. Was our predicament really my fault? Or was it my sister's?

Victoria continued to explain her theory. "And then there's the whole death thing. I mean, sure, anybody could kill anybody with the right opportunity and resources, but you've said it yourself. Rebecca can cause mass destruction. I've seen that park you all were at two years ago. There are still crevices in the ground from the earthquake she caused. And now…" She hesitated, restarting her sentence. "And now she's trying to kill Maria—someone who's already destined to die soon. Why would she try to get to her before her time? It doesn't make sense to me. Theoretically, Maria's destiny is already woven."

There was a long pause as she sat in silence, pondering. I was still struggling to process. Finally, she asked, "Blake said Rebecca thinks evil spirits are after Paige? What if an evil spirit is after *Rebecca*? A spirit that wants the Immortal Ones dead?"

I rubbed my eyes, blinking the room back into my blurry sight. This was tiring. It all was. "You think the captivators sent an evil spirit to infect Rebecca? Can they do that?"

Victoria unwrapped a gum wrapper and slid a stick into her mouth. She shrugged. "Maybe all the Chosen Ones are connected somehow. Maybe they're reaching Rebecca through *their* Chosen One." She smacked her lips together, chewing the gum.

I thought about her theory for a second. It at least made a little sense. The captivators hadn't bothered us since December, even when they had to know it was us spreading the cure. They hadn't stormed into any of our homes with guns blazing to intimidate us at all. That seemed strange, considering Maria hadn't been back to Indianapolis since our last brush with them. But maybe that was why they were waiting. They wanted Maria too. What if they somehow used their Chosen One to infect Rebecca? To make her think she was protecting us by going after Maria?

Wait, no. That didn't make sense either. If anything, the captivators would want her alive. At least before the baby's born.

"None of this is making sense," I said, standing to pace. "I feel like we're just spitting out theories."

Victoria rolled her eyes, standing to place the book back on the shelf. "Well, something is upsetting the balance. All I know is there's a cosmic order to things. Triple deities exist in all kinds of religions and cultures to explain the balance of what the Hindus call creation, preservation, and destruction. And something's off. Rebecca's leaning a little too heavily on the destruction side."

A sudden cacophony of sounds coming from downstairs made me jump. It sounded like several pans and utensils had crashed to the ground. I consciously took a breath. If someone didn't put the metal slats in the correct spots when setting the sandwich stations, the pans tended to fall. It reminded me of the game Don't Break the Ice. That was probably all it was.

But then someone screamed.

Victoria and I glanced at each other for a split second before racing out of the apartment and down the stairs. I couldn't see much at first. The stairs led to the back of the kitchen, where large appliances and walls blocked our view. Warm sandwiches sat on plates near the order window, abandoned before someone had a chance to add toppings. Breathing heavily, I skidded to a stop just short of the counter, shocked by the sight that met me. Victoria rammed into me, unable to stop herself in time, and we both hit the side of the counter.

"You hurt my sister, and I swear to God, I'll kill you! I'll kill you right now!" Ursula shouted, a knife at the back of Rebecca's neck. My sister wasn't so innocent herself. She had her own knife at Savanna's. The entire scene was unsettling to say the least.

Rebecca's voice was almost a growl, but I couldn't see her face from where I was standing. "Drink the water," she said slowly, but forcibly.

All four adults had swarmed around them, standing helplessly with their eyes wide.

"How do you beat Destruction at her own game?" Victoria whispered to me, referencing the Hindu trinity she had mentioned upstairs.

Mom tried to reason with Rebecca. "Honey, please. You don't want to do this."

Savanna stared ahead at the glass of water in front of her. Something wasn't making sense. Why would Rebecca care if Savanna was drinking water?

Victoria turned, glancing back at the kitchen, seeming to spot a clue I had missed. "Shit. I think that's rue water."

I shook my head, not recognizing the term. "Rue water?"

"It's like the holy water of Hoodoo. Except it's also an abortive. She's trying to kill the baby." My heart pounded violently in my throat, the sound drowning out the chaos. Victoria quickly rounded the corner to join the crowd of adults and their pleas. Nothing they were saying talked my sister down.

I ducked behind the counter, attempting to clear my head. I needed to focus. Sure, my powers were a little more useless than normal while Savanna was pregnant, but I could still do some things. At least, I hoped I could. Catching sight of the tub of knives Victoria kept under the register, an idea occurred to me. Early on in Savanna's pregnancy—before we even knew about it—I could touch one object and every identical object in the room would disappear. The thing was, I couldn't intentionally do it. I had to try to dematerialize one knife without thinking about the rest. I couldn't exactly let my powers know my plan. Grabbing a knife from the bin, I gripped it tight, willing it away.

All the other knives in the bin dissipated, including the one in my hand. I leapt up, looking to see if Rebecca and Ursula's knives had also disappeared. They were both staring at their empty hands in shock. *Yes!* Who said my powers were useless?

Savanna recognized the opportunity in their distraction. She grabbed the water, splashing it on

Rebecca, then slid her left foot to hit Rebecca's legs as my sister leapt in surprise. Rebecca lost her footing, falling on her butt as Mom and Mr. Porter swarmed her, pinning her down as she screamed. Something smelled like it was burning. I glanced at the oven in the kitchen, but there was nothing on it to burn. Leaping over the counter, I rushed to Savanna, who was hyperventilating from the unexpected threat to her life. Ursula and Ms. Jones had beat me to her side, asking her if she was okay. She nodded as Mrs. Porter stood between them and Rebecca, shrinking into a prowling black panther to help keep the two sides separate.

I stood behind my sister as she continued to scream. Red welts appeared on her white skin. Mom and Mr. Porter shushed her, trying to get her to calm down, but she was practically rabid. Victoria came to stand beside me, staring at the scene in incredulity. Attempting to kill Maria was one thing, but Savanna…?

Mr. Porter struggled against Rebecca's movements, but luckily for him, my sister's age made her a little easier to restrain. She didn't have the power to phase through his grip, nor telekinetically remove it. I also knew if she really wanted to kill Savanna or my child, she could. Something was holding her back. Even if it was something small.

"I remember now," Mr. Porter said between grunts. "I remember the legend."

Rebecca stopped fighting, tears rolling to the floor. Mom stroked her hair as my sister twisted her head, trying to hide behind her restrained arm. Mr. Porter let go so she could, apparently deciding the threat had receded. I placed myself near the pacing panther, adrenaline coursing through my veins. I wasn't going to be as easily persuaded.

Mom inspected the red welts on Rebecca's arm. "Please tell me you have some salve," she asked, peering at Victoria.

Victoria nodded, hesitating before heading to the back.

Mr. Porter rubbed his forehead, crossing his legs. "There's an old druid tale. The tale of Onora, I think. It's a cautionary story that warns against gifting powers to another. Onora gives her powers to everyone in the village and one by one, they all go mad." He met my eyes, his mouth slightly agape, before sliding his gaze to Savanna, his dark eyes almost pleading. He swallowed. "She's not thinking straight."

Victoria returned with a small tub of salve, handing it to Mom.

"So what do we do?" Mom asked, unscrewing the lid.

Mr. Porter sighed. "Most, if not all, the cures I'd like to try probably won't work on a Chosen One. Persuasion dust definitely doesn't." He watched as Mom spread the salve on Rebecca's blistering arm. "I think we'd have to consult the Chosen One for the witches."

"And who might that be?" Mom asked.

Mr. Porter appeared defeated, rubbing half his face in exhaustion. "I don't know."

Savanna's hands clutched her necklace, her voice shaky. "Can you at least bless my necklace so I can get out of here?"

I felt the urge to hug her, to hold her, to protect her, but she was surrounded by everyone else trying to do the same. And honestly, what was I going to do? I was of better use trying to help find a cure for Rebecca's mental instability.

My throat tightened as Savanna's hands moved to unclasp the necklace, dangling it in front of her. "I accidentally broke it earlier."

I leaned over the panther, holding out my hand. She dropped the necklace in my palm, her glassy blue eyes meeting mine. I didn't have to hear her thoughts to know what she was thinking. When the good guys start attacking, is anywhere safe? I gulped. I should have warned her about Rebecca, but I didn't want to scare her. Besides, I thought it was more likely Rebecca might try going after Maria again instead of going after our baby.

I glanced at the empty glass on the ground, crouched, and gingerly picked a piece of it up with my other hand. Would rue water even have worked?

Mr. Porter stood, holding out his hand for the necklace, but I had lost myself in a spiral of anger, the shock of the event wearing itself off. The truth was suddenly as clear as the glass I was holding. Rebecca had tried to harm Savanna. She had tried to kill our child. Our child. It still felt weird to even think in those terms. I turned on my heels, twisting toward my sister. She had curled into a fetal position, facing our mom. Her innocent-like form triggered a rumble of anger through my stomach and into my chest. I shook. How dare she. How dare she try to gain sympathy with her crocodile tears.

Stepping toward her, I sucked in a salivary breath, preparing to yell at her. The glass dematerialized in my hand as I'd prepared to chuck it near her head, the sudden involuntary disappearance distracting me enough to lift my head in time to see the entire stack of identical glasses behind the counter disappear too. Damn it.

"Bradley." Mr. Porter's hand was on my chest, attempting to shove me back. My breathing grew heavier, menacing. I wanted to say something—anything—to make my sister pay, but I couldn't think of anything strong enough. I let Victoria's dad shove me all the way out the door until we were outside, the tinted windows making it impossible to view the scene we had left behind. His hand reached to unfurl my fingers, untangling Savanna's necklace from my grip. "Harming your sister is not going to help the situation."

He stepped back, cupping the necklace in his hands and whispering through his fingers. I waited, attempting to catch my breath, my chest heaving.

"That necklace isn't going to protect Savanna if Rebecca keeps this up," I said through clenched teeth, barely attempting to curb my anger as I started to pace.

"It'll protect her from the people who matter."

I stomped my foot, turning on my heels to stare at him. "We're not safe anymore!"

Mr. Porter's eyebrows drew in as he shook his head. "Don't say that."

"Why? It's true!" I shook my head, beginning to pace again. "We should be at a safe house or on the road. I don't know why we're trying to make it work here."

"You don't stand a chance without Rebecca helping protect you."

"Protect us?" I scoffed, waving my hand toward the shop. "Did that look like she was trying to protect us? Face it. We're just going to have to try to make it without her."

Mr. Porter started to roll his eyes, but stopped himself, digging in his pocket for something. "We'll deal with Rebecca. We'll find a cure. But for now…" He procured a woven brown leather bracelet with a silver-colored centerpiece. A clear lid was clasped over the center, showing a small collection of herbs like what was in Savanna's necklace. "You were right earlier. Maybe you should have this to keep you from being tracked by the captivators."

I scowled, taking the bracelet, and examining it. "I'm not really a jewelry kind of guy."

Mr. Porter cocked an eyebrow. "You want to live? Wear it. It won't protect you from your sister, but it will make it more difficult for the captivators to find you. You'll be virtually invisible to them."

I was still angry, but I shoved it on my wrist just the same. "Whatever." Then I swiveled toward the street and started walking. No way was I going to ride in the same car as Rebecca.

23 // I CONFRONT SERENA'S RUMORS
JAY-JAY

"**W**hy'd you do it?" I asked, sliding into the chair across from Serena in the newspaper room.

She glared at me for a second, pursing her lips, before her round eyes fell back to the letter she was reading. She tapped a pencil on her chin, squinting at the handwriting. Serena was part of the department that handled the letters to the editor. Normally, I wouldn't interrupt, but I'd waited all day to get her alone.

I grabbed a nearby pad of paper and dug a pencil out of my backpack. Pretending to write my own letter, I read the words aloud as I thought of them. "Dear Editor, I want to talk about boundaries. You see, I have this friend. Well, maybe she isn't exactly a friend. It's complicated. Anyway, this 'friend' has trust issues like you wouldn't believe. Because she has trust issues, she finds it necessary to go through my personal belongings. I'll be the first to say I have nothing to hide, so this wasn't a big deal at first. But then she hacked into my computer. She didn't ask, and she didn't warn me. Which, okay, again, whatever. But then she used the information she found to spread a nasty rumor about me. As a result, the girl I was dating broke up with me. So let me ask you this. How can I set boundaries with someone who has no boundaries? And where is a reasonable place to set that boundary? Signed, Outed and, dare I say, Violated?"

I thought I saw her wince, but when I got a better look at her face, her expression was still passive, her eyes still on the letter. I knew she wasn't reading it anymore. Her eyes had stopped moving across the page.

"Well?" I prompted. "Do you have anything to say for yourself?"

Her grip tightened, the paper crinkling between her fingers. Her jaw moved like she was grinding her teeth as she rolled her eyes. "I didn't hack your computer."

"Like hell you didn't."

She dropped the letter, smoothing it out on the desk. Her voice was quiet, her tone unusually timid. "Are you really gay?" I thought I saw a little bit of blush in her light brown cheeks as she pursed her lips.

I blinked. Confused. Why would she need me to confirm something she already thought she knew? This was Serena. She didn't ask questions. She used every other means to learn all she could about a person and then assumed everything she found was true. She was cocky with her knowledge, not hesitant. "No."

She finally looked at me, her eyes round and… hopeful? I scowled. I hadn't initially pegged her as homophobic. Not when she was friends with Seth.

Especially not when she stayed friends with Seth after Seth kissed her. Oh yeah. I saw that. I mean, I wasn't physically there, but I had a vision. I knew what happened before Seth ran away last December. So why did Serena care if I was gay or not? Was it such a relief to believe I was straight? Maybe then she wouldn't have to second-guess being around me.

I leaned forward, angry but trying not to show it. I don't think I was doing a very good job. "Pan isn't synonymous with gay," I clarified.

Her eyelids fluttered as she jerked away from me. "Oh my God." Her mouth had fallen open, her words loud enough to draw the attention of some of the people near us. Her reaction made me uncomfortable, my skin clammy. She really did hate me.

"That better be a good story you're cookin', Jay-Jay," our adviser shouted from across the room as he stood over another person's shoulder. He was staring at their computer screen, not looking at us.

I held up the pad of paper and my pencil to abate him. He glanced over and nodded before returning to the student he was helping.

Serena lowered her voice only slightly. "Jay-Jay, I was just making stuff up. I didn't hack your computer. I didn't realize I could actually be right."

She what? I shook my head, confused by her words. "You weren't," I argued. "And now Alyssa won't speak to me."

She crossed her arms, snorting as she leaned back in her chair. "Alyssa doesn't speak to anyone."

"Yeah, well, she spoke to me." And I knew. I knew why Alyssa didn't speak to just anyone. She had a condition called selective mutism. She couldn't just speak when she wanted to. It was like her tongue wouldn't let her. I wasn't about to blab that to Serena so she could use it to torture her further—even if Alyssa broke up with me for a totally panphobic reason. "And she's not okay with dating someone who sometimes likes guys, which is ridiculous because it's not like I'm some douchebag who will cheat on her because 'I'm secretly gay.'" I made sure to use air quotes around those last three words. To be fair, Alyssa hadn't exactly explained her reasoning for dumping me. Maybe it didn't have anything to do with that, but it sure felt like it. "That's not how it works."

Serena squinted, arcing her pen in the air like she was physically pointing out her words. "So you like guys *and* girls?"

I shrugged. "And anybody in between."

"But not at the same time?" she asked, lifting an eyebrow.

I groaned, placing my hands on the table. "Let me ask you this. Do you ever have a crush on more than one person at once? It doesn't even have to be a major crush. You just wouldn't be opposed to dating them if they asked you out? You wouldn't date them at the same time unless you're polyamorous, of course," I quickly clarified, waving my hands. "But like, you don't go around having eyes for one person and one person only, right? You keep your options open?"

She pursed her lips, continuing to squint as she thought. Her pause made me nervous. This wasn't an uncommon phenomenon, was it? Savanna's friends always talked about liking multiple guys at once. They would even rank them. In front of me. And explain their rating in excruciating detail. Let me tell you, seeing some of those guys in classes the next day was… awkward. I didn't know how Serena handled knowing all these secrets about people. Maybe that was the point. She didn't handle it. Instead, she went around gossiping her knowledge away.

Finally, her gaze came back to me. "I think I know what you mean."

I sighed in relief, swallowing the extra saliva that had gathered in my mouth. "Okay. Well, I'm not any different. The only difference is that my pool of potential crushes is bigger."

Serena smiled almost mischievously. "You know I don't believe that."

I blinked. I thought I had gotten her on the same page.

She explained, "Because if that were true—if your pool of potential crushes is bigger—than Alyssa wouldn't have been the first and only person you've asked out or dated."

I leaned back in my chair, trying to come up with a witty response, but she was kind of right. Alyssa *was* the only person I'd asked out and dated. I rolled my eyes. "I don't know if you've noticed," I said, tapping the tabletop, "but I'm kind of a geek around here." I sighed dramatically. "And geeks are just not chic."

She lifted an eyebrow, laughing. "Did you just use the word 'chic' in a sentence?"

I rolled my eyes, crossing my arms defensively. "Are you going to make fun of everything I say?"

She nodded, still cackling. When she finally calmed down, she placed her hands flat on the table, spreading her fingers. She sucked in a breath. "I was trying to figure out what made Alyssa so special—why Maria chose her."

"By outing me?" I scoffed.

Her eyes met mine, glistening in an almost pleading way. "No." Her gaze dropped to her hands. "Well, okay. I did do that, but not on purpose. I didn't actually have proof. I didn't hack your computer. I just wanted to get her to crack—to spill her secrets. And I thought if I made her lose faith in you as a boyfriend..." Her voice trailed off.

I hope she knew how illogical that sounded. But then again, she always seemed smart until she tried to implement a plan solo. That's when her plans tended to bite her in the butt. I took a breath, trying to keep myself from snapping. I had a theory about why Maria had chosen Alyssa and her family to be extra guardians.

"Alyssa can see through things," I explained, not meeting Serena's eyes. I was afraid if I looked into them, I would get mad all over again and talk way above the acceptable decibel level.

Serena snorted. "So can most molecular manipulators. That doesn't make her special, Jay-Jay."

I shook my head. "No. Like, she can see through a layer of everything all the time. She can't turn it off. I suspect she could look even further if she wanted to. It's almost like she has X-ray vision."

Serena shifted in her seat. "X-ray vision?"

We shared a knowing look. I suspected we both had the same idea—Alyssa wasn't just here to keep an eye on Savanna. She was here to keep an eye on the baby. Literally. "Too bad she wasn't at Wich Wharf yesterday," I said.

Serena blinked, seeming confused. "What happened?" Holy crap, she hadn't heard. I smiled spitefully, a tad smug that she wasn't completely in the loop.

"Remember that rue water Mr. Porter sprayed on us a while back?"

Serena's eyes widened. I assumed she was remembering his admittance that it caused miscarriages. "But that stuff wouldn't work on Savanna. He said so."

I shrugged. "He *assumed* so. My mom said it burned Rebecca's skin after Savanna tossed it on her."

Serena's face twisted in confusion. "Why would Mr. Porter have rue water anywhere near Savanna?"

I shook my head. She needed to wait for the whole story. "He didn't. Rebecca brought it out to serve to Savanna. According to my mom, Savanna took a sip, thought it tasted strange, and spat it out. That's when Rebecca went berserk. She held a knife to her throat and everything, trying to get her to drink the rest."

Serena was silent for a while as she struggled to process. It was hard to wrap my mind around too. Rebecca wasn't violent. At least, not to any of us. So why was she trying to kill Bradley and Savanna's unborn child? Did she think it would solve all their problems?

"Why would the Fates suddenly want that baby dead after pulling all the threads to make it happen in the first place?" Serena asked, gazing ahead, her eyes unfocused. I imagined the gears in her brain grinding, working overtime to try to make it make sense. The thing was it didn't make sense. That was the problem.

I glanced down at the table, tapping my pencil on the pad of paper. "Apparently, she tried to kill Maria last week too."

Serena gasped, her hands covering her mouth. Seems Rebecca trying to kill an unborn child wasn't nearly as shocking as Rebecca trying to kill a fully grown Immortal One. She slowly lowered her hands, a theory occurring to her. "Can a Chosen One kill an Immortal One?"

My breath hitched in my throat at the possibility. Theoretically, if anyone could end the life of someone deemed "immortal," it would be a Chosen One. It would be fate itself. I gulped. "Maybe that's what activated the rue water. The fact that Rebecca had given it to Savanna could have been enough to cause a miscarriage. If anybody else had given it to her, maybe it would have done nothing, like Mr. Porter had theorized." I shook my head. This was all starting to give me a headache.

Serena crossed her arms against her chest. "So Rebecca's dangerous to them."

I nodded, catching her up to the present. "Bradley wants to leave."

I hadn't seen Bradley in some of our shared classes all day, but I knew he was around. He was at lunch, broody and quiet, refusing to let go of Savanna's hand. I didn't have any classes with Savanna in the mornings, and part of me suspected he had gone to hers, but I also didn't think Frank would have enabled that. Maybe he'd been with Frank all day instead.

"No wonder he was all clingy at lunch," Serena noted. "I suspect he'll want to trade seats with me in algebra later so they can hold hands." She scowled, muttering something I couldn't comprehend under her breath.

"Just..." I hesitated as I decided how I wanted to phrase my words. "Keep a lookout for any signs that they might run. They're not going to get far without us, and it's not safe for them to be out on their own."

"You don't have to tell me twice," Serena mumbled, picking up her letter and returning her attention to her newspaper duties.

We all had to be on high alert now.

24 // IT'S TIME FOR US TO RUN
BRADLEY

"**O**lga said I could stay with her," Savanna whispered, staring at the floor. We were standing outside her locker after school. I could barely hear her over lockers slamming, foot traffic, and shouts of the other students.

We were standing so close, our breaths in each other's faces. I didn't want to hit her with my movement. I shook my head ever so slightly. "No." I drew back enough to see her blue eyes more clearly, my hand on the locker behind her to keep my balance. I missed being able to embrace her the way I could before she was pregnant. Now her stomach acted as a spacer, and it reminded me of those nuns on television who use measuring tapes at school dances, telling their students they must leave room for Jesus. It might have been a funny thought if I was in the headspace to take a joke, but we were really in trouble now.

The one person who could theoretically kill me, Savanna, and our child wasn't on our side anymore. If the Fates created the fated and the Immortal Ones, they could just as easily take them out.

Savanna sighed, still not meeting my gaze. She flicked a stray tear from below her eye. "When did we get here?" she asked, her words scratching at my insides. "There was a time I would have gladly sipped that water if I thought it would work." She shook her head, letting out a sob, her hands pulling her hair back at the roots. "Why do I care?" Her eyes finally met mine, my stomach flipping inadvertently at the pain in them.

I didn't have an answer for her. I hadn't been part of the abortion discussion, having been out of town when she and her mom had discussed options. Even though I hadn't originally considered it, that didn't mean I wasn't okay with her decision. Even if the pill had worked, I would have been okay with it. If it had worked, we wouldn't be standing here. Our lives wouldn't be so messy. We wouldn't be living in as much fear as we were. Nobody would be considering running or relocating. We could finish high school like normal teenagers. We wouldn't have to be parents so young. We could have waited for a better time to create life, if we thought there was a better time. But sometimes futures were fragile. Life was fragile. We were basically fighting over our spilled blood.

I didn't like the idea of Savanna living with Olga. And that wasn't because Olga lived three hours away. Being near Olga, especially in her hometown, meant being near Chad. If he was still locked up, maybe I'd feel better, but I knew from Olga he'd been released from his court-mandated inpatient program over a year ago. He'd gotten out on a technicality. Savanna in Itasca living a block away from the guy who tried to murder my brother wasn't safer than if we stayed in Indianapolis, even with the larger diviner presence in the Chicago area. Being around more diviners hadn't saved my brother. And it wasn't going to save Savanna.

Someone banged the locker next to us with a stack of books. "Get a room, you two." I flinched, my muscles tightening as I tried to stay focused on Savanna. She must have noticed my struggle because she tugged my hand, making me follow her outside.

"Look, I get why you don't want me staying with Olga." Savanna took a breath, probably to prepare for her argument.

I cut her off before she could continue. "You don't know why," I said, trying to shake the idea of Chad harming her from my mind. There were other reasons it was a bad idea. "Olga may tell you it's fine, but that is because she's somehow managed to bully her parents into letting her live in their house, despite the fact that she has ruined her family's reputation in the community. She is defiant, rebellious, and has no sense of safety.

"Her mom is very religious, and not like Jay-Jay's mom or your mom are, okay? That woman uses prayer and the Bible as a weapon. She equates a lot of normal behaviors to demonic activity. And if you walk into her house, pregnant and fifteen? She's... well, I don't know what she's going to do, but I can't imagine it to be good.

She isn't like those Christians who believe in helping and loving everyone. She's the ugly stereotype. Sending you to Olga's house would be like sending you back to your dad. Maybe worse. Why do you think Olga was sent out of state for a summer after what happened with my brother and Chad?"

Savanna let go, crossed her arms, and leaned against the brick wall of the school. She scuffed the sole of one of her shoes against the pavement, her jaw set, her blue eyes not meeting mine. "It would still be better than staying here."

"No, it wouldn't," I argued.

She stomped, her eyes flashing. "You don't own me!"

I stepped back, shocked that she was fighting so hard for this. It was a dumb move. She had to see that. "If we separate," I said, remembering the time I'd flown to San Diego without her, "one or both of us is going to get sick."

She narrowed her eyes. "Did Maria tell you that?"

It took me a little too long to remember that she hadn't known about the coughing fit I had the second the plane left the tarmac last December. "When I left you to go to San Diego, I felt like I was hacking up a lung. It didn't go away until I came back to Indianapolis." A memory sparked in my mind—one she would remember too. "And when I broke up with you, remember? I stopped being able to breathe. I was coughing up blood. And my hand that had healed itself? It unhealed and then healed again. And when I got to the nurse's office, my blood sugar levels had skyrocketed." I licked my lips, getting to the point. "We can't separate."

She hit me on the arm so quickly, I didn't have time to defend myself. "Then why did you tell me in the hospital that we might have to go our separate ways?" she screamed.

My jaw dropped, and I reached for the bruise that was sure to form on my arm. I tried to come up with a viable explanation on the spot. In the moment, separating had seemed inevitable. And to be honest, I'd forgotten about the whole angering fate thing. Plus, maybe I thought the consequences would wear off after the baby was born. I don't know. "Because I'm a dumbass," I argued, trying to appear like I was on her side so she would stop fighting me. "I was basically on my deathbed. Give me a break." Okay. Maybe that was an exaggeration. And I immediately regretted my choice of words when Savanna blanched, her face blanking for a second, her brown skin somehow twinging toward green.

I could see someone approaching us from the corner of my eye. They had removed themselves from the steady stream of students who were heading to the parking lot. Assuming it was a diviner tailing us, I turned, spotting the least likely diviner—Liam Brown. He looked concerned, his dark blond eyebrows drawing together as he readjusted the backpack strap on his shoulder.

"I know I'm going to regret asking this," he said, stopping a foot from us, "but what's going on?" The Browns were the only area diviners who had managed to stay mostly out of the loop on our drama. Although the Browns had helped us search for Seth in December, they hadn't met us at the football field when we found her. They hadn't been there to witness any of the chaos that had ensued that night between us and the captivators. The Browns had gone home to their partially ignorant life. I wasn't sure if that was safe, but we didn't cross paths enough for me to feel like we needed to pull him into our mess.

Savanna covered her eyes, breathing for a second to collect herself as I struggled to summarize our predicament in as short a sentence as I could. "It's not safe for us here."

Liam hooked his thumbs into his belt loops. "Tell me something I don't know."

I looked at Savanna, blowing through my nose as she uncovered her face. Her hands dropped to fiddle with her necklace. "My charm doesn't protect me from Rebecca."

His eyes narrowed, his eyebrows pulling even closer. I knew what she had said would sound strange to him. "And you need protection from Rebecca why?" he fished.

"She tried to kill her," I blurted out, waiting for the shock to hit him. He'd met my sister. In fact, he was around her more than I was when we first attempted to take down Priori Labs. He'd seen her in action. Rebecca was tame. Even in a fight, she usually tried to minimize injury.

Liam's brown eyes widened, his jaw slack. He looked more terrified than we did, but maybe that was because we were usually in a state of fear as opposed to his slight privilege of removed bliss.

"I hate being powerless." Savanna shook her head. "If I had my powers, I could take her."

"No, you couldn't," Liam and I said at the same time. I could swear the fear was causing her not to think straight.

She glared back at us, her arms still crossed over her belly. "I'm not useless."

"No one said you were," I snapped.

Liam waved his arms, trying to steer our attention away from each other. "Hey, you can argue another time. I think I might have an idea, but it depends on whether or not Rebecca can track you. Can she?" He glanced at Savanna as he asked this, but I was the one who answered. She was my sister after all.

"Not yet. She hears singing when she is around Maria, but I don't think she does around Savanna. I don't know how long that will last, though. I wouldn't be surprised if she felt a pull. That's how the last Chosen One found Maria, or rather, her parents. Rebecca's never needed to find us before. Our hangouts are too predictable."

Liam nodded, quiet for a moment as he thought. When he spoke, his voice was lowered almost conspiratorially. "Would she look for you in a synagogue?"

Savanna exhaled, relief flashing across her face like his simple question held the answer to all our problems, but I was still wary. What if I was wrong? What if Rebecca *could* track us? She could crumble the place to the ground. I gulped.

Maybe it was still our best bet. Liam was right. She probably wouldn't think to look for us in a synagogue. She may be the Chosen One, but she wasn't a mind reader.

Liam and Savanna were both staring at me, probably waiting for my face to look like I was on board. I sighed, nodding reluctantly. "I guess we could hide there. Temporarily."

"We?" Savanna asked, lifting an eyebrow. It annoyed me that she was surprised by my choice of words. Why wouldn't we both go into hiding? Couldn't she see we were in this together?

"I'm not leaving you alone." I glanced at the dwindling cars in the pickup lane. Mom knew not to bother picking me up. After what happened, I'd gone home and packed a bag. I'd been staying at Frank's place ever since. He'd be looking for me soon.

I gazed at the parking lot, spotting Jay-Jay leaning against his car. He wasn't facing us. Instead, he was watching a group of guys in the back row jump on someone's Jeep. Savanna followed my gaze. "He's going to freak if I disappear. Plus, my stuff's at his house." She cringed apologetically at Liam. "Do you mind picking me up there?"

Liam shrugged. "I need time to run it past my rabbi anyway."

Savanna sent him a small smile, pushing away from the wall. I watched her as she made her way toward the parking lot. She stopped only after a couple of steps, spinning around to cover her mouth. "Shoot. I have a doctor's appointment tomorrow."

I winced, my heart stuttering. "Can you skip it?"

She dropped her hands, draping them over her stomach. "I don't know." Her eyes pleaded with mine, like I would have the answer to my own question. She realized I knew even less about pregnancy than she did, right? How important were those appointments anyway? "Aren't they just gonna take an ultrasound picture, make sure there's a heartbeat, and send you on your way?" I asked.

She puffed out her cheeks then blew out her lips. "It's called a sonogram, and no. Sometimes they take blood, sometimes they do other exams, sometimes they want to talk to me for like an hour 'cause the nurses think I'm stupid." The more she explained, the more visibly annoyed she got. She groaned. "Whatever. I'll ask Ms. Jones what she thinks." She spun on her heels, picking up her pace toward Jay-Jay.

Liam looked at me, his lips pressed tightly together, his eyebrows raised. His voice sounded strained when he finally opened his mouth to speak. "I'll talk to my rabbi. He's known for occasionally letting people who are escaping persecution stay in the basement of our synagogue. How long do you think you'll need to hide?"

I shrugged. *Forever*, I thought. This wasn't going to end with Rebecca. I swallowed, attempting to be more optimistic. I doubted that answer would be helpful to Liam or his rabbi. "Just until Mr. Porter can cure Rebecca's madness."

He nodded, still looking perplexed, but he didn't ask me to elaborate. He nodded his head toward the lot. "You want a ride?"

I nodded, digging my cell phone out of my pocket. "I have to let Frank know where I'm going. Give me a second." If I ditched him, I'd never hear the end of it. I pressed a few buttons, typing out the text message, and hit send. Part of me thought he'd hate the plan. Frank was usually insistent on playing guardian. He took a while to respond as Liam and I stood there, waiting for what seemed like five minutes.

"Maybe you should have called," Liam suggested, rocking on his feet.

I ignored him, staring at the screen. Finally, a response came in. It was only one word: *Go.*

25 // I SPEAK TO MY BROTHER'S GHOST
BLAKE

When the opening dialogue of *The World Ends with You* flashed on my Nintendo DS screens for the first time, I thought the writers had somehow taken my brain out of my skull and copied it into the game. Witnessing Neku Sakuraba's life was like looking into a crystal ball and seeing my reflection twisted in the glass. He could hear thoughts, except his power seemed to come from a mysterious pin. With it, he was given seven days to save himself before the Reapers erased him from existence.

Surviving video games is way better than surviving real life. Mostly because even if you die, you get to start all over and try again. If you die in real life, well… you're just dead. And that sucks.

Today, I was fighting alongside Shiki Misaki, some redheaded fashion designer girl. I had the sound cranked in my headphones to drown out the chaos that was happening at Wich Wharf. Mom had dragged us all there after school because she had to work but also because Mr.

Porter thought he had found a locator spell to track the third Chosen One.

Someone lifted the headphones off my ears as I was midbattle, and everyone's inner and outer shouts flooded my ears, interrupting my concentration. Neku flashed on the screen as he was struck by the enemy. I paused the game as Paige dropped my headphones on the table. "Tell her I don't have an evil spirit controlling me!" She pointed at Rebecca, who had her arms folded across her chest, her glare so dangerous I thought it might burn a hole in Paige's skull.

I scowled and grabbed my headphones, preparing to put them back over my ears. This argument sprawled over several days. Now nobody knows where Bradley and Savanna are. They hadn't been showing up to school either, which had Mom and Dad worried that they'd run.

I knew they hadn't, though. When you hear thoughts, you kind of get to know everyone's secrets. Frank was pretending to know nothing, but I'd heard it slip in his mind. The important part was they were safe, and Rebecca had no idea who to interrogate for information because nobody around her had admitted to knowing anything.

Paige looked at Mom. "Please tell me we will fix her before my birthday on Sunday."

Mom gently set her shuffled tarot cards on her table. "You know I can't see around your sister."

I slid the headphones back on my head, eager to break my connection to everyone's blended thoughts.

Seth's managed to break through just before I covered my ears: "If this doesn't get solved by her birthday, this is going to be bad. She's going to take it so personally." I groaned, her thoughts making me feel guilty. Shutting off my game, I removed my headphones.

Paige stomped over to Mom's table and slumped in a chair, burying her face in her hands. Her thoughts gave me goose bumps. "Everyone thinks I'm a failure. I'm a failure. What if I *am* being controlled by an evil spirit? What if that's why I can't keep my thoughts straight? What if Rebecca's right and everyone's only freaking out because the solution to save me is just as bad? I'm the reason Bradley won't come home. Not Rebecca. What if it's better that I wasn't here? Maybe I don't deserve to turn fourteen." She was sobbing now, and Mom turned to her in concern. Good. She should be concerned. I hated being the tattletale. Paige really was getting bad again.

Mr. Porter laid out a large map of the world in the center of the cement floor. He handed an unlit white candle to his daughter and one to his wife, then held the last one out for anyone to take. Seth grabbed it, determined to do anything to help Paige.

"Rebecca," Mr. Porter said, beckoning her to his side. His thoughts were nervous, unsure whether she would go along with the plan.

My sister stood unmoving. "I'm not supposed to get close to other vursitorja."

"This isn't a summoning spell," he explained patiently. "You won't have to get close to them, but I need you to be in the circle when we cast it."

Rebecca stared at him for a long moment. I couldn't hear her thoughts. They weren't breaking through her wall like they had been. "It's not a trick?" she asked.

I snorted. Mr. Porter smiled and raised his eyebrows. "As if I could overpower you."

She seemed to accept that answer, shuffling to his side. He grabbed her shoulders, steering her until she was standing in front of the map. I stood to get a better look as we all crowded around. Only Paige had stayed in place.

Mr. Porter raised his voice so he could be heard over the nervous chatter. "I need those who have candles to pick a corner of the map and stand there." Seth sidestepped to the nearest corner as Mrs. Porter made her way around the map. Victoria and her dad had already chosen their corners. "Everyone else besides Rebecca, I want you to form a circle around us and join hands. It is important that you not break the circle until the spell is done. Do you understand?" He gazed around us as we all nodded. We joined hands as we spread ourselves around the center of the room. It was lucky my whole family was there. Without Paige, we were struggling to reach each other. Mom and Dad had Tuesday's small hands, trying hard not to tug her too much between them.

Mr. Porter smiled when we had finished arranging ourselves. "Let us begin." He snapped his fingers, fire lighting at the tips as he held them to the wick. When the candle lit, he reached toward his daughter, using his candle to light hers. Victoria then lit her mom's and she lit Seth's. With his free hand, Mr. Porter grabbed Rebecca's shoulder, squeezing it as he muttered a series of strange words. Even as a mind reader, I couldn't be sure of the language. His thoughts hadn't exactly announced it, and I only knew English.

He stopped chanting for a second to give instructions. "We are going to light each corner of this map at the exact same time. Try to make it as precise as possible." He let go of Rebecca, returning to his chant as all four of them bent to their corners, watching him intently. Holding the flame near his edge of the map, Mr. Porter lifted his fingers, counting backward from five. When he hit one, all corners of the map lit at once. The flame spread across the paper. The chanting continued as smoke filled the air, the smell causing Tuesday to cough.

My eyes watered as the map was destroyed. I closed them, peeking every few seconds until the fire disappeared. When I reopened my eyes, only a tiny piece of the map hadn't been burned.

Mr. Porter stopped chanting, leaning in to read the location. I heard it in his thoughts before he said it out loud. "Maputo." He smiled. The noise he made almost sounded like a laugh as he looked at Rebecca. "Your counterpart is in Mozambique."

Rebecca didn't look nearly as enthusiastic. Her arms were still crossed. "So? I'll warn him not to come here."

Mr. Porter raised his eyebrows. "Him?"

Some of us exchanged nervous glances. I could hear their silent questions. "How does she know that? You mean to say, she could have told us the entire time who he was?"

Rebecca shrugged. "His name is Elzo."

Dad let go of Tuesday's hand as Mom bent to pick her up. She was getting a little big to be held all the time, but I noticed there was something about holding a child that calmed Mom.

Mr. Porter tilted his head. "Can you contact him?"

Rebecca gritted her teeth, her shoulders reaching up to her ears. "We're not telepathic."

Dad walked up from behind Mr. Porter, his expression stern. She was definitely in trouble. "Bex—"

"Don't call me Bex!" my sister screamed, the extinguished candles on the floor relighting on their own, the flames reaching almost to the ceiling. We all jumped back to keep from catching on fire.

Dad barely flinched, but I could hear his thoughts racing, panicking. "I'm not losing another child," he thought, images of Jesse in the hospital taking over. His thoughts then flashed to Bradley—to what I assumed was the forest in New Mexico where he had been taken as a kid. Then he thought of Paige's suicide attempt, seeing my oldest sister unconscious on the floor. He moved on to less serious memories, like the many times Bradley had run away or disappeared for days on end. The phone call he got from Frank about Paige's drinking. The night we learned Savanna was pregnant. Then, there was the moment I told them about Rebecca trying to kill Maria. Then the day Dad got the call she tried to kill Savanna and her baby.

When he laid it all out like that, I wondered how much more we could take as a family when our problems were trying to tear us apart. *What is family?* I thought. Because to me it seemed we were chaos, holding on to each other by our fingertips. Love drove us to overlook all the messiness. That thought made my eyes burn and my throat hurt. I didn't know why.

Dad cleared his throat. "What are you doing to this family?" he asked, sounding like he was getting ready to ground her. "Hm?" he prompted when she didn't answer. He grabbed her arm, lifting it in front of her face. "Do you see this?" There were still red splotches dotting her skin from the rue water Savanna had splashed on her. It turned out my sister was allergic to the very thing she had tried to use as poison. Dad dropped her arm, stepping back to gesture at the room. "Look around."

Rebecca barely turned her head. I couldn't see her face from where she was standing.

Dad repeated himself, angrier. "Look." My sister turned, seeming to count us with her eyes as she slowly twirled. "Who is missing?" Dad asked.

I heard several people answer him with their thoughts before Rebecca whispered, "Bradley." She stopped moving, staring straight at me. The danger in her eyes made me back away. She was the only person in the room I couldn't read. I didn't know what she wanted. Her nostrils flared. "You know."

Everyone stared at me—a mix of worried thoughts and relieved hopes all came at me at once. My heart started to pound. I quickly shook my head, panicking. "No, I don't," I denied, afraid she would try to hurt me next. Some of the hopeful thoughts went away, replaced by doom and gloom.

Dad interrupted our staring match, still addressing Rebecca as he pointed in Paige's direction. "I want you to look at your sister."

Rebecca didn't break our eye contact.

"Look at her!" Dad raised his voice to military commander level.

Rebecca flinched, turning her head to watch our sister dry her tears. Dad's next words almost sounded like they should have come from her inner voice. "You are doing that to her. You are hurting her. You need to stop this nonsense before somebody ends up dead."

Rebecca was now the one crying. He'd broken through her uncaring expression. Tears slid down her cheeks. "The spirit of a Bulgarian serial killer is doing that." She sniffled. "He escaped the spirit realm and is going after teenage girls." She wiped a tear from her cheek with the back of her hand. "I checked the suicide rates on a school computer. They're getting higher. Trust me. I wouldn't be doing this if I thought the spirits were lying to me. I'm not cursed. I'm trying to help." Her eyes met mine again, anger flooding her tone. "Tell them."

Suddenly, her wall went down. I could hear all her thoughts, all the voices, all her knowledge. It hit me like an ocean wave, attempting to drown me in words. I lost my footing, my legs hitting the back of a chair, and I fell into it as I tried to make sense of the jumbled disaster that was in my sister's mind.

"We are in the spirit realm," one voice whispered. I shivered at the spookiness. It was like hearing a ghost. A similar voice added to it. "Tell her we see no problems here. Tell her the spirit she saw wasn't real. Hurry, before it's too late." Another voice wailed. "This is useless. She cannot hear us over the madness!"

Rebecca's memory focused in on the story she had told—her walking the empty halls of her school, speaking to a spirit who told her she had to kill an Immortal One to restore balance to the universe. I saw how convincing the spirit was, but the added ghostly voices of what I assumed were the past Chosen Ones warned me not to believe it.

"You don't hear them?" I asked, unable to focus my eyes on anything with all the memories flooding my vision. I couldn't see Rebecca's face.

"Hear who?" she asked.

"The Chosen Ones!" I shouted over the loud voices flooding the room. "Liesel and—"

One of the voices scoffed, offended by the name. "I am Devi!"

"D-Devi," I corrected.

It was quiet on Rebecca's end, although I could barely hear her voice anyway through the chatter. Her thoughts raced, confused about what I claimed to hear. "Devi?" she asked. "I haven't heard her voice in ages."

"Something tells me you haven't heard any of the Chosen Ones in ages," I said as more of their voices shouted at me.

One stood out to me suddenly. "Blake? Is that you?" Jesse. My muscles tightened. "Tell her to stop," he begged, his voice sounding like he was near tears.

I could barely make my mouth move, the words scratching my throat on the way out. "J-Jesse says to stop." There were several gasps in the room, barely audible over the chaos.

"You can hear Jesse?" Rebecca's hand was on my arm. I thought I heard Mom crying.

"When was the last time you heard him?" I asked, my throat feeling like it was closing, making it hard to breathe. I missed Jesse so much. I wished I could see him. I wished he wasn't just a disembodied voice.

Rebecca's hand tightened over my wrist. "Weeks." I thought I felt water on my skin.

"I think I made her sick," Jesse said in a small, broken voice. I nodded like he could see me, even though I couldn't see him. "She needs to talk to Elzo. His ancestors"—his childish voice tripped over that word—"know a spell to fix her. Please. Before it's too late."

"That's what we're trying to do," I answered him aloud.

"Tell her," Jesse begged.

I opened my mouth, but words didn't come out. I needed to say goodbye. I needed to shut out the voices. But I didn't want to say goodbye to Jesse. Not again. Water splashed my cheeks. I knew I was crying. I hated to cry. "T-turn—" I stopped. I couldn't make myself ask Rebecca to turn it off, to put her wall back up. It wasn't fair. She got to speak to Jesse whenever she wanted. She got to keep him all to herself.

Rebecca must have understood what I was too scared to ask. In an instant, the sounds were gone. I tried to stand, stumbling as my legs wobbled. I wanted to get to my headphones, to turn all the other voices off too. I needed silence, but I was crowded by family.

Rebecca still had my wrist, but it was Dad who pulled me into a hug. "It's okay," he said, rubbing my back and squeezing me tight. Rebecca's hand got squished between us as I cried into his shirt, drowning in his cologne.

After a while, Rebecca managed to free her hand. "I want to hear him again. I want to talk to Jesse."

I sniffled, trying to collect myself enough to tell her how to fix her problem. "Then talk to Elzo."

26 // I'M ONLY TRYING TO SAVE THE UNIVERSE
REBECCA

Our eyes are windows to each other's worlds. That's the only way I know how to describe it.

Whenever teachers and textbooks talk about Africa in school or in church, it is almost always described as desert and poverty. At our old church, the pastor used to call it a demonic wasteland and how we needed to send missionaries to save the people who live there. Teachers at school talk about it like it is a place to time travel to, where there are no roads and no internet and people have to walk miles to get to where they need to go. They talk about donating rice and clean drinking water, as if the whole of Africa is out of touch with the rest of society. In pictures, Black children are unclothed and have large bellies and skinny bones, as if they are always living close to death. Maybe that is true in some areas, but Maputo, where Elzo is from, looks like the cities I know in America. Well, except for the beach. I've never been to a beach, unless you count the ones along Lake Michigan.

I've seen Maputo through his eyes. I've seen murals painted on cement walls, beautiful hotels along the ocean, people drinking and glowing in a dark and noisy nightclub. It is not always a happy place, though. Despite the beauty of Maputo, I read on the internet that Mozambique is one of the poorest countries in the world. I have seen Elzo's people begging on the streets, hungry and unhoused. I have seen his boyfriend shed a tear at the rising cost of food in the supermarket.

A few months ago, I woke from a nightmare. Men and women were in the streets of Maputo, desperate for food and shelter and, most of all, change. Someone lit a building on fire. Police shot into the crowd. Elzo had to get a bullet removed from his leg. I saw in the news later that week that the leaders of his country had decided not to make gas more expensive as they had planned to do. I couldn't help but feel relief for him.

I've never needed Elzo. His life is in a faraway land where his family carves beauty into wood and dances to the beat of handmade drums. Elzo is special to his people because he can talk to the ancestors. He seems to be a leader, but not the kind who is in charge of a country or laws. He is a leader in the way people treat him. Those who come to him for advice and guidance remind me of those who used to come to our house asking my mom for the same things. I can't hear his experiences—only see them through his eyes—but I've come to think of him as a healer.

I don't need healing.

I am jealous of Elzo. He hasn't lost the ability to hear his ancestors. I hadn't noticed the fading voices until Blake mentioned Liesel and Devi. The truth was, I didn't miss them. It was hard to live a normal life when old men and women were constantly judging it. Carrying spirits as old as four thousand years to witness typical middle school drama invites a series of comments worse than bathroom sink gossip. God forbid some girl was applying red lipstick. And the pants on women? You'd think I'd taken some of them to a horror show.

"Why are all you girls wasting time in school?" One of them liked to ask. Repeatedly. "When I was your age, I was preparing for marriage."

I could tune it out—and sometimes I did—but I knew they were there. Always.

But then Blake brought up Jesse. Him I did miss. Realizing that I had barely noticed his absence made me sick. But Jesse had to know it was for a good cause. He had to know I was trying to save Paige. He had to understand. As I began to reconsider my actions—if not for anyone but Jesse—the room grew cold. My family disappeared. So did the Porters. I was alone in the cold empty restaurant.

The singing began.

I knew who was coming this time. Having been pulled into the spirit realm on multiple occasions by now, it wasn't strange. The girl with the golden hair stood where my brother and dad had been. This time her hair was tangled, her clothes torn. I didn't think it was possible to harm a ghost's appearance, but perhaps there was a way. After all, the veil between our worlds was thinning.

She breathed heavily, as if ghosts needed lungs to live. "I have spotted him," she said, panting. "But his foothold in your world is too strong. He latched on to your sister."

Fear made my skin tingle. My heart rate rose. My blood felt cold underneath my skin as I turned to where my sister had been sitting. The chair was empty now. The sight made my knees weak, as if her lack of presence was somehow telling of the future. If I didn't do something, surely she would be gone soon.

"She's getting bad again," I whispered, nearly choking on my words. Jesse would have to wait. The living were more important.

I'd lost a sibling before. Nobody prepares you for it because it's not supposed to happen. Moms and dads will sometimes mention that one day they will be gone—grandparents too—but they never say anything about siblings. The idea of death didn't preoccupy me like it seemed to preoccupy other people, but if I were to have guessed the order of our deaths, I would have assumed the oldest went first. Bradley would go, then Paige, then me. It wasn't supposed to be the other way around.

I was in school when Jesse got shot. They had sent the kids from the lower elementary school on field trips while everybody in the upper grades took a standardized test. Blake's class was probably in his school's gym, playing games before their buses were to arrive. Jesse's bus had left first thing for the science fair at Bradley and Paige's school. I was sitting in front of a computer in the lab, reading a short story and answering questions. In the middle of the test, the principal had entered and whispered into my teacher's ear. It was bad news, I knew it. Their expressions made my skin prick with goose bumps. My teacher caught me watching her, but instead of directing me back to my screen like she had all hour with the other students, she pressed her fingers to her lips, twisting them into a strange expression I couldn't comprehend. Her eyes glistened.

She didn't tell me what happened. Instead, I made myself concentrate on the test because everybody had made a big deal about it for weeks, and I had to finish no matter what. Anxious theories had run through my mind as I clicked through the questions. Had somebody died? Was someone sick? I thought of my classmates and their families and tried to guess whose parent or sibling had been injured. Maybe it wasn't anyone I was related to. Maybe it was another teacher or an accident at another school. Maybe it was someone from my teacher's family.

When I finished the test, I raised my hand to ask if I could go to the bathroom, but instead, my teacher crouched next to me and said in a sweet, delicate voice, "Sweetheart, someone is waiting for you in the office. You can go ahead and grab your stuff out of the classroom, okay?" Her fingers played with a few strands of my hair.

I jerked away. This seemed serious. And it really seemed like it had more to do with me. "Am I in trouble?" I whispered, trying not to distract the classmates who were still testing. I pointed to the screen. "I promise I didn't cheat. I just sometimes look around when I think, that's all."

My teacher was quick to reassure me. "No, no." But she didn't elaborate as she stood, pointing to the door. "Go on."

I trudged to my classroom, shaky from anticipation. After I gathered my things from my classroom, I headed to the front of the school. In the office, Mr. Burnett was sitting in a chair next to a distraught-looking Blake. My neighbor scrambled to his feet when he saw me, his shoulders droopy, his mouth open a little. His shockingly blue eyes were unusually wide and glassy. He reached his arms toward me, barely touching my shoulders. "Rebecca," he said, enunciating every syllable of my name. "Something has happened to Jesse."

I thought he was dead. The stomach drop, tumble, and roll that wavered through me was somehow a worse experience than when he actually died. I don't know how to explain it. Maybe it was because if he had been killed by the bullet, I would have had no way to say goodbye. I wasn't even sure what he looked or dressed like the last time I'd seen him that morning. I didn't know the last words I'd said to him. Maybe it was because it was so unexpected, like if Mr. Burnett had ripped the rug from underneath my feet.

The day Jesse really died, I was there to say goodbye. And it hurt, but I expected it. I had his last words sewn into my memories for eternity. I had pictures and artwork. But it wasn't long after his death when it felt like I could speak to him after. I thought maybe I was hallucinating at first, but repeating his words seemed to make Mom happy to hear. Now I know it was never goodbye for me.

It won't be the same for Paige.

I can talk to the ancestors, but only if they were chosen. The past Chosen Ones can talk to other spirits, but they can't bring them to me. Jesse could talk to Paige, but I wouldn't be able to talk to her. I would have to be brought into the spirit realm, which I've never done on my own. It seemed the spirits always called me personally.

I looked back at the golden-haired ghost. She brushed at the torn clothing along her arm. "I don't know how long I will last before the killers get to me. They have already weakened and injured several of my friends. Every day I have seen their victims cross the divide between your world and mine. It's only a matter of time. Your sister will be next if you don't do something to stop the madness."

I sucked in a deep breath, a renewed sense of urgency taking over. This needed to stop. This needed to stop right now. Clenching my fist, I nodded slowly, letting her know she could release me from her realm. She faded away, my family and the Porters reappearing in their places. Blake peered from behind Dad's arm, waiting for my decision.

I couldn't take Maria again. The teleporters had orders not to come here since my last attempt. Without them, there was no way I could make it to San Diego on my own. Well, maybe there was, but it would involve a lot of threats. That left Savanna, who was no doubt hiding with my brother.

I swiveled on my heels, looking at the small scrap of the map that centered around Maputo. If Mr. Porter could find Elzo through me, surely he could find a blood relative. Bending to pick it up, I studied the design, then let it flutter to the ground. In that moment of freefall, I willed the map to reform, holding my hand over the empty space. The burnt pieces appeared like flecks of ash quickly magnetizing to form the rest of the paper. As it spread over the space, the color seeped in, continents forming. I couldn't help but smile a little at what I had done as the last pieces clicked into place. Recreating the world was amazingly godlike.

"What are you doing?" Mr. Porter asked warily as I snapped my fingers to bring the candles back to their previous roar.

I didn't answer him. I didn't have time to convince him that what needed to be done was the right thing. It wasn't just Paige's life on the line. It was thousands of girls around the world. Thousands who could be mapped.

I wasn't a witch, but maybe I didn't need to be. Maybe if I concentrated enough, I could find where my brother and his girlfriend were hiding. I crouched, leaning over the center of the Western Hemisphere. Placing my palm on the Midwestern United States, I closed my eyes, breathed, and waited.

It took a moment, but something finally felt like it was pulling me. The sensation was the same tug Liesel had once described when she discovered a pregnant Magdalena in the camps. It was that invisible string attached to my tummy. I smiled, knowing I was getting closer to my intent.

As I waited, I remembered Liesel's story. I know she hadn't told the whole story of how the Nazis realized Magdalena had been telling the truth about her unborn child. They had tried to kill her—sent her straight to the chambers. But something kept her lungs regenerating.

"Do you believe me now?" Maggie had asked when they came to clear the naked, blue-tinted bodies. "You can't kill me."

That was true. They couldn't. But someone like me? I was Fate itself. I could cut any string.

I opened my eyes, willing the map to zoom in like it was computerized. To my amazement, it did, showing all of Indianapolis. The pull got stronger, pulsating in my stomach. Everyone around me was silent. I'm not sure they knew what to say. Or maybe they were too busy trying to figure out what I was doing. I moved my hand over my neighborhood, the pull feeling weaker. It was like playing a game of hot and cold. Running my hand up north, I felt the pull get stronger. I knew I was getting warmer when I hit the border between Indianapolis and the suburb of Carmel. I willed the map to zoom in further, revealing street and business names, my eyes stopping on a small Star of David. I led my finger to the spot where a synagogue stood. The pull in my stomach became so strong it was actually painful. *There.*

I pulled away before the pain got unbearable, releasing myself from the pull of the string.

"No!" Blake shouted as I stood. He must have seen where I had pointed. It gave him away. No one else had seemed concerned. Nobody else knew who was hiding at the synagogue.

I turned to him as he shoved away from Dad. "You could have told me," I said. Why couldn't I get him to understand?

"So you can be a murderer?" Blake shouted.

I flinched at the label. Murderer? That made me sound so… terrible. Like the Bulgarian serial killer that was after Paige. And we were not the same.

"Rebecca." Dad stepped between us. I knew he was serious because he didn't use any of his beloved nicknames. "You know the only way you're killing that baby is by killing Savanna and, by default, Bradley. Are you telling me that you will gladly kill your own brother to save your sister?" Dad pointed at Paige, who had stopped crying and instead was watching us with wide eyes.

I stared back at my sister, taking in her messy dark hair and her glimmering dark eyes—eyes she inherited from Mom and Grandpa. I considered Dad's words. It was well-known that fated couples died together. But as a Fate, couldn't I avoid that? Couldn't I create a loophole? I had to try. I couldn't just watch my sister be destroyed.

"It's not just her I'm saving," I said, hoping Dad would hear me—*truly* hear me. "It's the world."

27 // NOTHING EVER GETS BETTER
PAIGE

My sister truly had a god complex. I mean, it was obvious by the way she was acting. And it terrified me. Especially since she was using me and whatever the hell was messed up in my brain to justify *killing* someone. What. The. Hell.

I tugged at my hair, pulling a strand between my teeth to gnaw.

Mrs. Porter shapeshifted into a massive Great Dane, moving to guard the door. Of course this didn't seem to bother Rebecca, who merely leaned against one of the large windows. My sister sat a little straighter, crossing her arms. "You think that's going to stop me?" she smirked, raising an eyebrow. "I'm a Fate."

Her dangerous confidence almost made her unrecognizable. Rebecca had always been kind of my opposite. She was, like, sweet and stuff, and I mean, while I could be sweet too, it wasn't the same kind of sweet. It wasn't the innocent sweet.

Rebecca lifted her hand and placed her palm on the glass. Mrs. Porter barked as the window disappeared.

"Sayonara." Rebecca lifted her leg, stepping over the ledge and onto the sidewalk like a badass teenager from a nineties rom-com. She might as well have had highlights and an eyebrow piercing. Maybe even a secret tattoo.

Mrs. Porter growled, padding a few steps, although she didn't seem very committed to chasing after her, especially after Mom yelled at her to stop. She halted, her puppy-dog gaze meeting Mom's.

"Don't hurt her," Mom said softly. The dog's ears flattened, a whine replacing her bark.

Rebecca wasn't smiling as she reached back inside to grab her backpack off a chair. "You will thank me for this. I promise."

Fat chance.

Everyone watched her leave, looking as helpless as I felt. I rubbed my forehead like it would somehow erase the headache that was forming.

"She can't get far. She's just a kid," Dad insisted.

I closed my eyes. Why did that seem like such a dumb comment? Sure, the teleporters at the safehouses had been warned to stay away from her, but someone as powerful as her could surely find an alternative solution.

I opened one eye to see Mr. Porter nodding. He stroked the stubble on his chin. "Are there any bus routes that can get her to Carmel?"

Dad looked at Mom, his question unspoken. Blake rolled his eyes, and I assumed it was because he knew they didn't know. We avoided public transportation most of the time, although Bradley seemed to think he could take the bus whenever he wanted.

Seth cleared her throat, stuttering out an answer. "I-I think there's one out of Irvington, and then she would have to take one that's heading north, b-but with all the stops, it'll take her two hours."

Blake narrowed his eyes at her but didn't say anything. What did he hear up in her peculiarly undamaged brain?

Mr. Porter sighed, seeming almost relieved. "Okay, that gives us time. We can beat her if we drive."

"And then what?" Sage asked. "You think a witch and seven and a half diviners can take her? You heard her—she's a Fate. I bet she could kill us all with a snap of her fingers." She shook her head. "No. I'm not going up against that." I rolled my eyes. She always wanted out of whatever action plan came out of a conversation like this. It didn't even have to be life-or-death. If I wanted to go to a party, she always put her foot down, like she was the boss of me or something. Sage didn't know how to have any fun.

"We're not her targets," Dad reminded her. "You all stopped her before. You can do it again."

"I have a feeling she wasn't trying too hard the last time," Victoria said. "She didn't want to kill Savanna. She just wanted to kill her baby. I don't think Rebecca was prepared for Savanna not swallowing the water. She seemed to be panicking. She wasn't ready to slit her throat. But this time? She must have been psyching herself up for it all week. She's bringing her A game."

"Then what are we going to do?" Mom asked, her voice thin and hollow. Blake turned to her like he was analyzing whatever thoughts she had. He reached to hold her hand as everyone continued to argue over their plans to stop our sister. Mr. Porter ran upstairs, mumbling something about fetching items for a spell. Almost suddenly, Blake yanked his hand out of Mom's. That's what he gets for inducing a vision, I guess.

"Someone needs to call Frank so we can warn him," Dad said. "Brad has his phone turned off so we couldn't track him." I didn't have to wonder why Dad wasn't calling Frank himself. He hadn't exactly been nice to Frank the last few weeks. Not since, well... look. Okay. The whole me drinking thing was not as bad as everyone was making it out to be. I just... I don't know... I wanted to shut off the thoughts in my head for a little bit. So what?

Victoria slid her phone's keyboard out, mouthing Frank's name as she dialed.

I sank in my chair, staring at the little archway to the kitchen. *What if I end this now? She'll have no one to save.*

I felt someone's gaze on me but didn't check to see who it was. I dared a peek from the corner of my eye to see Mom sit next to me. It wasn't long until Seth eventually came to stand behind me as well, and her proximity made me self-conscious. Geez. It was like they didn't trust me.

As Mr. Porter walked out from behind the counter with a wooden box in his hands, Victoria finished her call with Frank and immediately started dialing another number. "I'm calling Alyssa too. Her family came here specifically to protect Bradley and Savanna. They're going to want to know about this."

Sage shook her head, protesting. "But we're not supposed to all be together in one place. That captivator woman will think we're planning something major, and we don't have Maria and her force field to protect us this time."

Victoria held the phone up to her ear, waiting through the dial tone. "My dad can spell the building like he did with this place."

"This place is spelled?" Sage asked, glancing at the ceiling in uncertainty. I hadn't known that either, but I wasn't going to question it. Of course a building that was home to a witch was spelled.

Mr. Porter shook his head. "It takes at least three witches to put a protection spell on a building. We don't have three witches."

Victoria nodded, frowning. She must have reached Alyssa's voicemail because she muttered something about how Alyssa never seemed to answer her phone. "Don't worry," she breathed, seemingly more to herself than anyone. "She always answers her texts." She started typing furiously.

Her dad set the box on the counter, unlocking it with a small iron key. "Okay, I…" he started to say as he lifted the lid, then stopped. After a significant pause, he lifted a piece of folded white paper, blinking at the handwriting. Clearing his throat, he read the outside lettering. "For Rebecca," he said, wonder in his voice.

I didn't move from my chair as several of the others immediately gathered around, trying to peer over and around his shoulder and arms to get a better look. It was like they all needed proof that what he was holding was real. I mean, I wasn't sure how a random letter to my sister was going to solve anything, but whatever.

Mr. Porter shakily unfolded it. He cleared his throat, continuing to read aloud, "Dear friends, I hope this letter finds you well. I am sorry it has taken me so long to send this, as I didn't have a proper address. Rebecca has helped me see through her eyes enough now to have seen the numbers and title of your establishment, as well as the street name."

Wow. Well, that was creepy.

Mr. Porter continued to read, "So hello, owners of Wich Wharf in Indianapolis, USA. My name is Elzo Sambine from Maputo, Mozambique."

I perked up. Mozambique? Was this the Chosen One Rebecca didn't want us to find?

"I am one of the chosen."

Yep.

"I believe Rebecca is ill. My people here call it something that roughly translates to 'the undoing.' It occurs when someone is given an ability they were not born to have. The afflicted suffer from hallucinations and are slowly driven to the kind of madness that causes murder and mayhem. Entire villages can be slaughtered. Long before my time, when the Portuguese came to my country, it was a bloody disaster. A woman with great power thought she could share it with her people. She performed a spell to split her power among trained soldiers. While they were able to defend themselves for a year or two, they began to go mad. They were thirsty for blood and turned on those they loved. I see a similar issue afflicting Rebecca. Soon, you will not be able to stop her."

Cue the *dun dun duuun.*

"For centuries, my ancestors have worked on a spell to reverse the effects," Mr. Porter read. "They tested it when Kenya gained independence a few years before I was born. Nobody had any ill effects. They did not go mad. Perhaps they did not have time to. Their abilities died when my predecessor did. They were still tied to her life.

"I know Rebecca's situation is different. The person whose powers she possesses has died. Their death did not affect her. Despite this fact, I hope the spell I have written for you here might reverse her madness."

Mr. Porter stopped reading aloud, silently scanning whatever else was written on the page. He chewed the inside of his cheek. "I don't know if we have time for this," he finally said as he reached the end of the instructions.

"Well, how long do you need?" Dad asked.

Mr. Porter sighed, his shoulders sagging. "Two hours."

Dad looked at Seth. "You said it would take her two hours to get to the synagogue if she took the bus?"

I turned to look at her as she nodded, her eyes wide. She glanced at the clock on the wall. "We've lost ten minutes, though."

Victoria stepped back from the crowd. "We'll just have to hold her off, then. Distract her until the spell is ready."

Mom bit her lip as Mr. Porter nodded. He grabbed a handful of red and white candles from the box before grabbing a paperclip and bending it out of shape. He used it to carve words into the wax of each candle, starting with "Protection Savanna Huckleberry Protection," and doing the same with several of the other candles, except changing the name every time.

Victoria walked over to the box, peering inside before lifting an old Polaroid camera. "Do you need pictures?" she asked him. He nodded, still busy carving names.

Blake seemed to know what she wanted before she asked. He stared at the camera lens, waiting impatiently for her to snap the picture. She pressed a button, activating the flash. He blinked his eyes as the little printer attached to it spat out the photo. Victoria pulled at it, waving it in the air as she stepped in front of the next person, explaining her need for their photo. I guess it had something to do with making sure the protection spell protected the right people.

Mrs. Porter transformed out of her dog form so her daughter could snap her photo. She jangled her keys in her hand, ready to drive whoever to Carmel.

"Chastain," Mom said, addressing Dad. She picked up Tuesday by the armpits, handing her over to him. "Stay here with Markus." He managed a feeble smile, taking Tuesday in his arms. Did he hate being left out of the fighting?

Mom dug her own keys out of her purse seconds after Victoria snapped her photo.

"Paige?" Victoria waved the camera at me. I didn't move, returning my gaze to the kitchen. No way did I want my picture taken. I could not look anywhere near decent right now. Seth nudged me, but I crossed my arms. She didn't need to snap my photo if I wasn't out there in need of protection. "I'm not going."

"Um," Seth said nervously. "We kind of need all hands on deck."

I shook my head, squeezing my arms. They didn't need me there. I was just going to distract Rebecca, remind her why she was doing the unspeakable. "This is my fault."

Sage groaned. "Did you not hear the letter? None of this is your fault. She's sick. She has this 'undoing,' or whatever."

I slid farther in the chair. "Whatever."

Victoria snapped the photo anyway, and I grimaced. I hoped she burned that photo.

"We need to hurry," Mom said, heading to the door. "We need to beat my daughter to that synagogue."

28 // I DAYDREAM OF A BETTER LIFE
SAVANNA

"Tell me about your necklace," Matilda, an elderly Jewish lady, asked as she carried a loaf of braided bread to a table in the dining hall. She'd spent the last hour finishing her cooking before Shabbat while discussing how the synagogue opens the dining hall during certain holidays to feed those who were hungry and unhoused. This wasn't one of those holidays, but she was determined to walk me through her usual Friday practices as if I were her own granddaughter. She seemed lonely, like she didn't really have any family of her own. I was afraid to ask what happened to them.

I lifted the charm enough to see it in my line of sight. "It's Saint Sara e Kali," I explained. "She's the patron saint of the Roma."

Matilda nodded, centering the bread. "I thought maybe you were Roma."

"Spanish Kale," I said, impulsively feeling the need to be specific, despite most gaché knowing nothing about the different ethnic and cultural practices among vitsas. Although my parents hadn't replicated much of my mother's upbringing, I still held tightly to my ancestry. "My dad's of Polska Roma descent, but he was raised by gaché and my mom fled her community." After hearing myself say it out loud, I felt the need to defend her choice. Gaché often saw some of our practices as restrictive or abusive, and I didn't want to accidentally contribute to the stereotype. "Not for bad reasons or anything, it's just… my parents had to move."

It felt weird to defend them now that they had abandoned me. I think it's why their decisions hurt so bad. I still loved them. They gave me life. They raised me. They protected me.

Part of me expected Matilda to say something bad about them. I mean, all she knew was that I was a pregnant teenager who'd been kicked out of my home. I hadn't exactly explained the whole "I'm a murder target" thing. She didn't even know my real last name. I was too afraid someone would track down my parents and give them a piece of their mind, which kind of defeated the whole witness protection angle.

Matilda gestured to the kitchen. "Help me, will you?" she asked. I grabbed a few plates she had pulled earlier from a cupboard as she removed a chicken from the oven. It smelled like lemon and garlic, and I wrinkled my nose. I was glad most of my morning sickness had disappeared months ago, but smells still seemed to cloud the air so pungently that I often hated being around food.

She glanced at the clock—it was close to five—before moving the chicken to a serving platter. Bradley should be returning any minute. Liam's family had taken him to a grocery and drug store over an hour ago.

"You are welcome to join our Erev Shabbat service after dinner if you'd like. It starts at six in the chapel," Matilda said.

I nodded, unsure if I wanted to go. Judaism was so foreign to me, and I had no previous context for it. My sixth-grade English teacher had made us read *Number the Stars*, but that wasn't exactly about the religion per se as it was about the Holocaust. Part of me was curious, but another part of me felt like crashing. My feet hurt, and I was exhausted.

Someone knocked on the emergency exit door. Setting the plates back down, I opened the door. I'd noticed throughout the week that the people at the synagogue always kept the doors locked. I wondered how much of that had to do with antisemitism and hate crimes.

Shoving the door open, I spotted Bradley with a plastic sack over one arm and a paper bag in another. Liam stood next to him with another paper bag, his family behind them. I tried to move out of their way and still hold the door open as they shimmied their way inside. Mrs. Brown held what looked like a pot of soup, and she hurried to set it on the counter. Mr. Brown nodded to me as he passed, followed by a kid I hadn't met before. The kid looked too much like a thinner curly-haired version of Liam to not be his brother.

"You must be Jaime," I said, trying to be polite as I closed the door behind him.

He nodded, his Adam's apple bobbing as he swallowed. "Um, yeah," he confirmed. "Hi." He held out his hand for me to shake, and I did so before suddenly remembering Bradley mentioning that Jaime was psychic. Too used to Jay-Jay and his hatred of physical contact, I yanked my hand out of his grasp midshake.

"Oh my God, I'm so sorry," I said, apologizing. Then I covered my mouth, remembering I was in a Jewish synagogue. Did they find that phrase offensive like some of my Catholic relatives did? I couldn't be sure.

Jaime paused for a second, his mouth agape, his hand still in midair. His eyes weren't unfocused like Jay-Jay's or Clarinda's were whenever they had a vision, so for a second, I thought I had saved him from whatever terrible thing he could see. He must have been more shocked than anything. After a few seconds, he closed his mouth, dropping his hand. "D-do you have a problem with handshakes?"

I almost laughed—I was so relieved. "No, no. I have this psychic friend who hates being touched. I totally just projected that onto you. I'm sorry."

Jaime smiled, pointing to my necklace. "I thought that thing blocked my abilities."

"Oh my—" I bit my lip, clasping the charms as I stopped myself from saying it again. "I totally forgot." I shook my head, letting go of the necklace to brush a few strands of my hair out of my face. "Pregnancy brain, I guess."

He shrugged. "No problem."

Seeing Matilda carry the chicken into the dining room, I walked back to the counter to grab the plates. "Everything good?" Bradley asked, removing a loaf of sliced bread from a bag. I blinked at the kitchen around us as everyone else found something to carry to the table. Bradley set the loaf down, reaching to grab a jar of peanut butter as he waited for my reply. Even with my nerves acting as a driving force in my life, the image of Bradley unloading groceries in a kitchen seemed so ordinary and domestic that I kind of wanted to cry with relief. For a second, I let my imagination get the better of me. What if there was such a thing as a world free from the hell we were always being put through? What if our relationship hadn't been so messy and complicated? What if instead of pretending Bradley wasn't ever going to leave again, this was reality? We were bonded—in life, in love, in… whatever the hell we wanted to be. And we had our beautiful girl and a house to ourselves and—

I stopped my thoughts in their tracks, my heart sinking as I reminded myself of our reality. Bradley always left. Even when he said he didn't. Even when I knew he loved me as much as I loved him. Even after being together again after an awkward four months of "it's complicated." I wasn't sure I could believe him anymore. But I didn't want to tell him that. Because maybe my saying it *would* make him leave. And at that moment, standing in a kitchen as he unpacked groceries, I caught a glimpse of a life we would never have. I wanted to cherish it.

Instead of answering Bradley, I turned on my heels and walked to the dining room with a pile of clean plates in my hand. Forcing a smile, I felt a little like a 1950s housewife. And while normally I would have fought the sexist image, it seemed preferable to dying.

That was when lights from a police cruiser shined through the windows.

Everyone kind of froze in place, looking sideways at each other as if they needed permission to unfreeze. I set the pile of plates on the table, the only one in the room daring to move more than my head, before Liam unfroze, bending to see a figure coming toward one of the windows. "I think that's Officer Lantern."

Everyone seemed to take the same relieved breath as Liam left to unlock the nearest door. We could all hear the hinges screech, a clap of thunder ominously announcing Frank's entrance. I took another look at the sky through the window. It seemed to be getting darker—too early for sunset. A storm must have been on its way.

Frank had been dropping our homework off daily, but tonight he looked more stressed than usual. In fact, I didn't see a single sheet of paper in his empty hands. His eyes landed on the half-set table of food. Something resembling guilt briefly flashed in his expression. "I'm sorry to interrupt your evening."

"Is something wrong, Officer?" Matilda asked, gripping the back of a chair for support.

Frank's gaze flickered to me before scanning the room. "I need to borrow Bradley and Savanna for a sec."

I stepped forward, but Mrs. Brown stuck her arm out in front of me. "Are they in trouble?"

Liam headed back toward the kitchen, probably to get Bradley.

Frank took a deep breath, adjusting his belt. "Uh, well," he squinted to the ceiling, seemingly struggling to come up with a reply. I realized he was likely struggling because of the two gaché in the room and the fact that Liam's parents hadn't exactly been filled in on the entire truth of our situation.

I put my hand on Mrs. Brown's arm, gently pressuring her to lower it as Liam returned with Bradley. "It's okay. I'm just going to go talk to him for a second." Bradley glanced between me and Frank, confused. Mrs. Brown lowered her arm, and I reached for his hand, waiting for him to grab it before leading him toward Frank. The closer we got to him, the closer he inched to the hallway. We rounded the double doors, barely out of everyone's sight as Frank turned to nervously peer out a window.

"Your location's been made," he said quietly, jumpstarting my heart for the fast track.

Bradley and I squeezed each other's hands. "What? By who?" Our words echoed each other's.

"The captivators?" Bradley tacked on.

Frank shook his head. "Worse."

I managed a quick shallow breath, letting Rebecca's name tumble out with my exhale. "We have to leave. We can't let her destroy this place looking for me. People are going to be showing up for the service soon." I stepped toward the exit door, but Bradley's grip held me back.

Frank took another deep breath, holding out his hand like he meant to calm me, but it was doing the exact opposite. "Listen. The Sullys are on their way. They've got a two-hour head start on Rebecca. Bradley's family and the Porters are still at the shop working on a protection spell. They should be heading this way soon. We have time to come up with a strategy."

I shook my head. "Two hours? We're not that far from Indy. We're practically on the border."

"We think Rebecca's taking the bus. She's eleven and she can't teleport, so unless she's conjured herself a moped and a driver's license, she shouldn't get here till closer to seven." Frank said quickly, then licked his lips. "Now I got a buddy who's been posted as security a few times at the area synagogues, and he says the Friday night services usually only last twenty minutes. I'm thinking we can get everyone in and out before she shows. You two, though"—he gestured between us—"need to get out of here in case our bus theory is wrong, and she really did conjure some kind of vehicle."

Bradley snorted. "She can't drive."

Frank jerked his head in a weird nod. "That's what I thought, but if we're being honest, underestimating your sister hasn't done anyone any good."

Bradley huffed before nodding. "Okay." He let go of my hand, placing his on the lower part of my back, trying to guide me toward the door. Planting myself in place, I refused to move. I had definitely changed my mind. Bradley glanced back at me, questions burrowing in his brown eyes. "What's wrong?"

I crossed my arms, leaning away from him and against the wall. "I'm not leaving these people."

Bradley shook his head, incredulous. "We're putting them in danger if we stay."

"We've already put them in danger," I argued. "Rebecca's already on her way here." I swallowed hard at the truth. She was the only person in the world who could potentially end me. Still, I couldn't make myself run. "If she gets here before Frank expects her to, and she doesn't see me, she could expel every single life in this building looking for me."

Bradley was quiet for a minute, his nostrils flaring. I expected him to argue, but instead, he kept standing there, his eyes on mine, breathing until he had calmed whatever anger was building inside him. He glanced at Frank, finally opening his mouth. "If she shows during the service…"

I closed my eyes for a second, breathing a sigh of relief. When I opened them again, Frank had his gaze on the ceiling, his lips moving like he was counting something. "We have fourteen diviners to distract her." He looked back at Bradley. "I got a call on my way here. Markus has a spell he thinks might stop Rebecca's delusions, but it's going to take time to prepare. We will need to stall her until he can get here with the cure."

Bradley raised his eyebrows, biting his thumbnail for a second before releasing it. "Well, if the captivators show, that'll definitely be a distraction." He let his hand fall to his leg with a slap. Right. Fourteen diviners all heading in the same direction—north and out of city limits—was sure to grab their attention. He raised his hand again. "Why don't we just light a beacon telling them we're here?" He shook his wrist, jiggling the bracelet on it. "What is the point of these?"

Frank held his hands up defensively. "Relax. Even if they show, they can't see you. You'll be invisible to them."

"But not to you guys," Bradley argued. "If someone so much as looks at us, we're dead."

I shook my head. A strange calm had taken me over, and I wasn't sure why. Something about Bradley freaking out maybe? "We won't be *dead,*" I corrected. "They need us alive."

Bradley dropped his arm, holding it straight while he gripped his elbow with his other hand. His voice was less panicked and more serious as he whispered, "We're gonna wish we are."

Oh. His words felt like ice as they pierced my heart, pumping cold liquid into my bloodstream. The baby shifted, uncomfortable with the change. Even with our powers gone, I knew which memories were occupying his thoughts. Bradley would never say it in a million years, but I'd seen in his memories the full extent of what Garrett had done to him in the RV. I struggled to swallow through my newly raw throat. "That's not going to happen," I croaked, tears stinging the back of my eyes. Not to him.

He shook his head, no longer meeting my eyes. He seemed to be trying to look at the wall, but he was failing, staring instead at my stomach. "They show up, we run. No looking back."

I nodded vigorously, agreeing with him. "Of course."

29 // WHEN DID MY SISTER BECOME THE DEVIL?
BRADLEY

Savanna's newfound ability to go from one emotion to another in a matter of seconds never failed to catch me off guard. Her nod slowed, her foot tapping the floor. "I'm gonna go eat now," she announced as if we weren't about to be under siege. She seemed to be trying to smile, but it looked more like she was constipated as she maneuvered around us toward the dining hall.

I waited till she was out of sight before turning back to Frank. "My sister is going to get us killed."

"Can't argue with you there."

I huffed, the frustration I had been holding back for Savanna's sake practically leaking out of my pores. "Even if Mr. Porter manages to cure her, she is going to lead the captivators straight here. They're going to think we're trying to leave, and they will come for us."

There was a knock on the door, and I could see through the window it was the Sullys. Frank walked over to open the door for them. My stomach sank as Alyssa followed her parents inside.

"And so it begins," I muttered under my breath, leaning against the wall in defeat, once again wishing I was older… wishing I could make my own decisions without adults taking over… wishing I had a driver's license so I could just grab Savanna and go… wishing staying at the synagogue or with a couple of nice Jewish families was enough to hide us, to solve all our problems. Instead, everything kept getting worse.

I ground my teeth, listening to Frank fill the Sullys in on his stupid plan. When I got sick of feeling helpless, I left to rejoin Savanna, Matilda, and the Browns.

By the time we were cleaning the dishes, Victoria and her mom had arrived, claiming my mom and most of my siblings weren't far behind. I barely acknowledged their greetings as I headed to the bathroom to check my blood sugar.

As I stood by the sinks, pricking my finger, the normalness of this action almost felt like a safe haven from the impending doom. I'd been trying so hard— harder than I ever had before—to try to live my life without getting sucked into the bad stuff. For a while, I thought I was winning by doing that—by focusing on the present. I wanted to be strong for Savanna while she was falling apart. I didn't think we'd be useful to anyone if we were both focusing on the negative. It almost seemed like we had switched places—outlooks on—life. She had spent the last several months having things—vices—

taken away from her. She was preparing for everything else, including her life, to fall away. And for what? Creating life? What a cruel and stupid punishment.

I guess that's why I'd been acting the way I'd been, because if I didn't take it better than she was, there wouldn't be hope for any of us.

I read the number on the monitor, crosschecking it with my pump. They were both miraculously average. I'd managed to input just the right number of carbs before eating into my pump to keep my sugar from spiking or falling.

I wondered where I'd be if the cure had worked. Would I still be in this bathroom doing ordinary day-to-day things as if the world wasn't crumbling around me? Would I have missed out on the one familiar thing somehow keeping me stable? I think some people would find it ironic that I'd find a disease that had hospitalized me on more than one occasion comforting. I guess I can't really explain it in a way that will make anyone who hasn't been in my shoes understand. Maybe it's for the same reason I sometimes find sadness or anger comforting. I don't really know life without it.

I glanced at my reflection in the mirror, noticing the bags under my eyes. I guess that was the physical proof that this week hadn't been a vacation. I stared, letting my vision blur as my eyes dried uncomfortably. My throat burned as I swallowed. Would I still look the same in three months? I blinked, allowing my vision to refocus on my face. I didn't think I looked young, but I guess perspective is everything. I'd turn sixteen by the time the baby was born. Maybe then I'll look slightly less like I could be my child's older brother. Or maybe it won't even matter because I'll be dead.

Taking a deep breath, I pulled away from the sinks and trudged out the door. I spotted a large metal Star of David on the wall, and it taunted me. I didn't believe in God. Sure, there were supernatural aspects to the world that I couldn't ignore, but even if God exists, it seemed He never interfered.

Savanna cleared her throat. She was leaning against the wall. She tilted her head, smiling slightly through her exhaustion. "Do you want to go to the prayer service with me?"

I looked down at the necklace drooping just above her chest. With the number of times she played with it, I was surprised the etchings on her charm hadn't rubbed off. I knew she'd been searching for a higher power, something to place her hopes in. I nodded despite not wanting to. God was the only card we had left to play if there was such a being.

She took my hand, peeling herself from the wall. "Let's go."

★

We sat next to Matilda and the Browns, but not before Liam fastened a kippah to my hair. I felt like I was pretending to be somebody I wasn't, but I'd been determined to show Savanna I was capable of going through the motions with her. I didn't want to be the same guy who kept leaving because he felt uncomfortable. I didn't want her to keep thinking she would have to go through things alone.

The service opened with singing. I couldn't understand a word of Hebrew, but I tried to remain respectful, though I was lost for most of the service. I kept having to watch everyone else to figure out if I was supposed to be standing or sitting. There were several points where the women would cover their eyes. Savanna seemed to be catching on quicker than I was, mimicking Matilda and Mrs. Brown with ease. After that, an English prayer was read, but it was immediately followed by more singing or chanting in Hebrew. I glanced at Liam, who, like his mom, was mouthing all the words by memory while his younger brother and father read from a booklet.

I noticed the service wasn't well-attended. At least compared to the Sunday morning Christian services I'd been to. There were maybe no more than fifteen other people in the chapel.

Outside, the non-Jewish diviners loitered in the parking lot, on the lookout for my sister. I hoped she took her time so that the fifteen service attendees had a chance to leave. It would be nice if they didn't have to witness a supernatural attack outside their synagogue.

The assistant rabbi started to list off names to be prayed for. I was shocked to hear Savanna's and my names on the list. Who had added us? And for what? Was it Matilda who thought we were homeless? I guess in some senses, we were.

Savanna squeezed my hand as the rabbi finished listing off names. Her touch made me realize I was holding my breath, and slowly, I let it go, wishing prayers were magic.

When the service ended twenty minutes later than Frank had told me it would, I anxiously stood in the lobby, waiting for the congregants to leave. Savanna leaned into me, her mouth close to my ear as her hands unclipped the kippah from my hair. "I think we're gonna be alright," she said before she turned to Liam, holding up the piece like she wasn't sure what to do with it. He took it before she addressed Matilda. "I think Bradley and I are going to stay with his parents tonight."

Matilda smiled, her hands covering her cheeks. "Oh, that's wonderful."

I frowned. She had no idea how not wonderful that was. Or how big of a lie Savanna had just told. There was no way we would stay with my parents.

"Lying in a synagogue?" I whispered to Savanna as we neared the door, following a few people in the crowd. Others mingled in the lobby, socializing as they normally would. I didn't know how to get them to leave.

She shrugged. "Some lies are good lies."

I snorted, unconvinced, before I spotted a fire alarm near the door. I glanced back at the small crowd of mingling people. *Should I pull it?* What were the chances they would go home? I shook the thought out of my head. It would probably just bring everyone out to the parking lot, directly in plain sight.

Savanna followed my gaze and sighed. "If we're inside with them, Rebecca might hurt them trying to find us. I don't want these people and this place to be destroyed." She tugged on my arm, one hand on the door. "We need to be in plain sight."

I squeezed her hand, holding her back like she had done earlier with me. "That's a death sentence," I said through gritted teeth.

Savanna inhaled sharply, biting her lip. She knew I was right. I could see it in her shining blue eyes. Still, she insisted. "I have faith that Mr. Porter will get the potion here on time. He can fix Rebecca before anything bad happens."

I shook my head. Had the prayer service clouded her judgment? I wasn't going to let her be a martyr. We couldn't afford to be martyrs. I squeezed her hand even tighter.

"Look," she said, repositioning her feet. "I hate being useless. I'm not going to sit around and hide while everyone risks their lives for us. That's not fair."

I swallowed, saliva running down my parched throat, and closed my eyes. "Nothing about our lives is fair." Hiding was something we'd have to get used to.

I felt her lips on my cheek, her breath warm against my skin. "I can't explain it, but I *know* we're going to make it. The universe is on our side." Damn it. She really wasn't thinking straight.

Before I could tug her back toward the inner crowd, she ripped her hand out of my grasp, hurrying through the door and into the late spring air. I chased her, which was way too easy since she ran slower than usual. I grabbed her arm, which prompted a sharp "Let me go!" from her.

Mom and Frank heard us first, their heads swiveling in our direction. Frank was on the phone. "I gotta deal with something. Keep driving." He hung up, jogging with Mom to where I was trying to gently redirect Savanna. Gentle was hard with her, though. She'd always been stronger than me in more ways than one, and pregnancy didn't diminish a cent of that strength.

"Bradley, Bradley, let her go," Mom said through ragged breathing as she reached us, holding her hands out.

I stopped fighting, Savanna once again ripping her arm out of my grasp.

Frank spoke fast. "Markus is about twenty minutes out. He's got the potion. Rebecca maybe has ten min—"

He didn't get to finish his sentence. A large, silver-plated knife soared through the air, barely in my peripheral vision before it paused, floating an inch in front of me. It had stopped only centimeters from Savanna's nose.

Savanna and I immediately stepped back, Frank drawing his gun and aiming in the direction it had soared from. Sage, her face stuck in concentration mode, had her palm facing the knife. When we were clear of it, she let go, gasping from exertion as it clattered to the cement. Mom swiped it from the ground as the rest of us turned to see Rebecca standing between two cars.

Ten minutes my ass. That would be the second time Frank got his calculations wrong.

"Don't shoot!" Mom ordered, her free hand flying toward Frank.

Frank didn't move, his voice low. "You think I like having my gun pointed at a child?"

The rest of the diviners ran toward us, gathering around as Rebecca tilted her head, her tongue running along the tips of her teeth. A chill ran up my spine as I grabbed Savanna's hand, tugging her farther back into the newly formed crowd of diviners.

Alyssa's mom stepped to the front, a large, human-sized shield materializing in front of her, the band wrapping around her arm. Victoria eyed it before doing the same, shielding half of the front line. I couldn't see Rebecca after that, but she sounded angry as she shouted, "You think that will stop me?" Then she laughed, almost evilly.

The large glass windows behind us shattered. Several of us ducked, and I could hear a few screams from inside. My skin stung where a few of the pieces hit me, but I didn't have time to be distracted by it. Savanna had fallen to her knees, dragging me with her. My heart stopped, feeling like a piece of dead weight in my chest, when I saw her back. A large shard had pierced her skin, lodging itself just below her left shoulder blade.

"Savanna!" I shouted.

She coughed, wheezing as blood dripped from her lips and onto the pavement.

Alyssa huddled next to us, her hand wrapping around the shard as Frank shouted, "Don't pull it—"

She yanked it out. Savanna screamed in agony. I opened my mouth to yell at Alyssa, but she pointed to the spot where she'd taken it out, dropping the shard in the bushes behind us. Blood wasn't gushing from the wound. In fact, through the tear it had created in her shirt, I couldn't see a scratch on her.

Savanna's scream turned into a series of gasps. Her eyes closed. I sat back, barely breathing through the relief. Why was her self-healing working? Could Rebecca only kill her if there was no intervention? The glass had to be accidental. At least, the part where a shard had lodged itself into Savanna's back. Did she have to do that on purpose for it to work? Either way, I was grateful for the self-healing. It gave us an advantage.

Frank returned his attention to Rebecca, keeping his gun aimed. "Stop this or I *will* shoot!"

Mom shot him a look of betrayal.

"No, you won't," Rebecca replied. I still couldn't see her, my rapidly beating heart having returned to my chest. I missed the days when my sister was afraid to use her power.

Footsteps pounded toward us. I turned to see the Browns running from the front steps of the synagogue. Mrs. Brown slid past me, her arm around Savanna. "Are you okay, sweetheart?"

Savanna nodded. "Yeah, yeah. Nothing a little self-healing can't fix."

"Self-hea—?" She ran her hand over the back of Savanna's shirt, confused by the lack of injury.

Alyssa shifted to the other side of Savanna so Mr. Brown could fit in between us. "I got you kids," he assured us, touching his fingertips together and pulling his hands apart, a purple sphere glowing between them.

"Holy crap," I said between pants. I glanced at Liam. He hadn't told me his father had a force field. There was no way he could get it to be as big as Maria's had been at the football field, but I watched as he managed to expand it over Savanna and me. To say I felt a million times safer would be an understatement.

A familiar growl escaped the crowd near the front, immediately causing me to lose my sense of safety. I couldn't see the creature completely through the shield, but it was large and catlike, its fur a tan color. Once again, my heart dropped.

Savanna squeezed my hand. "Close your eyes," she said quietly, watching me carefully. I'd been doing better with my flashbacks since I started therapy, but that didn't mean they had completely gone away. Because we didn't exactly see many mountain lions in Indiana, working on my fear of them hadn't exactly been a priority. Most of my sessions in the last few months mostly centered on Savanna's and my present situation.

I obeyed her, closing my eyes and trying to breathe through my mouth. It was just Mrs. Porter. The lion wasn't there to hurt me. But still, I saw the one from my nightmares prowling between the yellow-leaved trees of the forest in my mind.

"You have a force field around you," Savanna reminded me. "You're safe."

I tried to believe her, nodding as though I could possibly take her advice. I missed the ability she used to have—the one where she could force my mind to replay the good memories to overshadow the bad. Sweat slicked my skin, the goose bumps reminding me of the fall weather during those days in the Sangre de Cristo Mountains.

"Is he afraid of the cougar?" Mr. Brown asked.

I felt Savanna shift as if she were trying to put her weight on any place but her knees. "He's had a bad experience with one."

I took another deep breath, opening my eyes just in time to see another knife hurl toward the large cat.

What was it with my sisters and knives?

30 // I'M NOT SURE WHETHER TO BE THANKFUL OR TERRIFIED
SAVANNA

Paige ran between the shields, leaping over the mountain lion and landing in a somersault on the pavement. Mrs. Chambers screamed and jerked forward, and for a second, her reaction echoed my fears. Paige had dived straight into the path of Rebecca's knife. Letting go of Bradley's hand, I stood to get a better look as Paige's arm extended outward, the silver extending from her fist glistening in the sunset. She had caught it. It was such a badass move. I wished I had been the one to do it.

Mrs. Chambers gasped as her older daughter lifted herself from her knees to stand at full height, her dark hair having loosened from her braid. The breeze fluttered, blowing at the strands. Rebecca looked flustered, stepping back a bit, her brown eyes wide, her mouth gaping. She clearly hadn't expected Paige to do that either.

Frank dared to lower his gun.

I couldn't see Paige's face, but her hand seemed to be shaking as she stepped forward. "You wanna kill Savanna?" she shouted. "You will have to go through me." She moved her hand so the knife was in front of her where I couldn't see.

Rebecca's eyelids fluttered for a moment as she assessed her sister's threat. She suddenly didn't seem so scary, her teeth biting into her lip. Silence existed between them for a long moment.

Paige stepped closer. "You hurt her, and everything you have done to try to save me will have been for nothing."

"Paige?" Mrs. Chambers called in a worried voice. Paige didn't move, her spine rod straight. Seth inched around the crowd, seeming to try to get closer to Paige without her noticing. I wasn't sure why she was trying to be stealthy.

Frank glanced at his watch. "We still have twelve minutes," he muttered unhappily.

Mrs. Porter reshifted her form, melding from a mountain lion to a bird, flapping her wings until she was circling above them. I glanced at Bradley, checking to see if he'd regained his composure. He was still on the ground, peering between his fingers at what he could see of the scene. No one wanted to hurt Rebecca, but it was obvious holding her off was going to be difficult. Paige seemed to know how to be a distraction.

"You know," Paige said, her voice wobbling, "you totally suck as a sister right now." She chuckled dryly, but Rebecca didn't respond, her gaze transfixed on her sister.

Paige took another step. "You think I don't know something is wrong with me?"

Mrs. Chambers held her hands close to her chin. "Nothing is wrong with you," she responded, only loud enough for a few of us to hear. Blake shook his head, rubbing his eyes tiredly.

Rebecca finally spoke. "So you agree?" she asked, drawing out the words, slow and deliberate.

Paige nodded, her voice tight and thick. "I feel everything so strongly all the time. It never stops."

"It's the spir—"

"No!" Paige stomped her foot. "This didn't just start when Bradley got Savanna pregnant."

My hand instinctively flew to my stomach, like I wanted to shield the baby from the judgment that always seemed to come when someone mentioned our predicament.

She continued, "I have been like this for so much longer." She was only a few feet from her now. "I was trying to hide it. I was trying to pretend to be normal. But think about it. You know me. Sage knows me. Seth knows me. Mom knows me. Everyone who knows me will tell you I have always been an emotional nightmare."

Mrs. Chambers shook her head, but she didn't say anything, and I couldn't see her face. I didn't understand why she wouldn't agree. I'd only known Paige for almost two years, but she had almost always come off exactly as she was describing herself. She was intense about her ideas to the point where she couldn't shut up about them. Through Bradley's memories, I'd seen days where he'd hardly see her because something upset her so much she wouldn't leave her room. Objects flew around the room when she felt angry or betrayed.

I'd heard Bradley's dad chalk it up to normal teenage stuff. "She's just being a girl," he'd say. *A girl.* As if all teenage girls overdosed on pills in their free time.

I glanced at Bradley as he stood. Did mental illness run in his family? Or was it a direct result of all the trauma they'd been through? Would it be something I'd have to watch for in our child as she grew? Should I be learning to recognize the signs? I followed his gaze to Blake, who flinched as if someone had called his name. He turned to meet Bradley's eyes, his face ashen. "What's she doing?" Bradley asked aloud.

Blake winced. "Seth has her."

We all looked back at Seth, who was practically on Paige's heels. Mrs. Porter was watching her almost literally like a hawk.

Frank's police radio crackled, emitting a voice that spoke in coded language before listing the synagogue's address. He tilted his head, his hand hitting the button on his radio. "This is Officer Frank Lantern. I am on scene and the situation is being handled."

"Copy that," the voice responded.

"Someone inside must've called in an emergency," Frank muttered.

I glanced behind me at the synagogue but couldn't see anyone. My heart sank at the view of the front, the large windows gone. This looked like a targeted attack, and they didn't deserve it.

Paige's voice made me turn back to the scene. "This is what it's about, right? Saving me? What if you had nobody to save?" I couldn't see the knife, but her words immediately hit me with a bad feeling. It wasn't just me either. Most of the group had begun to run forward, either slipping between or running around the large shields to get to her.

Rebecca screamed as Seth wrapped her arms around Paige. The knife fell to the ground as the glass from several of the surrounding cars shattered. A police siren bleeped in the distance, followed by Frank swearing. They all crowded around Paige, instantaneously forgetting about Rebecca. Huge mistake.

I gulped as Mr. Brown's shield flickered, and through the purple haze, I could see Rebecca standing on the hood of an SUV. Her nostrils flared as she held her balled fists near her ears. Moving her hands in front of her, she unfurled her fingers only slightly. The ground shook dangerously beneath us. Everyone struggled to keep their balance. Bradley and I shared an intense, wide-eyed look before a large fissure erupted from the ground. The crack raced toward us.

Mr. Brown faltered as he saw it coming, his shield dissolving as he tried to shove us both out of the way. The ground opened beneath him, gravity attempting to take him with it. I instinctively reached for his hand, but missed, nearly tumbling into the large crack in the cement. He managed to grab the ledge as I screamed.

"Dad!" Jaime shouted, but he was stuck on the other side of the fissure with Bradley and Liam.

Frank attempted to rush to us, but another fissure opened to separate me from the rest of the group. Victoria and Mrs. Sully dropped their shields, trying to use them to bridge the gap, but Rebecca only made the fissure wider. I swore I heard Victoria call her a name I'd rather not repeat.

"She's fine. Just a few scars," Alyssa said from somewhere deep inside Paige's concerned entourage. I was surprised her voice was loud enough for me to hear.

I got down on my knees again to see if I could help pull Mr. Brown off the edge, but it was no use. I couldn't get in the right position. "Rebecca, stop this!" I screamed.

An arch that looked almost like it was made out of ice began forming from the nose of the SUV to my trapped corner. Rebecca traipsed onto it as if it were a bridge, the ice melting away behind her, as if her feet emitted heat. Frank shot a bullet near the ice in front of her, but it bounced off, failing to penetrate. Luckily, it bounced into the hole instead of hitting someone.

"Damn it," he growled, and I caught Clarinda's furious gaze as she temporarily averted her attention from her other daughter.

When Rebecca reached my corner, all traces of the arch had disappeared. She cocked an eyebrow, one of her infamous knives materializing in her hand. Something flew toward me in my peripheral vision, hitting my shoe as it slid across the cement. I glanced down, realizing it was the knife Paige had been holding earlier. I didn't dare look to see who had tossed it, but I bent to grab it. Probably one of the telekinetics. Backing against the bushes, I braced myself as Rebecca charged me. She swiped the knife through the air. Dodging the attempts, I found myself backed as far as I could go, the window ledge pressing against my calves. I pressed the sole of one of my shoes to the wall, preparing to propel my way forward. My weight distribution had been thrown severely off by the pregnancy, making it difficult to calculate how much strength I needed to throw into my action. Still, I sprang forward, aiming my knife at her right shoulder.

She wasn't nearly as skilled a fighter as I was, and it was blatantly obvious when she swiped her armed hand out instead of keeping it in. The blade of my knife hit the outside of her shoulder, but I couldn't manage to push the blade far enough in to do any real damage. She yelped, dropping the knife as I yanked the weapon out. Her mom screamed as she stumbled back into plain view, her lower lip wobbling. Rebecca reached her other hand to feel her wound as a cry escaped her lips. Blood dribbled down her arm.

"Just because I'm pregnant doesn't mean I can't win a fight," I said, anger searing through me. I leaned over her as she continued to stumble back until she eventually lost her footing, falling on her butt. "Half an inch to the right, and you'd be bleeding out." I motioned the movement to my own collarbone, showing her where I could have fatally stabbed her.

The police siren grew louder, a familiar black SUV rolling into the lot.

I turned my back to Rebecca, bending to pick up her knife. She screamed—a visceral cry in the twilight.

"Look out!" Bradley shouted.

"I can't hold on much longer," Mr. Brown groaned at about the same time.

I turned back to her just as she aimed a new knife at my stomach with her nondominant hand. I barely had time to react. Metal struck metal as I pushed my knife up, brandishing hers out of her grip. She groaned, backing up a few inches as she lifted her only good hand, palm facing toward the sky as her fingers curled in. The ground shook again, and Mr. Brown lost his grip as several people screamed. The cement beneath my feet cracked and crumbled, something I couldn't fight with my knives. I closed my eyes, bracing myself for a fall.

"No!" The scream came from a little girl as the shaking ceased.

I opened one eye, then the other as Rebecca turned in the direction of the voice. I froze, recognizing the girl

I'd seen in Priori Lab's security cameras a year and a half ago. She was a little bit older now—maybe five or six—as she stood in front of Wystan and the captivator woman from the lab… Griselda Day.

Rebecca quickly backed away from me, her feet getting closer and closer to the nearest fissure. Something about this girl seemed to scare her. "Y-you can't be here," she stuttered. "We're not supposed to be this close to each other." I remembered the security footage from the lab, having seen Rebecca and the girl nearly burn each other's skin off through mere touch. Seconds later, they'd been blown apart by an invisible force that had shaken the whole building. At the memory, I tried to put as much distance between me and Rebecca, backing behind the bushes.

The blond-haired woman jerked her head in my direction, scrutinizing me, or at least trying to. I knew by her unsteady gaze that she couldn't see me. The protection amulet was working. I held my breath as I clutched the necklace. She smirked, stepping forward as she crossed her arms, her gaze flickering between me and Rebecca. "So Daphne was correct. Your hallucinations are targeting the one person we need alive." She clucked her tongue disapprovingly. "Well, we can't exactly have that. You understand?"

I held back a scoff. Of course the people wanting to steal and torture my unborn child had come to try to save me. The tables truly had turned.

The woman crouched to the little girl's height. "Do you see Savanna, my dear?"

I shook my head at Daphne as she turned to look at me. It was clear she could see me, by the way her eyes met mine. Crap. I guess the amulet didn't work on Chosen Ones. Holding a finger to my lips, I hoped to Saint Sarah she got the message not to narc. She tilted her head, squinting one of her eyes as one side of her upper lip curled. She didn't get the message, lifting her finger to point at me. "She's right there," she said, as if it were obvious. Ugh. Why were little kids always the worst at keeping secrets?

"What are you talking about?" Bless Mrs. Chambers, but her pretending not to see me wasn't fooling anyone.

Griselda heaved a dramatic sigh. "Wystan," she said in an annoyed voice.

Wystan lifted his hand, snapping his fingers. I winced, knowing he was the one who could make anyone see anything. But nothing happened. It was anticlimactic. I glanced around, waiting for something in my line of vision to change. Instead, I caught Bradley's gaze. He held his arm up, pointing to his bracelet, and I sighed in relief. We were immune. But that meant—

Mrs. Chambers screamed, dropping to her knees as her hands patted the empty air. Nobody else seemed to react to the sound but Bradley and me. They must all have been stuck in their own personal hallucinations. Even

Rebecca seemed lost in an illusion, her eyes transfixed on something in the air.

"Stop!" Bradley shouted, running at Wystan before stopping himself.

Wystan chuckled, turning to look in the direction of Bradley's voice. "Guess we found Public Enemy Number Two."

Griselda smiled. "Perhaps we can make a trade. His life and Savanna's life for"—she paused, glancing around—"everyone else's." She side-eyed Wystan. "Do you think you can make that work?"

Wystan grinned wider, fixating his gaze on Rebecca. Bradley's sister cupped her hands in the air as if she had caught a butterfly, peeking into her hands to study it. "I gotta know what she's been seeing first." He glanced at Daphne, an eyebrow quizzically raised. "Ghosts?"

She didn't notice he was asking her, too distracted by everyone's wild reactions, especially Mrs. Chambers's. A car drove slowly into the other end of the parking lot as Daphne returned her attention to Rebecca, taking a step closer. She blinked rapidly, as if the sun was in her eyes, which didn't make sense since it had mostly set. "I want to know what that is," she said, picking up her pace. Wystan ran out to grab her arm just before she stepped too close to a fissure. He crouched, peering nervously at Rebecca as she stumbled to her right as if something had shoved her aside.

The car stopped on Rebecca's and my side of the lot, not bothering to fit into a space. Mr. Porter dashed out of the driver's seat, a potion bottle in his hand. "I brought the cure," he announced, trying to address Frank in particular. Frank redrew his gun, aiming it directly at Mr. Porter's chest. "Don't!" I screamed, breaking my silence. Mr. Porter held his hands up, barely keeping the bottle in his grasp.

Wystan stood, rolling his eyes as he snapped his fingers again. Everyone blinked as if they were coming out of their individual hallucinations. Frank immediately lowered his gun. "Markus?"

"What cure?" Wystan asked, sounding a little frustrated.

Mr. Porter sized him up, starting from his feet to his head. "Who are you?"

Griselda came to stand next to Wystan and Daphne, one eyebrow cocked. "It's so rude of us not to have introduced ourselves. We're—"

Rebecca interrupted, her eyes transfixed on the three captivators, "Griselda Day. Danger intuitive. Born in Tennessee twenty-six years ago. The second of two children." Her eyes flickered to Wystan. "Wystan Reece. Illusionist. Born in Illinois twenty-five years ago. The first of three children." Then she lowered her gaze to Daphne. "Daphne Nicholson-Reece. Lie detector. Matrona of the druids or captivators. Born in Kansas six years ago. The first of one child."

Daphne smiled at the mention of her name, revealing a missing tooth. "And you're Rebecca Chambers. Materializer." She said that last word with punctuated syllables. "Vursitorja," she stumbled over the Romani word, "of the diviners. Born in New Mexico eleven years ago. The"—she held three of her fingers up—"third of five kids." She giggled, seemingly proud of herself for being semi-able to recite whatever knowledge she had of Rebecca.

Mr. Porter let out a low, impressed whistle. "Well, that's just—" his own nervous laughter cut him off as he stepped closer to the fissure dividing most of the diviners from Rebecca and me. "Let me just get this cure to Rebecca so she can stop killing everybody." His foot hit dead air and he worked to balance himself, looking down at the trench. "Which, uh, which one of you did that?"

Almost all of us glanced at Rebecca as he studied the scene more closely, noticing the crumbled pavement in front of me and the scattered broken glass.

Wystan narrowed his eyes, motioning toward the potion bottle. "What's in that?"

Griselda lifted her head almost regally. "Yes, I'm sure Clay would like the recipe if it is what you say it is."

"Well, uh"—Markus glanced nervously around before handing the bottle to Frank—"unless this Clay you speak of is a witch, I doubt it will do much good."

"Well then, I guess we'll just have to capture ourselves a witch," Griselda said, grinning evilly.

Frank pulled back his hand, gripping the bottle like he was about to throw it at Rebecca. Her eyes widened as she tried to run out of the way, but she'd essentially trapped herself in our small corner. The way the fissures were drawn, it was like a giant game of inescapable foursquare. Frank released the bottle, stopping it midair with his telekinesis when she ducked. He caused the bottle to slam to the ground in front of her feet, breaking the glass and releasing a weird light blue smoke into the air.

Rebecca coughed, breathing it in as she tried to wave it away. She blinked, turning her head like she was seeing us for the first time. "What—?" She cringed, her hands gripping her hair at her scalp. I noticed Blake wince, stepping closer to the cars to get some distance.

Paige peered at her brother between her arms as she stayed huddled on the ground. "The voices must be back," she guessed aloud.

"Rebecca?" Mrs. Chambers walked to her edge of the fissure, watching her daughter with wide concerned eyes and a wobbly chin.

Tears sprouted from her daughter's eyes as she released her hair, taking in stuffy, sniffling breaths. She turned to me, then glanced at Bradley. "I'm so sorry."

EPILOGUE
WYSTAN

I glanced down at my daughter, ruffling her thin brown hair. We hadn't come here to fight, hence the lack of an armed entourage. I crouched beside her, pulling her to me. "Feel better now?" I asked.

She nodded, sucking on her fingers as she watched her diviner counterpart hug an invisible Savanna. We'd cut our arrival almost a little too close for comfort. The matronae were the only ones capable of ending the life of anyone deemed immortal. While we were fine with Rebecca targeting the diviners, we hadn't banked on her targeting the one person we needed most. The lore always stated that the matrona of the diviners possessed a powerful urge to save the immortals. It was in her favor to keep the universe in balance. So imagine our surprise when Daphne told us Rebecca had tried to kill our main diviner of interest.

I stood, leaning toward Griselda and lowering my voice. "Should we be concerned that they've somehow managed to make Public Enemies Number One and Two invisible to us?"

Griselda smirked, placing one hand on my daughter's shoulder. "That's what we have Daphne for." Her green eyes danced over the crowd, landing on the witch. He was helping one of the teenage girls to her feet. I thought maybe the girl might have been Paige—one of Bradley's sisters—but it had been so long since I'd seen her, and there were at least three other girls her age in the crowd. "The witch puts an interesting card on the table, though. I thought the real ones had fled the country after the trials." She cocked an eyebrow. "If the Tale of Onora translates to the diviners, we're going to need a witch who knows how to make that cure."

"Should we try to take him?"

She shrugged, squaring her shoulders. "For now, he's of more use to us as the Immortal's protector. If my calculations are correct"—she moved her gaze to the spot where I thought Savanna might be standing, noticing Rebecca had let go of her and was talking to someone who'd fallen through one of the cracks—"we still have three more months of this waiting."

I scowled. "They could be gone by then."

Griselda grimaced in agreement. "Yes, well, if we take them now, we won't be able to hide them. If Cyrus sees we've brought them to the lab, he'll have them executed. He is not happy about what they did to his stocks."

We watched as a man in his fifties climbed a rope ladder, heaving himself over the edge and onto the correct elevation. "You okay?" he groaned, glancing at the space where Savanna must be standing.

"You might want to brace yourselves," Rebecca warned, holding a hand over the crack the man had climbed out of. He scrambled toward the bushes as several of the diviners stepped away. The ground began to rumble under our feet. Griselda and I tugged Daphne back toward the SUV as the cracks closed and disappeared.

Daphne turned around, looking up at me with pleading green eyes. "I want to go home."

Home. To her, home was back in Kansas. It was an eight-hour drive.

Griselda smiled at her, crouching to her height, and tapping her nose with her finger. "You, my little matrona, have just given me an idea." I glanced at Griselda questioningly. She caught my eye, smirking, and reached for the driver's side door. "There is one place our enemies can't penetrate."

I felt the same smile tug at my lips. She was right. Forget Priori. Penn Valley had the real estate and the security to pull our operation off. "That school?" I asked, hopeful.

She nodded. "It's time to move forward."

"Believe half of what you see and nothing of what you hear."

> — *Edgar Allen Poe, The System of Dr. Tarr and Prof. Fether*

ALPHABETICAL INDEX
OF DIVINERS

ALPHABETICAL INDEX OF CAPTIVATORS

ACKNOWLEDGMENTS &
ABOUT THE STORY

This has been a wild year, and wow, it's probably a miracle you are holding this book in your hands.

I finished writing the rough draft shortly after attending my first comic convention in the spring of 2022. I'm glad because life got busy. I found myself at four more conventions in the following months. My priorities shifted from writing to selling. Then, rather suddenly, I lost my day job.

As an independent author, I don't make money from my writing. In fact, I spend significantly more than I make.

I'm not complaining. My goal was never to make a living off my stories; especially, this series. In the past, when I received a small amount of royalties, I forwarded the amount to charity. However, it did make it more difficult to get more books through the editing and publishing process.

This book was no exception.

Over Our Spilled Blood is my favorite book of the series so far. I got to explore one of my favorite tropes as well as spend some extra time in other characters' heads. I spent many years building up to the events in this book and the next and am so relieved to finally have reached this point in the story.

I got to introduce some new characters, concepts, storylines, and settings in this book. The first that I want to take note of is the introduction of the Porters and their witchy sandwich shop chain. Since I began writing this version of the series, I wanted to somehow include a sandwich shop. One of my first jobs was at a sandwich shop in Overland Park, Kansas, where I had the best boss and some amazing coworkers. I want to thank JP, especially, for making that experience memorable and positive enough for me to want to include a tidbit of it in my books.

I don't remember what originally inspired Savanna and Bradley's teen pregnancy storyline. It was something I added to the original series when I was around eleven or twelve years old, having decided to turn it into a series in the first place. The original plot was fully contemporary fiction, and the concept of teen pregnancy and pregnancy in general had always fascinated me. I do remember that as I was adding it to my notes for what was originally the second book in the series, I was thinking about a family member who had been through a similar situation. My childhood was filled with comments that used their situation as a cautionary tale, muddled with judgments and rumors. Ever since, I have always felt a deep reverence toward teen parents; especially, young mothers.

When I began writing this version of the book, Roe v. Wade was rumored to be overturned. In fact, it *did* get overturned, sparking outrage across the United States. In my rage, Savanna's story became one of few choices, including a lack of freedom.

While abortion laws have been ever-changing throughout history, at the time this book was finally published (in 2023), Indiana's laws completely banned abortion, which is far more restrictive than it was at the time of Savanna's pregnancy in 2008. Her story could have been much uglier if set in today's world. In fact, many stories are.

I want to acknowledge all teen parents, whether they became parents by choice or circumstance, as well as all the people who chose to end a pregnancy or give their child up for adoption. I admire your strength and bravery.

On that note, I want to especially thank the teacher at my high school who oversaw the Teens as Parents (TAPs) program. Although I was not a teen parent, I had her for a different, yet equally important class. She was one of my best teachers and was admired by many of my classmates, parents or not. Mrs. Nancy McRoberts is retired now, but having heard from many of her TAPs students, I do highly encourage public schools in the United States who do not have this program to consider incorporating it. It was definitely a life changer for many of them. For some, it may have been their only means of support.

Speaking of support, I want to thank my editors, Jessie Campbell and Rita Ray, for sticking with me this far into the series. My writing is better because of them.

I'm thankful for my cover designer and illustrator, KT Barnes, for also sticking with me this far into the series. She reads every book before designing the cover and has been a great person to bounce ideas off.

I also want to thank my best friend Nery, for being one of my biggest cheerleaders.

I continue to be grateful for the people in my life who inspired character names. These people included my cousin Markus, my childhood friend Miranda, a childhood family friend Calvin, and cousins once removed Bradly and Issac. My mom's college friend Nancy, whom I've never met, also inspired a character's name. My character Alyssa's name is a spoof of my own.

This is the first book I've written that includes a character with selective mutism. Alyssa has always been an important character to me since her inception, and because of that, we share a diagnosis. When I first created Alyssa as a teenager, I was not diagnosed with any of my mental illnesses or disabilities. I created her to be everything I wanted to be but was too shy to be. When I did this rewrite as an adult, I reimagined her a bit. I wanted teens who were like me to see themselves in a character.

I wanted to give a name to her anxiety so that readers who didn't have a diagnosis could have a chance at finding one via their connection to her. I also wanted readers who couldn't relate at all—and perhaps viewed people like me through eyes like Serena's—to be able to give a name to the similar anxiety and demeanors they may witness in the real world. Perhaps that too, could help diagnose those who slipped through the cracks like I had. Perhaps more children, teenagers, and adults could receive the help they deserve.

Thank you to everyone who has been on this journey with me. My heart is buried in this book.

OWN VOICES RECOMMENDATIONS

Two of the major themes in this series—racism related to the Romani people and type one diabetes—were not written from the author's personal perspective. However, they were depicted with a great amount of research. As the author, I would like to urge my readers to actively add Own Voices books to their reading lists and bookshelves as authors like me can only provide limited views on certain subjects.

For a growing list of Own Voices books depicting type I diabetes or the Roma, please visit
https://linktr.ee/ekbarnesauthor

x

ABOUT THE AUTHOR

It would not be false to claim that E.K. Barnes has enjoyed creating and writing stories for most of her life. In fact, the Diviner's Legacy series was first thought up when she was only ten years old. E.K. grew up in a family of creatives, surrounded by musicians and artists. Since she was young, she was always drawn to stories of adversity. If the story didn't match or exceed the anxiety she felt on a daily basis, she didn't care much for it. Struggling with undiagnosed mental illnesses for most of her childhood, E.K. preferred to live in her imaginary worlds. She owned and operated *Scribe Stash*, a personalized subscription box service for readers and writers from 2017 to 2018. Since the publication of her second book in 2021, she has often been seen at multiple comic conventions in the Midwestern United States.

E.K. is a member of the Independent Author Network. She is a 2014 graduate of Olathe Northwest High School in Kansas and has been a student at Johnson County Community College, MidAmerica Nazarene University, and Southern New Hampshire University.

She currently resides in Kansas with her dog, Nikki.

https://linktr.ee/ekbarnesauthor
Instagram & Tik Tok: @ekbarnes_author